The 7 Deadly Sins
SAMPLER

The 7 Deadly Sins
SAMPLER

Foreword by Al Gini

Selected and edited by Daniel Born,
Mike Levine, and Donald H. Whitfield

THE GREAT BOOKS FOUNDATION
A nonprofit educational organization

With generous support from Harrison Middleton University,
a Great Books distance-learning college

Published and distributed by

 THE GREAT BOOKS FOUNDATION
A nonprofit educational organization

35 E. Wacker Drive, Suite 400
Chicago, IL 60601
www.greatbooks.org

With generous support from
Harrison Middleton University,
a Great Books distance-learning college
www.chumsci.edu

9 8 7 6 5 4 3

Library of Congress Cataloging-in-Publication Data
The seven deadly sins sampler / edited by Daniel Born, Donald H. Whitfield, & Mike Levine; foreword by Al Gini.
    p.cm.
ISBN 978-1-880323-19-9 (alk. paper)
1.   Short stories, American. 2. Short stories, English. 3. Deadly sins—Fiction.
    I. Born, Daniel. II. Whitfield, Donald H. III. Levine, Mike.

PS648.S5S48 2007
823'.0108—dc22   2007004940

Cover and interior illustration: Lisa Haney
Book design: Think Design Group LLC

About the Great Books Foundation

The Great Books Foundation was established in 1947 by two University of Chicago educators, Robert Maynard Hutchins and Mortimer Adler. An independent, nonprofit educational organization whose mission is to help people learn how to think and share ideas, the Foundation promotes the reading and discussion of classic and contemporary texts across the disciplines, and publishes books and anthologies for readers of all ages. It also conducts hundreds of professional development courses each year in Shared Inquiry,™ a text-based Socratic method of learning that helps participants read actively, pose evocative questions, and listen and respond to others effectively in dialogue.

*Spelling and punctuation have been modernized
and slightly altered for clarity.*

Contents

Foreword

The Seven Deadly (Yet Delicious and All Too Human) Sins

Al Gini

Growing up, I reached the conclusion that we are a glorious species and we know it. Individually and collectively we have achieved wondrous things: scaled great heights, performed heroic deeds, harnessed the power of the sun, and discovered cures for age-old maladies. Our machines have taken us to the moon and beyond. And yet during my formative years I also heard a very different message, one that I continue to ponder. This came from priests, parents, and sometimes the police. The message was brutal. I learned that I was a scoundrel and a sinner.

Sin. In his book *Whatever Became of Sin?* (1973), the noted psychiatrist Karl Menninger tried to rehabilitate this simple three-letter word as a concept worthy of serious thought. Menninger knew very well that many educated people—including his clients—had traded in the language of the confessional for that of the therapist's couch. More than thirty years later, not much has changed. And even if our particular age of anxiety and terror has put the portentous word *evil* back into circulation, the effect has been to make parsing varieties of sin appear even more frivolous and archaic.

The idea of sin as one that might help in the development of ethical standards continues to fall out of favor.

According to the theologian George Otis Jr., "Sin has lost its prominence and . . . popularity as a sermon theme." Though we may still hear homilies about moral corruption, misdeeds, or social injustice, the notion of sin now carries an unmistakable whiff of medievalism. Even in the official *Catechism of the Catholic Church*, fully revised and published in English in 1994 and consisting of 2,865 numbered sections, the seven deadly sins, as such, are denoted by the more euphemistic phrase "capital sins" and dispensed with in a paragraph.

And yet the idea of the seven deadly sins has maintained remarkable staying power in popular culture. Elda Rotor, the editor of the Oxford University Press series The Seven Deadly Sins, points out that this fifteen-hundred-year-old list has informed "theological and philosophical tracts, psychology, politics, social criticism, popular culture, and art and literature." She refers to authors such as Chaucer, Dante, and Spenser, just a few in a vast pool of great writers who have made reference to these deadly sins throughout history. To her list one can easily add Faulkner, Kafka, Maugham, Melville, Mencken, Poe, and Rousseau—and this is just to get started. It should come as no surprise that literary voices are so effective in exploring the possibilities—and consequences—of transgressive acts. That these themes continue to resonate with today's readers should also come as no surprise. As Rotor notes, "Our contemporary fascination with these age-old sins, our struggle against or celebration of them, reveals as much about our continued desire to define human nature as it does about our divine aspirations."

According to biblical tradition, we are all sinners, doomed because of the first couple's disobedience in the Garden of Eden. The story says their sin became our heritage. St. Augustine, much influenced by the dualistic Manichean doctrine that the soul is good but the body is evil (even though he officially denounced that doctrine), goes even further when he announces that our propagation is "vitiated by sin" and that we are "bound by the chain of death, and justly condemned." In the Augsburg Confession, an early document of the Protestant Reformation, humankind is described as "full of evil lusts and inclinations from our mothers' wombs." To tone down the rhetoric a notch, one might say we succumb easily to our passions. More often than not we are driven by the body's appetites rather than by our rational faculties.

Whatever the cause of these passions and appetites, many thinkers through the ages have agreed that we need regulations, specific commandments that can steady our course and help us find a middle ground between Dionysian excess and Spartan austerity. In the Hellenic tradition of ancient Greece, the virtuous life was defined by balance and moderation; in the Hebraic tradition mediated through the Bible, the virtuous life was achieved by strict obedience to God. In the course of time, these two traditions fused, as Augustine sought to integrate his reading of Plato and Aristotle with his understanding of the scriptures. The Augustinian stamp on Christian theology highlights a draconian imperative: All is forbidden that is not specifically allowed, and all transgression will be severely punished.

But the story of the seven deadly sins properly begins with St. Gregory I, also known as Gregory the Great partly because of his prodigious work ethic during fourteen years as supreme pontiff. He reorganized the church's ecclesiastical and bureaucratic structure, established the Gregorian chant as the official liturgical music, and not least of all, established the catalog of the seven deadly sins that persists to this day. To be sure, he was not the first theologian to list "cardinal" or "capital" sins. The earliest such attempts originated in the monastic movement of the Eastern Church, when the fourth-century Egyptian monk Evagrius Ponticus drew up a list of eight deadly sins. A short time later the ascetic St. John Cassian of Marseilles introduced this list to Western monasticism.

Before Gregory became pope, he lived the life of a monk and served, for a time, as abbot of the monastery of St. Andrew in Italy. Cerebral and austere, he was drawn to John Cassian's list because he saw in it an opportunity to address temptations faced by those entering religious orders. By creating his final list of seven, Gregory hoped to offer a tool for contemplation, one to help monks maintain their ascetic regimen of chastity, poverty, and obedience. Gregory also knew very well that not only priests suffer from temptation. All people, he declared, could benefit from constant vigilance. Gregory offered his list of seven deadly sins to "serve as a classification of the normal perils of the soul in the ordinary conditions of life." Each sin, he suggested, simultaneously offers us an opportunity to concentrate on the vice and to meditate on the virtue and beneficence of its opposite.

GREGORY'S SEVEN DEADLY SINS

Sin	Latin Name	Also Known As	Corresponding Virtue
Pride	Superbia	Vanity, Arrogance	Humility
Envy	Invidia	Jealousy, Covetousness	Love
Anger	Ira	Rage, Fury, Hatred	Kindness
Sloth	Acedia	Laziness, Idleness	Zeal
Greed	Avaritia	Avarice, Materialism	Generosity
Gluttony	Gula	Addiction, Overindulgence	Temperance
Lust	Luxuria	Sexual obsession	Self-control

Writing in *Wicked Pleasures* (1999), the ethicist Robert C. Solomon speculates as to why seven sins prevailed over ten (to correlate perhaps with the Ten Commandments?), or for that matter, just a few. Even more curious, he thinks, is the fact that Gregory chose these particular seven, rather than a list of truly damnable and destructive infractions. According to Solomon, these seven "barely jiggle the scales of justice, and it is hard to imagine why God would bother to raise a celestial eyebrow about them." Gregory could have come up with a list eminently more vile, and Solomon wonders why "human viciousness and brutality—cruelty, savagery, indifference to human suffering, tyranny, ethnic hatred, religious persecution, and racial bigotry—don't even make the list."

But the genius of Gregory's list is precisely that his choices are so pedestrian, addressing, in Solomon's words, "rather routine and mundane features of human behavior." Who among us has not wrestled with moments of exaggerated self-importance, bowel-churning resentment in regard to the good fortune of others, or irrational feelings of hatred or revenge? Who has not demonstrated excessively lazy behavior or wanted too much? Who does not occasionally eat or drink to excess or entertain lascivious thoughts? These matters are not just philosophical abstractions to be debated and discussed; they are perennial issues of the human heart.

Certain critics argue that in contemporary culture, Gregory's code is highly subjective and outdated. According to a 2005 poll commissioned by the BBC, a majority of the British public no longer believes that the seven deadly sins have any relevance to their lives. The poll also offers an up-to-date list of cardinal sins that more closely reflects our global state of economic and ecological interdependence. The new "terrible seven" designate cruelty as the worst transgression of modern times, followed by adultery, bigotry, dishonesty, hypocrisy, greed (the only one of the original seven that makes this list), and selfishness. What the survey suggests is that in today's world, sins are not perceived as solitary activities with limited and unilateral impact; rather, they affect both the transgressor and the larger community.

Mahatma Gandhi argued that all virtues and vices be measured and weighed in relation to their impact on others. For him, individual actions usually have collective consequences, and there is no such thing as a person living a completely independent life. Hence sin is measured in terms of its impact on others. His list of sins, which also differs from Gregory's, might be more accurately called the "seven most deadly social sins."

TWO NEW LISTS OF SEVEN DEADLIES

BBC Poll	Mahatma Gandhi
Cruelty	Wealth without work
Adultery	Pleasure without conscience
Bigotry	Science without humanity
Dishonesty	Knowledge without character
Hypocrisy	Politics without principles
Greed	Commerce without morality
Selfishness	Worship without sacrifice

Yet one would be naive to ignore the larger social consequences of Gregory's original seven. As the psychotherapist Solomon Schimmel notes in *The Seven Deadly Sins* (1997), each sin spawns a larger, harmful social phenomenon: lust can lead to pornography; gluttony to substance abuse; envy to terrorism; anger to violence; sloth to indifference to the pain and suffering of others; greed to abuse of public trust; and pride to discrimination.

Whether or not you agree with Gregory's list, the seven deadly sins have endured the test of time—and continue to serve as a barometer of moral health. Gregory wanted to support and encourage the study of sin, and for him, understanding it is a summons to life. It is central to moral development. This goal is echoed by Menninger, who urged religious leaders to focus on sin, "to identify it, define it, to warn us about it, and to spur measures for combating and rectifying it."

Even those of us who are not religious understand intuitively the concept of sin. Sin can harm oneself as well as one's relationships with others, it often violates tribal or community laws and customs, and it sometimes manifests simply as a loss of control. At the most practical and secular level, Robert Solomon argues in *Wicked Pleasures,*

> what are (archaically) called the "deadly sins" have nothing to do with damnation or degeneracy but rather with *poor health.* They lead to a reduced lifespan, an unappealing appearance, the inability to attract a mate at the health club. What is deadly about the deadly sins is that, literally, they shorten our lives. Thus gluttony is really a code name for calories and high cholesterol. Lust is short for overdoing it, endangering one's health. . . . Sloth now means not getting enough exercise. Greed is taking on more than you can handle, inducing dangerous stress.

Solomon goes on to say that from a more philosophical standpoint, the seven deadly sins are deadly because their "apparent innocuousness" erodes our critical skills and anesthetizes our ethical sense. We need to take them seriously, not just because they involve wrongdoing, but because the habit of doing wrong has a major influence on the formulation of self-identity and character, the quality that Heraclitus said determines one's fate, and that, according to Aristotle, is the very foundation for an ethical life.

PRIDE

Gregory, as well as Chaucer and Dante, depicted pride as the deadliest of all the sins. The philosopher Baruch Spinoza claimed that pride is a "species of madness" because it misleads us into thinking that we can accomplish all things. As Henry Fairlie observes in *The Seven Deadly Sins Today* (1978), pride produces a distorted view of self and the world. Pride strips a person of the ability to maintain an objective outlook or make sound judgments. The writer and Trappist monk Thomas Merton argued that pride robs us of our humility and our basic concern for objectivity because we are constantly focused on self.

For St. Thomas Aquinas, pride is more than narcissism; beginning with an "inordinate desire to excel," it is also "characteristic of pride to be unwilling to be subject to any superior, and especially to God." The result is an exaggeration of our own abilities and rights. In Aquinas's view, pride "is the beginning of every sin." Indeed, many commentators have identified pride as the catalyst or trigger for the other six.

Of course, not all pride need be excessive, or even dysfunctional. In the Hellenic tradition of Homer and Aristotle, pride could be a virtue as well as a necessity. This virtue is about appropriate self-confidence and self-esteem. As Martin Luther King Jr. once expressed it, true self-esteem means being able to say, "I am somebody. I am a person."

ENVY

According to the writer Joseph Epstein, envy may be the most pervasive of all the sins. It is reflected in our competitive nature as well as in the contempt we sometimes feel toward those we perceive as our betters. In his book on the subject (*Envy*, 2003), Epstein says there may possibly have been "certain persons—saints, great national athletes, dazzlingly beautiful women, scions of billionaires—who have not known envy, but permit me to doubt it. To err may be human, but to envy is undoubtedly so."

Envy is not just desire or admiration, says Epstein; it is the inordinate desire for that which belongs to another. It can turn into active ill will toward others and the desire to strip rivals of their status, abilities, or possessions. Envy may even include the willingness to do harm and violence. In its most malicious form, envy can turn into hatred. To deeply envy another is to say, "I want your life (and—I hate you for having it)." The German philosopher Immanuel Kant argued that envy is an "abominable vice, a passion not only distressing and tormenting to the subject, but intent on the destruction of the happiness of others."

"Insidious gnawing envy" is "the vampire vice," says Don Herzog, in his essay on envy in *Wicked Pleasures*. It preys on our consciousness and disables our ability to be balanced in our assessment and judgment of others. "Envy," declares the political economist Adam Smith, "is that passion which views with malignant dislike the superiority of those who are really entitled to all the superiority they possess."

Envy also distorts our own self-image, making us feel inferior and dissatisfied with ourselves. As the novelist Angus Wilson so graphically puts it: "[Envy] has the ugliness of a trapped rat that has gnawed its own foot in its effort to escape."

ANGER

Anger is not just part of the human repertoire of emotions. In considering the biblical texts, the theologian Robert A. F. Thurman, author of *Anger* (2005), suggests that "the angriest person around seems to be God himself." First he gets mad at Adam and Eve for eating the forbidden fruit. He kicks the humans out of paradise, makes them suffer childbirth, illness, and death, and perhaps worst of all, requires that they struggle at manual labor to earn a living. Later, God gets mad at their son Cain and lets him know it, and still later, God destroys virtually every living thing, with the exception of Noah and his family and a few animals. There is the firebombing of the twin cities Sodom and Gomorrah, not to mention another wave of killing that God inflicts on the Egyptians for not letting his people go.

Some forms of human anger can be viewed as the righteous kind: the sort of rage that energetically confronts injustice and cruelty and demands reform. But human anger usually falls short of this idealistic standard. Too often, it is neither righteous nor rational. It can impede prudent conduct; unchecked, it can destroy both oneself and others. Anger need not be associated with hatred, rage, abusive violence, yelling, or offensive behavior—but usually it is. Anger generally involves the loss of self-control, and ignorance often feeds it.

SLOTH

The term *sloth* is now considered archaic, and one rarely hears it outside of academic conversations. In everyday language, slothfulness can mean idleness or laziness. Colloquially, being "laid back" sometimes qualifies as a personal quality, a wished-for state that is good in itself. But from a theological point of view, slothfulness constitutes a debilitating character defect.

The novelist Thomas Pynchon, in an essay titled "Nearer, My Couch, to Thee," notes that traditionally sloth "was supposed to be the progenitor of a whole family of lesser, or venial sins, among them Idleness, Drowsiness, Restlessness of the Body, Instability, and Loquacity." The real danger of such sluggishness is that it can deaden the will and narcotize our spiritual sense of awareness. It detaches the self from the world, but not in a meditative sort of way. It tends toward faintheartedness and a lack of desire for what is good, spawning inertia, torpor, and an inescapable sense of ennui.

The writer Dorothy Sayers put it this way: "[Sloth] is the sin that believes in nothing, cares for nothing, seeks to know nothing, interferes with nothing, enjoys nothing, hates nothing, finds purpose in nothing, lives for nothing, and remains alive because there is nothing for which it will die."

GREED

"Greed, for lack of a better word, is good," says high-flying financier Gordon Gekko (Michael Douglas) to a group of company shareholders in Oliver Stone's film *Wall Street* (1987). "Greed is right. Greed works."

For the economist Milton Friedman and his cadre of like-minded theoreticians, greed—defined as the pursuit of personal wants and desires within the context of healthy, legal competition—is the fundamental reason for our social and economic system's success. In Friedman's view, we have created the most successful consumer-based economy in the world because the unfettered marketplace gives people what they want or think they need to have.

Though many agree with Friedman, there have been notable dissenters. In *One-Dimensional Man* (1964), the political philosopher Herbert Marcuse argues that the capitalist pursuit of wants and desires has become a fetish, and that we now confuse the good life with the goods of life. For Marcuse, when the possession of things becomes one's metaphysical orientation toward life, product idolatry and consumerism begin to act as a warped substitute for authentic living. The philosopher and psychologist Eric Fromm argued that in modern society the terms *citizen* and *consumer* are synonymous, and all consumers identify themselves by the formula: I am what I have and what I consume. A life of product idolatry assumes that having more is being more, and if some is good, then more must absolutely be better.

The real issue regarding the sin of greed is perhaps not the acquisition of specific products or goods, but rather the issue of desire itself or, more accurately, obsessive desire. With no regard for justice, moderation, and logic, greed desires to possess more than is useful. And yet no matter how much is acquired, it never seems enough; and because it never seems enough, there is no real joy in possessing it.

As Henry Fairlie has noted, greed is "not so much the love of possessions, as the love merely of possessing. To buy what we do not need, more even than we need for our pleasure or entertainment, is a love of possessing for its own sake." Greed can never be fulfilled. Gandhi pointed out that the world has enough for everyone's need, but not enough for everyone's greed.

GLUTTONY

At first glance, gluttony seems to be the most innocuous of the seven deadly sins, and it probably runs neck-and-neck with lust as the most widespread of the seven. Historically, the sin of gluttony has been identified as excessive eating— and sometimes drinking. It can be argued that the early church's classification of gluttony as one of the deadly sins had mostly to do with rejecting the excesses of paganism. In *Gluttony* (2003), the writer Francine Prose comments on the lavish dinner parties in ancient Rome: these featured not only colossal amounts of food but also places where guests could regurgitate on a regular basis in order to continue eating and drinking over a prolonged period of time.

In America today, food remains at the core of our popular understanding of the sin of gluttony—and with real reason. Prose notes that one-third of all Americans are overweight, and 14 percent of American children are considered obese. At the time she was writing, obesity-related conditions contributed to 350,000 deaths a year; doctors estimated that 70 percent of cardiovascular disease was related to obesity. According to the American Medical Association, diabetes, a frequent companion of chronic obesity, is the fastest-growing disease in America.

Yet there is more to the sin of gluttony than poor health and untimely death. (It is worth observing that Aquinas liked his food well enough, and it was no accident that his nickname was "the dumb ox"—he tipped the scales at a hefty 320 pounds.) Prose interprets Aquinas's teaching on gluttony as having distinctly spiritual consequences, arguing that "it's not what we put in our mouths, but the *inordinate desire* for food, a longing so powerful and thoroughly involving that it comes between us and God." And she notes John Cassian's advice on this particular sin: "We cannot enter the battle of the inner man unless we have been set free from the vice of gluttony."

LUST

Lust is probably the most practiced—and written about—of the seven deadly sins. To begin with, its status is conflicted due to its complicated relationship to sexual desire itself. Some definitions equate lust with sex, while another secondary level of meaning frequently qualifies it as sexual desire of an "unbridled" or "intense" kind. (One might reasonably ask whether moderate lust is an oxymoron.) About sex itself there is less confusion. As I argue in *Why It's Hard to Be Good* (2005), "Sex can be performed alone, with another person, or in groups. From self-gratification to the basic one-on-one missionary position, to swinging and taking part in orgies—sex is a game that almost any number can play." In 1879, Mark Twain, giving a dinner speech for the Stomach Club (a gathering of American writers and artists) in Paris, commented on the solitary version this way: "To the lonely it is company; to the forsaken it is a friend; to the aged . . . it is a benefactor; they that be penniless are still rich, in that they have this majestic diversion."

Twain's humor had no place in the teaching I received on the subject during my teenage years. The sum total of Roman Catholic officialdom on sex could be reduced to one basic sentence: Don't do it until you're married, and then never for fun, and only when absolutely necessary.

The early church fathers and most of their ecclesiastical successors adamantly argued against the pleasures of the flesh. In much of Western Christian thought, the body has been perceived as an obstacle to spiritual growth and salvation, a prison that impedes and confuses the life of the mind and the perfection of the soul. Interpreters of the story of the fall in the Garden of Eden have generally chosen to perceive the body as part of the painful penalty for disobeying the word of God.

According to Augustine, the good soul finds itself trapped in the bad body. We must, he argued, triumph over our animal nature and free ourselves from sexual desire. Procreation is the only possible excuse for sex, which should be indulged in without lust or pleasure. Aquinas, who seconded Augustine on this point, routinely associated intercourse with such terms as filth, stain, foulness, vileness, and distaste, and asserted that any sexual activity that does not have reproduction as its aim is ungodly and immoral. The suspicion of the body is also a part of the Greek philosophical legacy, which generally privileged the psyche (mind) over the soma (body). For Socrates, Aristotle, and Plato, the acts of reasoning and contemplation are the highest activities a human can perform. And while the pleasures of the body—sensuality and eros—should not be disrespected, they do have the potential to distract us and to destabilize the function of reason.

For Gregory and his clerical associates, sexual desire speaks to the fallen state of humankind, and for Augustine venereal pleasures debauch the mind. Sexuality is the pursuit of intense pleasure that borders on ecstatic experience, beyond both reason and self-control. Desire can rob individuals of their autonomy and willpower, and like an addiction, it destroys rational faculties.

As a young man I was deeply troubled by this message. The severity of Augustine's teachings was in direct contradiction to the mounting urges and desires of my body. My torment led me to seek out spiritual advice from one of my theology professors, Father John Coughnin. I went to him and recited a litany of woes. To my surprise and horror, Father Coughnin burst into laughter.

"My God, lad," he said in his thick brogue, "you've swallowed Augustine's bait, hook, line, and sinker! Calm yourself! He's sold us all a false bill of goods. 'Deny the body!' 'Deny yourself!' 'Every dirty thought makes you dirty!'" Father Coughnin was rolling his eyes.

I must have appeared confused. Father Coughnin continued: "Listen to me. Augustine couldn't trust himself when it came to these matters, and he surely wasn't about to trust us. So he tried to deny human nature, but it can't be done. The simple fact is that the desires of the flesh don't go away until we're six days dead and six feet under. And thank God for that, otherwise we wouldn't even be here having this conversation!"

Now, getting older by the day, I realize that Father Coughnin's merriment wasn't just about the foibles of sex. He was laughing at the essential fluidity and fallibility of the human condition. We are, indeed, a glorious species with strong positive traits. And we are also a species prone to temptation and excess. Collectively, we are in a constant struggle to achieve moderation—the golden mean between extremes. The authors in this collection offer us many different ways of thinking about sin, sometimes with serious intent, other times with humorous effect. They don't necessarily present a set of settled opinions on the deadly sins themselves. They don't lay down laws. What they do is keep us thinking and imagining what the moral life might be. This may be the best way to think about Gregory's original intent. Socrates put it another way, his student Plato tells us, in words that ring down through the centuries with equal force: The unexamined life is not worth living.

About Shared Inquiry

Shared Inquiry is the effort to achieve a more thorough understanding of a text by discussing questions, responses, and insights with others. For both the leader and the participants, careful listening is essential. The leader guides the discussion by asking questions about specific ideas and problems of meaning in the text, but does not seek to impose his or her own interpretation on the group.

During a Shared Inquiry discussion, group members consider a number of possible ideas and weigh the evidence for each. Ideas that are entertained and then refined or abandoned are not thought of as mistakes, but as valuable parts of the thinking process. Group members gain experience in communicating complex ideas and in supporting, testing, and expanding their thoughts. Everyone in the group contributes to the discussion, and while participants may disagree with one another, they treat one another's ideas respectfully.

This process helps develop an understanding of important texts and ideas, rather than merely cataloging knowledge about them. These guidelines keep conversation focused on the text and assure all the participants a voice.

1. **Read the selection carefully before participating in the discussion.** This ensures that all participants are equally prepared to talk about the ideas in the work and helps prevent talk that would distract the group from its purpose.

2. **Support your ideas with evidence from the text.** This keeps the discussion focused on understanding the selection and enables the group to weigh textual support for different answers and to choose intelligently among them.

3. **Discuss the ideas in the selection, and try to understand them fully before exploring issues that go beyond the selection.** Reflecting on the ideas in the text and the evidence to support them makes the exploration of related issues more productive.

4. **Listen to other participants and respond to them directly.** Shared Inquiry is about the give-and-take of ideas, the willingness to listen to others and talk with them respectfully. Directing your comments and questions to other group members, not always to the leader, will make the discussion livelier and more dynamic.

5. **Expect the leader to only ask questions.** Effective leaders help participants develop their own ideas, with everyone gaining a new understanding in the process. When participants hang back and wait for the leader to suggest answers, discussion tends to falter.

How to Use This Book

The first set of questions following each story is *interpretive*—these questions call for the task of close reading. What is the specific language of the text meant to convey? Are there several interpretations, and can we justify our interpretation by appealing to the text itself? What key passages in the text help unlock its meaning? What passages are confusing and seem to defy understanding? In successful learning communities, close reading evolves into a rich give-and-take between participants who are able to summon specific passages in order to make a point. Thus the text does not get lost in the conversation between discussion participants, but is viewed as the principal voice in the dialogue.

The second set of questions ("For Further Reflection") is *evaluative*. These questions invite participants to weigh the significance or validity of the work in a larger context, and they are best contemplated after a thoroughgoing interpretive discussion has taken place.

Be aware that the temptation to skip interpretive questions and jump straight into evaluative judgments can short-circuit meaningful conversation. Watch out for untethered, rambling testimonials and personal anecdotes or unrestrained academic monologues. These developments can distract a group from genuine textual encounter and interpretation.

When grounded in a prior discussion of the text, on the other hand, evaluative questions can push participants to a deeper level of engagement. These questions demand the resources of wider observation, experience, and reading. In the best discussions, evaluative questions can lead to extended dialogues or, for students in the classroom, written essays that help develop thoughtful articulation of ideas and beliefs.

Pride

WILLIAM FAULKNER

William Faulkner (1897–1962) spent most of his life in his native state of Mississippi, largely shunning literary society and preferring to live and write in the small town of Oxford. Many of his novels and short stories are set in the fictional Yoknapatawpha County, which reflects Faulkner's deep familiarity with Mississippi and its people. From his early novels, such as *The Sound and the Fury* (1929), *As I Lay Dying* (1930), and *Absalom, Absalom!* (1936), through his later works, Faulkner constructed an elaborate chronicle of intertwined families enduring changes in the South brought about by the Civil War, Reconstruction, and the intrusion of the modern world. He was awarded the Nobel Prize in Literature in 1949. "A Rose for Emily" (1930) was the first of his stories to appear in a national magazine.

A Rose for Emily

1

When Miss Emily Grierson died, our whole town went to her funeral: the men through a sort of respectful affection for a fallen monument, the women mostly out of curiosity to see the inside of her house, which no one save an old manservant—a combined gardener and cook—had seen in at least ten years.

It was a big, squarish frame house that had once been white, decorated with cupolas and spires and scrolled balconies in the heavily lightsome style of the seventies, set on what had once been our most select street. But garages and cotton gins had encroached and obliterated even the august names of that neighborhood; only Miss Emily's house was left, lifting its stubborn and coquettish decay above the cotton wagons and the gasoline pumps—an eyesore among eyesores. And now Miss Emily had gone to join the representatives of those august names where they lay in the cedar-bemused cemetery among the ranked and anonymous graves of Union and Confederate soldiers who fell at the battle of Jefferson.

Alive, Miss Emily had been a tradition, a duty, and a care; a sort of hereditary obligation upon the town, dating from that day in 1894 when Colonel Sartoris, the mayor—he who fathered the edict that no Negro woman should appear on the streets without an apron—remitted her taxes, the dispensation dating from the death of her father on into perpetuity. Not that Miss Emily would have accepted charity. Colonel Sartoris invented an involved tale to the effect that Miss Emily's father had loaned money to the town, which the town, as a matter of business, preferred this way of repaying. Only a man of Colonel Sartoris's generation and thought could have invented it, and only a woman could have believed it.

When the next generation, with its more modern ideas, became mayors and aldermen, this arrangement created some little dissatisfaction. On the first of the year they mailed her a tax notice. February came, and there was no reply. They wrote her a formal letter, asking her to call at the sheriff's office at her convenience. A week later the mayor wrote her himself, offering to call or to send his car for her, and received in reply a note on paper of an archaic shape, in a thin, flowing calligraphy in faded ink, to the effect that she no longer went out at all. The tax notice was also enclosed, without comment.

They called a special meeting of the Board of Aldermen. A deputation waited upon her, knocked at the door through which no visitor had passed since she ceased giving china-painting lessons eight or ten years earlier. They were admitted by the old Negro into a dim hall from which a stairway mounted into still more shadow. It smelled of dust and disuse—a close, dank smell. The Negro led them into the parlor. It was furnished in heavy, leather-covered furniture. When the Negro opened the blinds of one window, they could see that the leather was cracked; and when they sat down, a faint dust rose sluggishly about their thighs, spinning with slow motes in the single sun ray. On a tarnished gilt easel before the fireplace stood a crayon portrait of Miss Emily's father.

They rose when she entered—a small, fat woman in black, with a thin gold chain descending to her waist and vanishing into her belt, leaning on an ebony cane with a tarnished gold head. Her skeleton was small and spare; perhaps that was why what would have been merely plumpness in another was obesity in her. She looked bloated, like a body long submerged in motionless water, and of that pallid hue. Her eyes, lost in the fatty ridges of her face, looked like two small pieces of coal pressed into a lump of dough as they moved from one face to another while the visitors stated their errand.

She did not ask them to sit. She just stood in the door and listened quietly until the spokesman came to a stumbling halt. Then they could hear the invisible watch ticking at the end of the gold chain.

Her voice was dry and cold. "I have no taxes in Jefferson. Colonel Sartoris explained it to me. Perhaps one of you can gain access to the city records and satisfy yourselves."

"But we have. We are the city authorities, Miss Emily. Didn't you get a notice from the sheriff, signed by him?"

"I received a paper, yes," Miss Emily said. "Perhaps he considers himself the sheriff . . . I have no taxes in Jefferson."

"But there is nothing on the books to show that, you see. We must go by the—"

"See Colonel Sartoris. I have no taxes in Jefferson."

"But, Miss Emily—"

"See Colonel Sartoris." (Colonel Sartoris had been dead almost ten years.) "I have no taxes in Jefferson. Tobe!" The Negro appeared. "Show these gentlemen out."

2

So she vanquished them, horse and foot, just as she had vanquished their fathers thirty years before about the smell.

That was two years after her father's death and a short time after her sweetheart—the one we believed would marry her—had deserted her. After her father's death she went out very little; after her sweetheart went away, people hardly saw her at all. A few of the ladies had the temerity to call, but were not received, and the only sign of life about the place was the Negro man—a young man then—going in and out with a market basket.

"Just as if a man—any man—could keep a kitchen properly," the ladies said; so they were not surprised when the smell developed. It was another link between the gross, teeming world and the high and mighty Griersons.

A neighbor, a woman, complained to the mayor, Judge Stevens, eighty years old.

"But what will you have me do about it, madam?" he said.

"Why, send her word to stop it," the woman said. "Isn't there a law?"

"I'm sure that won't be necessary," Judge Stevens said. "It's probably just a snake or a rat that nigger of hers killed in the yard. I'll speak to him about it."

The next day he received two more complaints, one from a man who came in diffident deprecation. "We really must do something about it, Judge. I'd be the last one in the world to bother Miss Emily, but we've got to do something." That night the Board of Aldermen met—three graybeards and one younger man, a member of the rising generation.

"It's simple enough," he said. "Send her word to have her place cleaned up. Give her a certain time to do it in, and if she don't . . ."

"Dammit, sir," Judge Stevens said, "will you accuse a lady to her face of smelling bad?"

So the next night, after midnight, four men crossed Miss Emily's lawn and slunk about the house like burglars, sniffing along the base of the brickwork and at the cellar openings while one of them performed a regular sowing motion with his hand out of a sack slung from his shoulder. They broke open the cellar door and sprinkled lime there, and in all the outbuildings. As they recrossed the lawn, a window that had been dark was lighted and Miss Emily sat in it, the light behind her, and her upright torso motionless as that of an idol. They crept quietly across the lawn and into the shadow of the locusts that lined the street. After a week or two the smell went away.

That was when people had begun to feel really sorry for her. People in our town, remembering how old lady Wyatt, her great-aunt, had gone completely crazy at last, believed that the Griersons held themselves a little too high for what they really were. None of the young men were quite good enough for Miss Emily and such. We had long thought of them as a tableau, Miss Emily a slender figure in white in the background, her father a spraddled silhouette in the foreground, his back to her and clutching a horsewhip, the two of them framed by the back-flung front door. So when she got to be thirty and was still single, we were not pleased exactly, but vindicated; even with insanity in the family she wouldn't have turned down all of her chances if they had really materialized.

When her father died, it got about that the house was all that was left to her; and in a way, people were glad. At last they could pity Miss Emily. Being left alone, and a pauper, she had become humanized. Now she too would know the old thrill and the old despair of a penny more or less.

The day after his death all the ladies prepared to call at the house and offer condolence and aid, as is our custom. Miss Emily met them at the door, dressed as usual and with no trace of grief on her face. She told them that her father was not dead. She did that for three days, with the ministers calling on her, and the doctors, trying to persuade her to let them dispose of the body. Just as they were about to resort to law and force, she broke down, and they buried her father quickly.

We did not say she was crazy then. We believed she had to do that. We remembered all the young men her father had driven away, and we knew that with nothing left, she would have to cling to that which had robbed her, as people will.

3

She was sick for a long time. When we saw her again, her hair was cut short, making her look like a girl, with a vague resemblance to those angels in colored church windows— sort of tragic and serene.

The town had just let the contracts for paving the sidewalks, and in the summer after her father's death they began the work. The construction company came with niggers and mules and machinery, and a foreman named Homer Barron, a Yankee—a big, dark, ready man, with a big voice and eyes lighter than his face. The little boys would follow in groups to hear him cuss the niggers, and the niggers singing in time to the rise and fall of picks. Pretty soon he knew everybody in town. Whenever you heard a lot of laughing anywhere about the square, Homer Barron would be in the center of the group. Presently we began to see him and Miss Emily on Sunday afternoons driving in the yellow-wheeled buggy and the matched team of bays from the livery stable.

At first we were glad that Miss Emily would have an interest, because the ladies all said, "Of course a Grierson would not think seriously of a Northerner, a day laborer." But there were still others, older people, who said that even grief could not cause a real lady to forget noblesse oblige— without calling it noblesse oblige. They just said, "Poor Emily. Her kinsfolk should come to her." She had some kin in Alabama; but years ago her father had fallen out with them over the estate of old lady Wyatt, the crazy woman, and there was no communication between the two families. They had not even been represented at the funeral.

And as soon as the old people said, "Poor Emily," the whispering began. "Do you suppose it's really so?" they said to one another. "Of course it is. What else could . . ." This behind their hands; rustling of craned silk and satin behind jalousies closed upon the sun of Sunday afternoon as the thin, swift clop-clop-clop of the matched team passed: "Poor Emily."

She carried her head high enough—even when we believed that she was fallen. It was as if she demanded more than ever the recognition of her dignity as the last Grierson; as if it had wanted that touch of earthiness to reaffirm her imperviousness. Like when she bought the rat poison, the arsenic. That was over a year after they had begun to say "Poor Emily," and while the two female cousins were visiting her.

"I want some poison," she said to the druggist. She was over thirty then, still a slight woman, though thinner than usual, with cold, haughty black eyes in a face the flesh of which was strained across the temples and about the eye sockets as you imagine a lighthouse-keeper's face ought to look. "I want some poison," she said.

"Yes, Miss Emily. What kind? For rats and such? I'd recom—"

"I want the best you have. I don't care what kind."

The druggist named several. "They'll kill anything up to an elephant. But what you want is—"

"Arsenic," Miss Emily said. "Is that a good one?"

"Is . . . arsenic? Yes, ma'am. But what you want—"

"I want arsenic."

The druggist looked down at her. She looked back at him, erect, her face like a strained flag. "Why, of course," the druggist said. "If that's what you want. But the law requires you to tell what you are going to use it for."

Miss Emily just stared at him, her head tilted back in order to look him eye for eye, until he looked away and went and got the arsenic and wrapped it up. The Negro delivery boy brought her the package; the druggist didn't come back. When she opened the package at home there was written on the box, under the skull and bones: "For rats."

4

So the next day we all said, "She will kill herself"; and we said it would be the best thing. When she had first begun to be seen with Homer Barron, we had said, "She will marry him." Then we said, "She will persuade him yet," because Homer himself had remarked—he liked men, and it was known that he drank with the younger men in the Elks' Club—that he was not a marrying man. Later we said, "Poor Emily" behind the jalousies as they passed on Sunday afternoon in the glittering buggy, Miss Emily with her head high and Homer Barron with his hat cocked and a cigar in his teeth, reins and whip in a yellow glove.

Then some of the ladies began to say that it was a disgrace to the town and a bad example to the young people. The men did not want to interfere, but at last the ladies forced the Baptist minister—Miss Emily's people were Episcopal—to call upon her. He would never divulge what happened during that interview, but he refused to go back again. The next Sunday they again drove about the streets, and the following day the minister's wife wrote to Miss Emily's relations in Alabama.

So she had blood kin under her roof again and we sat back to watch developments. At first nothing happened. Then we were sure that they were to be married. We learned that Miss Emily had been to the jeweler's and ordered a man's toilet set in silver, with the letters H. B. on each piece. Two days later we learned that she had bought a complete outfit of men's clothing, including a nightshirt, and we said, "They are married." We were really glad. We were glad because the two female cousins were even more Grierson than Miss Emily had ever been.

So we were not surprised when Homer Barron—the streets had been finished some time since—was gone. We were a little disappointed that there was not a public blowing-off, but we believed that he had gone on to prepare for Miss Emily's coming, or to give her a chance to get rid of the cousins. (By that time it was a cabal, and we were all Miss Emily's allies to help circumvent the cousins.) Sure enough, after another week they departed. And, as we had expected all along, within three days Homer Barron was back in town. A neighbor saw the Negro man admit him at the kitchen door at dusk one evening.

And that was the last we saw of Homer Barron. And of Miss Emily for some time. The Negro man went in and out with the market basket, but the front door remained closed. Now and then we would see her at a window for a moment, as the men did that night when they sprinkled the lime, but for almost six months she did not appear on the streets. Then we knew that this was to be expected too; as if that quality of her father which had thwarted her woman's life so many times had been too virulent and too furious to die.

When we next saw Miss Emily, she had grown fat and her hair was turning gray. During the next few years it grew grayer and grayer until it attained an even pepper-and-salt iron-gray, when it ceased turning. Up to the day of her death at seventy-four it was still that vigorous iron-gray, like the hair of an active man.

From that time on, her front door remained closed, save for a period of six or seven years, when she was about forty, during which she gave lessons in china-painting. She fitted up a studio in one of the downstairs rooms, where the daughters and granddaughters of Colonel Sartoris's contemporaries were sent to her with the same regularity and in the same spirit that they were sent to church on Sundays with a twenty-five-cent piece for the collection plate. Meanwhile her taxes had been remitted.

Then the newer generation became the backbone and the spirit of the town, and the painting pupils grew up and fell away and did not send their children to her with boxes of color and tedious brushes and pictures cut from the ladies' magazines. The front door closed upon the last one and remained closed for good. When the town got free postal delivery, Miss Emily alone refused to let them fasten the metal numbers above her door and attach a mailbox to it. She would not listen to them.

Daily, monthly, yearly we watched the Negro grow grayer and more stooped, going in and out with the market basket. Each December we sent her a tax notice, which would be returned by the post office a week later, unclaimed. Now and then we would see her in one of the downstairs windows—she had evidently shut up the top floor of the house—like the carven torso of an idol in a niche, looking or not looking or not looking at us, we could never tell which. Thus she passed from generation to generation—dear, inescapable, impervious, tranquil, and perverse.

And so she died. Fell ill in the house filled with dust and shadows, with only a doddering Negro man to wait on her. We did not even know she was sick; we had long since given up trying to get any information from the Negro. He talked to no one, probably not even to her, for his voice had grown harsh and rusty, as if from disuse.

She died in one of the downstairs rooms, in a heavy walnut bed with a curtain, her gray head propped on a pillow yellow and moldy with age and lack of sunlight.

5

The Negro met the first of the ladies at the front door and let them in, with their hushed, sibilant voices and their quick, curious glances, and then he disappeared. He walked right through the house and out the back and was not seen again.

The two female cousins came at once. They held the funeral on the second day, with the town coming to look at Miss Emily beneath a mass of bought flowers, with the crayon face of her father musing profoundly above the bier and the ladies sibilant and macabre; and the very old men—some in their brushed Confederate uniforms—on the porch and the lawn, talking of Miss Emily as if she had been a contemporary of theirs, believing that they had danced with her and courted her perhaps, confusing time with its mathematical progression, as the old do, to whom all the past is not a diminishing road but, instead, a huge meadow which no winter ever quite touches, divided from them now by the narrow bottleneck of the most recent decade of years.

Already we knew that there was one room in that region above stairs which no one had seen in forty years, and which would have to be forced. They waited until Miss Emily was decently in the ground before they opened it.

The violence of breaking down the door seemed to fill this room with pervading dust. A thin, acrid pall as of the tomb seemed to lie everywhere upon this room decked and furnished as for a bridal: upon the valance curtains of faded rose color, upon the rose-shaded lights, upon the dressing table, upon the delicate array of crystal and the man's toilet things backed with tarnished silver, silver so tarnished that the monogram was obscured. Among them lay a collar and tie, as if they had just been removed, which, lifted, left upon the surface a pale crescent in the dust. Upon a chair hung the suit, carefully folded; beneath it the two mute shoes and the discarded socks.

The man himself lay in the bed.

For a long while we just stood there, looking down at the profound and fleshless grin. The body had apparently once lain in the attitude of an embrace, but now the long sleep that outlasts love, that conquers even the grimace of love, had cuckolded him. What was left of him, rotted beneath what was left of the nightshirt, had become inextricable from the bed in which he lay; and upon him and upon the pillow beside him lay that even coating of the patient and biding dust.

Then we noticed that in the second pillow was the indentation of a head. One of us lifted something from it, and leaning forward, that faint and invisible dust dry and acrid in the nostrils, we saw a long strand of iron-gray hair.

QUESTIONS

1. Why do the men of Jefferson attend Miss Emily's funeral as "a sort of respectful affection for a fallen monument," while the women go "mostly out of curiosity to see the inside of her house"? (3)

2. Why is Miss Emily able to vanquish members of the new generation in Jefferson, "just as she had vanquished their fathers thirty years before about the smell"? (5)

3. Why does Miss Emily deny that her father is dead when the ladies of Jefferson come to offer their condolences?

4. In describing Emily's proud stance in public with Homer Barron, what does the narrator mean in saying that Emily's dignity "had wanted that touch of earthiness to reaffirm her imperviousness"? (9)

5. What changes the attitude of the ladies of Jefferson from feeling sorry for Emily's association with Homer Barron to saying that her behavior is "a disgrace to the town and a bad example to the young people"? (10)

6. What does the narrator mean in describing Emily as "dear, inescapable, impervious, tranquil, and perverse"? (12)

7. Why does Emily keep Homer's corpse?

FOR FURTHER REFLECTION

1. Who is the narrator of "A Rose for Emily"? Why does the narrator tell the story out of chronological order?

2. Why do the people of Jefferson seem to be so involved with Miss Emily, even though she has little direct contact with them?

3. How can pride make people believe that they can live as if nothing changes, either in their personal circumstances or in the society around them?

FLANNERY O'CONNOR

Flannery O'Connor (1925–1964) was born in Savannah, Georgia, and educated at the Georgia State College for Women. After receiving a scholarship in journalism at the University of Iowa, she decided to enroll instead in its master's program in creative writing, going on to become one of the Iowa Writers' Workshop's most famous alumni. She is the author of two novels, *Wise Blood* (1952) and *The Violent Bear It Away* (1960), and two story collections, *A Good Man Is Hard to Find* (1955) and *Everything That Rises Must Converge* (1965). Diagnosed with a form of lupus at age twenty-five, O'Connor spent the rest of her life on her mother's farm, writing and raising peacocks.

Good Country People

Besides the neutral expression that she wore when she was alone, Mrs. Freeman had two others, forward and reverse, that she used for all her human dealings. Her forward expression was steady and driving like the advance of a heavy truck. Her eyes never swerved to left or right but turned as the story turned as if they followed a yellow line down the center of it. She seldom used the other expression because it was not often necessary for her to retract a statement, but when she did, her face came to a complete stop, there was an almost imperceptible movement of her black eyes, during which they seemed to be receding, and then the observer would see that Mrs. Freeman, though she might stand there as real as several grain sacks thrown on top of each other, was no longer there in spirit. As for getting anything across to her when this was the case, Mrs. Hopewell had given it up. She might talk her head off. Mrs. Freeman could never be brought to admit herself wrong on any point. She would stand there and if she could be brought to say anything, it was something like, "Well, I wouldn't of said it was and I wouldn't of said it wasn't," or letting her gaze range over the top kitchen shelf where there was an assortment of dusty bottles, she might remark, "I see you ain't ate many of them figs you put up last summer."

They carried on their most important business in the kitchen at breakfast. Every morning Mrs. Hopewell got up at seven o'clock and lit her gas heater and Joy's. Joy was her daughter, a large blonde girl who had an artificial leg. Mrs. Hopewell thought of her as a child though she was thirty-two years old and highly educated. Joy would get up while her mother was eating and lumber into the bathroom and slam the door, and before long, Mrs. Freeman would arrive at the back door. Joy would hear her mother call, "Come on in," and then they would talk for a while in low voices that were indistinguishable in the bathroom. By the time Joy came in, they had usually finished the weather report and were on one or the other of Mrs. Freeman's daughters, Glynese or Carramae, Joy called them Glycerin and Caramel. Glynese, a redhead, was eighteen and had many admirers; Carramae, a blonde, was only fifteen but already married and pregnant. She could not keep anything on her stomach. Every morning Mrs. Freeman told Mrs. Hopewell how many times she had vomited since the last report.

Mrs. Hopewell liked to tell people that Glynese and Carramae were two of the finest girls she knew and that Mrs. Freeman was a *lady* and that she was never ashamed to take her anywhere or introduce her to anybody they might meet. Then she would tell how she had happened to hire the Freemans in the first place and how they were a godsend to her and how she had had them four years. The reason for her keeping them so long was that they were not trash. They were good country people. She had telephoned the man whose name they had given as a reference and he had told her that Mr. Freeman was a good farmer but that his wife was the nosiest woman ever to walk the earth. "She's got to be into everything," the man said. "If she don't get there before the dust settles, you can bet she's dead, that's all. She'll want to know all your business. I can stand him real good," he had said, "but me nor my wife neither could have stood that woman one more minute on this place." That had put Mrs. Hopewell off for a few days.

She had hired them in the end because there were no other applicants but she had made up her mind beforehand exactly how she would handle the woman. Since she was the type who had to be into everything, then, Mrs. Hopewell had decided, she would not only let her be into everything, she would *see to it* that she was into everything—she would give her the responsibility of everything, she would put her in charge. Mrs. Hopewell had no bad qualities of her own but she was able to use other people's in such a constructive way that she never felt the lack. She had hired the Freemans and she had kept them four years.

Nothing is perfect. This was one of Mrs. Hopewell's favorite sayings. Another was: that is life! And still another, the most important, was: well, other people have their opinions too. She would make these statements, usually at the table, in a tone of gentle insistence as if no one held them but her, and the large hulking Joy, whose constant outrage had obliterated every expression from her face, would stare just a little to the side of her, her eyes icy blue, with the look of someone who has achieved blindness by an act of will and means to keep it.

When Mrs. Hopewell said to Mrs. Freeman that life was like that, Mrs. Freeman would say, "I always said so myself." Nothing had been arrived at by anyone that had not first been arrived at by her. She was quicker than Mr. Freeman. When Mrs. Hopewell said to her after they had been on the place a while, "You know, you're the wheel behind the wheel," and winked, Mrs. Freeman had said, "I know it. I've always been quick. It's some that are quicker than others."

"Everybody is different," Mrs. Hopewell said.

"Yes, most people is," Mrs. Freeman said.

"It takes all kinds to make the world."

"I always said it did myself."

The girl was used to this kind of dialogue for breakfast and more of it for dinner; sometimes they had it for supper too. When they had no guest they ate in the kitchen because that was easier. Mrs. Freeman always managed to arrive at some point during the meal and to watch them finish it. She would stand in the doorway if it were summer but in the winter she would stand with one elbow on top of the refrigerator and look down on them, or she would stand by the gas heater, lifting the back of her skirt slightly. Occasionally she would stand against the wall and roll her head from side to side. At no time was she in any hurry to leave. All this was very trying on Mrs. Hopewell but she was a woman of great patience. She realized that nothing is perfect and that in the Freemans she had good country people and that if, in this day and age, you get good country people, you had better hang onto them.

She had had plenty of experience with trash. Before the Freemans she had averaged one tenant family a year. The wives of these farmers were not the kind you would want to be around you for very long. Mrs. Hopewell, who had divorced her husband long ago, needed someone to walk over the fields with her; and when Joy had to be impressed for these services, her remarks were usually so ugly and her face so glum that Mrs. Hopewell would say, "If you can't come pleasantly, I don't want you at all," to which the girl, standing square and rigid-shouldered with her neck thrust slightly forward, would reply, "If you want me, here I am—LIKE I AM."

Mrs. Hopewell excused this attitude because of the leg (which had been shot off in a hunting accident when Joy was ten). It was hard for Mrs. Hopewell to realize that her child was thirty-two now and that for more than twenty years she had had only one leg. She thought of her still as a child because it tore her heart to think instead of the poor stout girl in her thirties who had never danced a step or had any *normal* good times. Her name was really Joy but as soon as she was twenty-one and away from home, she had had it legally changed. Mrs. Hopewell was certain that she had thought and thought until she had hit upon the ugliest name in any language. Then she had gone and had the beautiful name, Joy, changed without telling her mother until after she had done it. Her legal name was Hulga.

When Mrs. Hopewell thought the name, Hulga, she thought of the broad blank hull of a battleship. She would not use it. She continued to call her Joy to which the girl responded but in a purely mechanical way.

Hulga had learned to tolerate Mrs. Freeman who saved her from taking walks with her mother. Even Glynese and Carramae were useful when they occupied attention that might otherwise have been directed at her. At first she had thought she could not stand Mrs. Freeman for she had found that it was not possible to be rude to her. Mrs. Freeman would take on strange resentments and for days together she would be sullen but the source of her displeasure was always obscure; a direct attack, a positive leer, blatant ugliness to her face—these never touched her. And without warning one day, she began calling her Hulga.

She did not call her that in front of Mrs. Hopewell who would have been incensed but when she and the girl happened to be out of the house together, she would say something and add the name Hulga to the end of it, and the big spectacled Joy-Hulga would scowl and redden as if her privacy had been intruded upon. She considered the name her personal affair. She had arrived at it first purely on the basis of its ugly sound and then the full genius of its fitness had struck her. She had a vision of the name working like the ugly sweating Vulcan who stayed in the furnace and to whom, presumably, the goddess had to come when called. She saw it as the name of her highest creative act. One of her major triumphs was that her mother had not been able to turn her dust into Joy, but the greater one was that she had been able to turn it herself into Hulga. However, Mrs. Freeman's relish for using the name only irritated her. It was as if Mrs. Freeman's beady steel-pointed eyes had penetrated far enough behind her face to reach some secret fact. Something about her seemed to fascinate Mrs. Freeman and then one day Hulga realized that it was the artificial leg.

Mrs. Freeman had a special fondness for the details of secret infections, hidden deformities, assaults upon children. Of diseases, she preferred the lingering or incurable. Hulga had heard Mrs. Hopewell give her the details of the hunting accident, how the leg had been literally blasted off, how she had never lost consciousness. Mrs. Freeman could listen to it any time as if it had happened an hour ago.

When Hulga stumped into the kitchen in the morning (she could walk without making the awful noise but she made it—Mrs. Hopewell was certain—because it was ugly-sounding), she glanced at them and did not speak. Mrs. Hopewell would be in her red kimono with her hair tied around her head in rags. She would be sitting at the table, finishing her breakfast and Mrs. Freeman would be hanging by her elbow outward from the refrigerator, looking down at the table. Hulga always put her eggs on the stove to boil and then stood over them with her arms folded, and Mrs. Hopewell would look at her—a kind of indirect gaze divided between her and Mrs. Freeman—and would think that if she would only keep herself up a little, she wouldn't be so bad looking. There was nothing wrong with her face that a pleasant expression wouldn't help. Mrs. Hopewell said that people who looked on the bright side of things would be beautiful even if they were not.

Whenever she looked at Joy this way, she could not help but feel that it would have been better if the child had not taken the PhD. It had certainly not brought her out any and now that she had it, there was no more excuse for her to go to school again. Mrs. Hopewell thought it was nice for girls to go to school to have a good time but Joy had "gone through." Anyhow, she would not have been strong enough to go again. The doctors had told Mrs. Hopewell that with the best of care, Joy might see forty-five. She had a weak heart. Joy had made it plain that if it had not been for this condition, she would be far from these red hills and good country people. She would be in a university lecturing to people who knew what she was talking about. And

Mrs. Hopewell could very well picture her there, looking like a scarecrow and lecturing to more of the same. Here she went about all day in a six-year-old skirt and a yellow sweatshirt with a faded cowboy on a horse embossed on it. She thought this was funny; Mrs. Hopewell thought it was idiotic and showed simply that she was still a child. She was brilliant but she didn't have a grain of sense. It seemed to Mrs. Hopewell that every year she grew less like other people and more like herself—bloated, rude, and squint-eyed. And she said such strange things! To her own mother she had said—without warning, without excuse, standing up in the middle of a meal with her face purple and her mouth half full—"Woman! do you ever look inside? Do you ever look inside and see what you are *not*? God!" she had cried sinking down again and staring at her plate, "Malebranche was right: we are not our own light. We are not our own light!" Mrs. Hopewell had no idea to this day what brought that on. She had only made the remark, hoping Joy would take it in, that a smile never hurt anyone.

The girl had taken the PhD in philosophy and this left Mrs. Hopewell at a complete loss. You could say, "My daughter is a nurse," or "My daughter is a schoolteacher," or even, "My daughter is a chemical engineer." You could not say, "My daughter is a philosopher." That was something that had ended with the Greeks and Romans. All day Joy sat on her neck in a deep chair, reading. Sometimes she went for walks but she didn't like dogs or cats or birds or flowers or nature or nice young men. She looked at nice young men as if she could smell their stupidity.

One day Mrs. Hopewell had picked up one of the books the girl had just put down and opening it at random, she read, "Science, on the other hand, has to assert its soberness and seriousness afresh and declare that it is concerned solely with what-is. Nothing—how can it be for science anything but a horror and a phantasm? If science is right, then one thing stands firm: science wishes to know nothing of nothing. Such is after all the strictly scientific approach to Nothing. We know it by wishing to know nothing of Nothing." These words had been underlined with a blue pencil and they worked on Mrs. Hopewell like some evil incantation in gibberish. She shut the book quickly and went out of the room as if she were having a chill.

This morning when the girl came in, Mrs. Freeman was on Carramae. "She thrown up four times after supper," she said, "and was up twict in the night after three o'clock. Yesterday she didn't do nothing but ramble in the bureau drawer. All she did. Stand up there and see what she could run up on."

"She's got to eat," Mrs. Hopewell muttered, sipping her coffee, while she watched Joy's back at the stove. She was wondering what the child had said to the Bible salesman. She could not imagine what kind of a conversation she could possibly have had with him.

He was a tall gaunt hatless youth who had called yesterday to sell them a Bible. He had appeared at the door, carrying a large black suitcase that weighted him so heavily on one side that he had to brace himself against the door facing. He seemed on the point of collapse but he said in a cheerful voice, "Good morning, Mrs. Cedars!" and set the suitcase down on the mat. He was not a bad-looking young man though he had on a bright blue suit and yellow socks that were not pulled up far enough. He had prominent face bones and a streak of sticky-looking brown hair falling across his forehead.

"I'm Mrs. Hopewell," she said.

"Oh!" he said, pretending to look puzzled but with his eyes sparkling, "I saw it said 'The Cedars' on the mailbox so I thought you was Mrs. Cedars!" and he burst out in a pleasant laugh. He picked up the satchel and under cover of a pant, he fell forward into her hall. It was rather as if the suitcase had moved first, jerking him after it. "Mrs. Hopewell!" he said and grabbed her hand. "I hope you are well!" and he laughed again and then all at once his face sobered completely. He paused and gave her a straight earnest look and said, "Lady, I've come to speak of serious things."

"Well, come in," she muttered, none too pleased because her dinner was almost ready. He came into the parlor and sat down on the edge of a straight chair and put the suitcase between his feet and glanced around the room as if he were sizing her up by it. Her silver gleamed on the two sideboards; she decided he had never been in a room as elegant as this.

"Mrs. Hopewell," he began, using her name in a way that sounded almost intimate, "I know you believe in Christian service."

"Well yes," she murmured.

"I know," he said and paused, looking very wise with his head cocked on one side, "that you're a good woman. Friends have told me."

Mrs. Hopewell never liked to be taken for a fool. "What are you selling?" she asked.

"Bibles," the young man said and his eye raced around the room before he added, "I see you have no family Bible in your parlor, I see that is the one lack you got!"

Mrs. Hopewell could not say, "My daughter is an atheist and won't let me keep the Bible in the parlor." She said, stiffening slightly, "I keep my Bible by my bedside." This was not the truth. It was in the attic somewhere.

"Lady," he said, "the word of God ought to be in the parlor."

"Well, I think that's a matter of taste," she began. "I think . . ."

"Lady," he said, "for a Chrustian, the word of God ought to be in every room in the house besides in his heart. I know you're a Chrustian because I can see it in every line of your face."

She stood up and said, "Well, young man, I don't want to buy a Bible and I smell my dinner burning."

He didn't get up. He began to twist his hands and looking down at them, he said softly, "Well lady, I'll tell you the truth—not many people want to buy one nowadays and besides, I know I'm real simple. I don't know how to say a thing but to say it. I'm just a country boy." He glanced up into her unfriendly face. "People like you don't like to fool with country people like me!"

"Why!" she cried, "good country people are the salt of the earth! Besides, we all have different ways of doing, it takes all kinds to make the world go 'round. That's life!"

"You said a mouthful," he said.

"Why, I think there aren't enough good country people in the world!" she said, stirred. "I think that's what's wrong with it!"

His face had brightened. "I didn't intraduce myself," he said. "I'm Manley Pointer from out in the country around Willohobie, not even from a place, just from near a place."

"You wait a minute," she said. "I have to see about my dinner." She went out to the kitchen and found Joy standing near the door where she had been listening.

"Get rid of the salt of the earth," she said, "and let's eat."

Mrs. Hopewell gave her a pained look and turned the heat down under the vegetables. "*I* can't be rude to any-body," she murmured and went back into the parlor.

He had opened the suitcase and was sitting with a Bible on each knee.

"You might as well put those up," she told him. "I don't want one."

"I appreciate your honesty," he said. "You don't see any more real honest people unless you go way out in the country."

"I know," she said, "real genuine folks!" Through the crack in the door she heard a groan.

"I guess a lot of boys come telling you they're work-ing their way through college," he said, "but I'm not going to tell you that. Somehow," he said, "I don't want to go to college. I want to devote my life to Chrustian service. See," he said, lowering his voice, "I got this heart condition. I may not live long. When you know it's something wrong with you and you may not live long, well then, lady . . ." He paused, with his mouth open, and stared at her.

He and Joy had the same condition! She knew that her eyes were filling with tears but she collected herself quickly and murmured, "Won't you stay for dinner? We'd love to have you!" and was sorry the instant she heard herself say it.

"Yes mam," he said in an abashed voice, "I would sher love to do that!"

Joy had given him one look on being introduced to him and then throughout the meal had not glanced at him again. He had addressed several remarks to her, which she had pretended not to hear. Mrs. Hopewell could not understand deliberate rudeness, although she lived with it, and she felt she had always to overflow with hospitality to make up for Joy's lack of courtesy. She urged him to talk about himself and he did. He said he was the seventh child of twelve and that his father had been crushed under a tree when he himself was eight year old. He had been crushed very badly, in fact, almost cut in two and was practically not recognizable. His mother had got along the best she could by hard working and she had always seen that her children went to Sunday School and that they read the Bible every evening. He was now nineteen year old and he had been selling Bibles for four months. In that time he had sold seventy-seven Bibles and had the promise of two more sales. He wanted to become a missionary because he thought that was the way you could do most for people. "He who losest his life shall find it," he said simply and he was so sincere, so genuine and earnest that Mrs. Hopewell would not for the world have smiled. He prevented his peas from sliding onto the table by blocking them with a piece of bread which he later cleaned his plate with. She could see Joy observing sidewise how he handled his knife and fork and she saw too that every few minutes, the boy would dart a keen appraising glance at the girl as if he were trying to attract her attention.

After dinner Joy cleared the dishes off the table and disappeared and Mrs. Hopewell was left to talk with him. He told her again about his childhood and his father's accident and about various things that had happened to him. Every five minutes or so she would stifle a yawn. He sat for two hours until finally she told him she must go because she had an appointment in town. He packed his Bibles and thanked her and prepared to leave, but in the doorway he stopped and wrung her hand and said that not on any of his trips had he met a lady as nice as her and he asked if he could come again. She had said she would always be happy to see him.

Joy had been standing in the road, apparently looking at something in the distance, when he came down the steps toward her, bent to the side with his heavy valise. He stopped where she was standing and confronted her directly. Mrs. Hopewell could not hear what he said but she trembled to think what Joy would say to him. She could see that after a minute Joy said something and that then the boy began to speak again, making an excited gesture with his free hand. After a minute Joy said something else at which the boy began to speak once more. Then to her amazement, Mrs. Hopewell saw the two of them walk off together, toward the gate. Joy had walked all the way to the gate with him and Mrs. Hopewell could not imagine what they had said to each other, and she had not yet dared to ask.

Mrs. Freeman was insisting upon her attention. She had moved from the refrigerator to the heater so that Mrs. Hopewell had to turn and face her in order to seem to be listening. "Glynese gone out with Harvey Hill again last night," she said. "She had this sty."

"Hill," Mrs. Hopewell said absently, "is that the one who works in the garage?"

"Nome, he's the one that goes to chiropracter school," Mrs. Freeman said. "She had this sty. Been had it two days. So she says when he brought her in the other night he says, 'Lemme get rid of that sty for you,' and she says, 'How?' and he says, 'You just lay yourself down acrost the seat of that car and I'll show you.' So she done it and he popped her neck. Kept on a-popping it several times until she made him quit. This morning," Mrs. Freeman said, "she ain't got no sty. She ain't got no traces of a sty."

"I never heard of that before," Mrs. Hopewell said.

"He ast her to marry him before the Ordinary," Mrs. Freeman went on, "and she told him she wasn't going to be married in no *office*."

"Well, Glynese is a fine girl," Mrs. Hopewell said. "Glynese and Carramae are both fine girls."

"Carramae said when her and Lyman was married Lyman said it sure felt sacred to him. She said he said he wouldn't take five hundred dollars for being married by a preacher."

"How much would he take?" the girl asked from the stove.

"He said he wouldn't take five hundred dollars," Mrs. Freeman repeated.

"Well we all have work to do," Mrs. Hopewell said.

"Lyman said it just felt more sacred to him," Mrs. Freeman said. "The doctor wants Carramae to eat prunes. Says instead of medicine. Says them cramps is coming from pressure. You know where I think it is?"

"She'll be better in a few weeks," Mrs. Hopewell said.

"In the tube," Mrs. Freeman said. "Else she wouldn't be as sick as she is."

Hulga had cracked her two eggs into a saucer and was bringing them to the table along with a cup of coffee that she had filled too full. She sat down carefully and began to eat, meaning to keep Mrs. Freeman there by questions if for any reason she showed an inclination to leave. She could perceive her mother's eye on her. The first roundabout question would be about the Bible salesman and she did not wish to bring it on. "How did he pop her neck?" she asked.

Mrs. Freeman went into a description of how he had popped her neck. She said he owned a '55 Mercury but that Glynese said she would rather marry a man with only a '36 Plymouth who would be married by a preacher. The girl asked what if he had a '32 Plymouth and Mrs. Freeman said what Glynese had said was a '36 Plymouth.

Mrs. Hopewell said there were not many girls with Glynese's common sense. She said what she admired in those girls was their common sense. She said that reminded her that they had had a nice visitor yesterday, a young man selling Bibles. "Lord," she said, "he bored me to death but he was so sincere and genuine I couldn't be rude to him. He was just good country people, you know," she said, "—just the salt of the earth."

"I seen him walk up," Mrs. Freeman said, "and then later—I seen him walk off," and Hulga could feel the slight shift in her voice, the slight insinuation, that he had not walked off alone, had he? Her face remained expressionless but the color rose into her neck and she seemed to swallow it down with the next spoonful of egg. Mrs. Freeman was looking at her as if they had a secret together.

"Well, it takes all kinds of people to make the world go 'round," Mrs. Hopewell said. "It's very good we aren't all alike."

"Some people are more alike than others," Mrs. Freeman said.

Hulga got up and stumped, with about twice the noise that was necessary, into her room and locked the door. She was to meet the Bible salesman at ten o'clock at the gate. She had thought about it half the night. She had started thinking of it as a great joke and then she had begun to see profound implications in it. She had lain in bed imagining dialogues for them that were insane on the surface but that reached below to depths that no Bible salesman would be aware of. Their conversation yesterday had been of this kind.

He had stopped in front of her and had simply stood there. His face was bony and sweaty and bright, with a little pointed nose in the center of it, and his look was different from what it had been at the dinner table. He was gazing at her with open curiosity, with fascination, like a child watching a new fantastic animal at the zoo, and he was breathing as if he had run a great distance to reach her. His gaze seemed somehow familiar but she could not think where she had been regarded with it before. For almost a minute he didn't say anything. Then on what seemed an insuck of breath, he whispered, "You ever ate a chicken that was two days old?"

The girl looked at him stonily. He might have just put this question up for consideration at the meeting of a philosophical association. "Yes," she presently replied as if she had considered it from all angles.

"It must have been mighty small!" he said triumphantly and shook all over with little nervous giggles, getting very red in the face, and subsiding finally into his gaze of complete admiration, while the girl's expression remained exactly the same.

"How old are you?" he asked softly.

She waited some time before she answered. Then in a flat voice she said, "Seventeen."

His smiles came in succession like waves breaking on the surface of a little lake. "I see you got a wooden leg," he said. "I think you're brave. I think you're real sweet."

The girl stood blank and solid and silent.

"Walk to the gate with me," he said. "You're a brave sweet little thing and I liked you the minute I seen you walk in the door."

Hulga began to move forward.

"What's your name?" he asked, smiling down on the top of her head.

"Hulga," she said.

"Hulga," he murmured, "Hulga. Hulga. I never heard of anybody name Hulga before. You're shy, aren't you, Hulga?" he asked.

She nodded, watching his large red hand on the handle of the giant valise.

"I like girls that wear glasses," he said. "I think a lot. I'm not like these people that a serious thought don't ever enter their heads. It's because I may die."

"I may die too," she said suddenly and looked up at him. His eyes were very small and brown, glittering feverishly.

"Listen," he said, "don't you think some people was meant to meet on account of what all they got in common and all? Like they both think serious thoughts and all?" He shifted the valise to his other hand so that the hand nearest her was free. He caught hold of her elbow and shook it a little. "I don't work on Saturday," he said. "I like to walk in the woods and see what Mother Nature is wearing. O'er the hills and far away. Pic-nics and things. Couldn't we go on a pic-nic tomorrow? Say yes, Hulga," he said and gave her a dying look as if he felt his insides about to drop out of him. He had even seemed to sway slightly toward her.

During the night she had imagined that she seduced him. She imagined that the two of them walked on the place until they came to the storage barn beyond the two back fields and there, she imagined, that things came to such a pass that she very easily seduced him and that then, of course, she had to reckon with his remorse. True genius can get an idea across even to an inferior mind. She imagined that she took his remorse in hand and changed it into a deeper under-standing of life. She took all his shame away and turned it into something useful.

She set off for the gate at exactly ten o'clock, escaping without drawing Mrs. Hopewell's attention. She didn't take anything to eat, forgetting that food is usually taken on a picnic. She wore a pair of slacks and a dirty white shirt, and as an afterthought, she had put some Vapex on the collar of it since she did not own any perfume. When she reached the gate no one was there.

She looked up and down the empty highway and had the furious feeling that she had been tricked, that he had only meant to make her walk to the gate after the idea of him. Then suddenly he stood up, very tall, from behind a bush on the opposite embankment. Smiling, he lifted his hat which was new and wide-brimmed. He had not worn it yesterday and she wondered if he had bought it for the occasion. It was toast-colored with a red and white band around it and was slightly too large for him. He stepped from behind the bush still carrying the black valise. He had on the same suit and the same yellow socks sucked down in his shoes from walking. He crossed the highway and said, "I knew you'd come!"

The girl wondered acidly how he had known this. She pointed to the valise and asked, "Why did you bring your Bibles?"

He took her elbow, smiling down on her as if he could not stop. "You can never tell when you'll need the word of God, Hulga," he said. She had a moment in which she doubted that this was actually happening and then they began to climb the embankment. They went down into the pasture toward the woods. The boy walked lightly by her side, bouncing on his toes. The valise did not seem to be heavy today; he even swung it. They crossed half the pasture without saying anything and then, putting his hand easily on the small of her back, he asked softly, "Where does your wooden leg join on?"

She turned an ugly red and glared at him and for an instant the boy looked abashed. "I didn't mean you no harm," he said. "I only meant you're so brave and all. I guess God takes care of you."

"No," she said, looking forward and walking fast, "I don't even believe in God."

At this he stopped and whistled. "No!" he exclaimed as if he were too astonished to say anything else.

She walked on and in a second he was bouncing at her side, fanning with his hat. "That's very unusual for a girl," he remarked, watching her out of the corner of his eye. When they reached the edge of the wood, he put his hand on her back again and drew her against him without a word and kissed her heavily.

The kiss, which had more pressure than feeling behind it, produced that extra surge of adrenaline in the girl that enables one to carry a packed trunk out of a burning house, but in her, the power went at once to the brain. Even before he released her, her mind, clear and detached and ironic anyway, was regarding him from a great distance, with amusement but with pity. She had never been kissed before and she was pleased to discover that it was an unexceptional experience and all a matter of the mind's control. Some people might enjoy drain water if they were told it was vodka. When the boy, looking expectant but uncertain, pushed her gently away, she turned and talked on, saying nothing as if such business, for her, were common enough.

He came along panting at her side, trying to help her when he saw a root that she might trip over. He caught and held back the long swaying blades of thorn vine until she had passed beyond them. She led the way and he came breathing heavily behind her. Then they came out on a sunlit hillside, sloping softly into another one a little smaller. Beyond, they could see the rusted top of the old barn where the extra hay was stored.

The hill was sprinkled with small pink weeds. "Then you ain't saved?" he asked suddenly, stopping.

The girl smiled. It was the first time she had smiled at him at all. "In my economy," she said, "I'm saved and you are damned but I told you I didn't believe in God."

Nothing seemed to destroy the boy's look of admiration. He gazed at her now as if the fantastic animal at the zoo had put its paw through the bars and given him a loving poke. She thought he looked as if he wanted to kiss her again and she walked on before he had the chance.

"Ain't there somewheres we can sit down sometime?" he murmured, his voice softening toward the end of the sentence.

"In that barn," she said.

They made for it rapidly as if it might slide away like a train. It was a large two-story barn, cool and dark inside. The boy pointed up the ladder that led into the loft and said, "It's too bad we can't go up there."

"Why can't we?" she asked.

"Yer leg," he said reverently.

The girl gave him a contemptuous look and putting both hands on the ladder, she climbed it while he stood below, apparently awestruck. She pulled herself expertly through the opening and then looked down at him and said, "Well, come on if you're coming," and he began to climb the ladder, awkwardly bringing the suitcase with him.

"We won't need the Bible," she observed.

"You never can tell," he said, panting. After he had got into the loft, he was a few seconds catching his breath. She had sat down in a pile of straw. A wide sheath of sunlight, filled with dust particles, slanted over her. She lay back against a bale, her face turned away, looking out the front opening of the barn where hay was thrown from a wagon into the loft. The two pink-speckled hillsides lay back against a dark ridge of woods. The sky was cloudless and cold blue. The boy dropped down by her side and put one arm under her and the other over her and began methodically kissing her face, making little noises like a fish. He did not remove his hat but it was pushed far enough back not to interfere. When her glasses got in his way, he took them off of her and slipped them into his pocket.

The girl at first did not return any of the kisses but presently she began to and after she had put several on his cheek, she reached his lips and remained there, kissing him again and again as if she were trying to draw all the breath out of him. His breath was clear and sweet like a child's and the kisses were sticky like a child's. He mumbled about loving her and about knowing when he first seen her that he loved her, but the mumbling was like the sleepy fretting of a child being put to sleep by his mother. Her mind, throughout this, never stopped or lost itself for a second to her feelings. "You ain't said you loved me none," he whispered finally, pulling back from her. "You got to say that."

She looked away from him off into the hollow sky and then down at a black ridge and then down farther into what appeared to be two green swelling lakes. She didn't realize he had taken her glasses but this landscape could not seem exceptional to her for she seldom paid any close attention to her surroundings.

"You got to say it," he repeated. "You got to say you love me."

She was always careful how she committed herself. "In a sense," she began, "if you use the word loosely, you might say that. But it's not a word I use. I don't have illusions. I'm one of those people who see *through* to nothing."

The boy was frowning. "You got to say it. I said it and you got to say it," he said.

The girl looked at him almost tenderly. "You poor baby," she murmured. "It's just as well you don't understand," and she pulled him by the neck, face-down, against her. "We are all damned," she said, "but some of us have taken off our blindfolds and see that there's nothing to see. It's a kind of salvation."

The boy's astonished eyes looked blankly through the ends of her hair. "Okay," he almost whined, "but do you love me or don'tcher?"

"Yes," she said and added, "in a sense. But I must tell you something. There mustn't be anything dishonest between us." She lifted his head and looked him in the eye. "I am thirty years old," she said. "I have a number of degrees."

The boy's look was irritated but dogged. "I don't care," he said. "I don't care a thing about what all you done. I just want to know if you love me or don'tcher?" and he caught her to him and wildly planted her face with kisses until she said, "Yes, yes."

"Okay then," he said, letting her go. "Prove it."

She smiled, looking dreamily out on the shifty landscape. She had seduced him without even making up her mind to try. "How?" she asked, feeling that he should be delayed a little.

He leaned over and put his lips to her ear. "Show me where your wooden leg joins on," he whispered.

The girl uttered a sharp little cry and her face instantly drained of color. The obscenity of the suggestion was not what shocked her. As a child she had sometimes been subject to feelings of shame but education had removed the last traces of that as a good surgeon scrapes for cancer; she would no more have felt it over what he was asking than she would have believed in his Bible. But she was as sensitive about the artificial leg as a peacock about his tail. No one ever touched it but her. She took care of it as someone else would his soul, in private and almost with her own eyes turned away. "No," she said.

"I known it," he muttered, sitting up. "You're just playing me for a sucker."

"Oh no no!" she cried. "It joins on at the knee. Only at the knee. Why do you want to see it?"

The boy gave her a long penetrating look. "Because," he said, "it's what makes you different. You ain't like anybody else."

She sat staring at him. There was nothing about her face or her round freezing-blue eyes to indicate that this had moved her; but she felt as if her heart had stopped and left her mind to pump her blood. She decided that for the first time in her life she was face to face with real innocence. This boy, with an instinct that came from beyond wisdom, had touched the truth about her. When after a minute, she said in a hoarse high voice, "All right," it was like surrendering to him completely. It was like losing her own life and finding it again, miraculously, in his.

Very gently he began to roll the slack leg up. The artificial limb, in a white sock and brown flat shoe, was bound in a heavy material like canvas and ended in an ugly jointure where it was attached to the stump. The boy's face and his voice were entirely reverent as he uncovered it and said, "Now show me how to take it off and on."

She took it off for him and put it back on again and then he took it off himself, handling it as tenderly as if it were a real one. "See!" he said with a delighted child's face. "Now I can do it myself!"

"Put it back on," she said. She was thinking that she would run away with him and that every night he would take the leg off and every morning put it back on again. "Put it back on," she said.

"Not yet," he murmured, setting it on its foot out of her reach. "Leave it off for a while. You got me instead."

She gave a little cry of alarm but he pushed her down and began to kiss her again. Without the leg she felt entirely dependent on him. Her brain seemed to have stopped thinking altogether and to be about some other function that it was not very good at. Different expressions raced back and forth over her face. Every now and then the boy, his eyes like two steel spikes, would glance behind him where the leg stood. Finally she pushed him off and said, "Put it back on me now."

"Wait," he said. He leaned the other way and pulled the valise toward him and opened it. It had a pale blue spotted lining and there were only two Bibles in it. He took one of these out and opened the cover of it. It was hollow and contained a pocket flask of whiskey, a pack of cards, and a small blue box with printing on it. He laid these out in front of her one at a time in an evenly spaced row, like one presenting offerings at the shrine of a goddess. He put the blue box in her hand. THIS PRODUCT TO BE USED ONLY FOR THE PREVENTION OF DISEASE, she read, and dropped it. The boy was unscrewing the top of the flask. He stopped and pointed, with a smile, to the deck of cards. It was not an ordinary deck but one with an obscene picture on the back of each card. "Take a swig," he said, offering her the bottle first. He held it in front of her, but like one mesmerized, she did not move.

Her voice when she spoke had an almost pleading sound. "Aren't you," she murmured, "aren't you just good country people?"

The boy cocked his head. He looked as if he were just beginning to understand that she might be trying to insult him. "Yeah," he said, curling his lip slightly, "but it ain't held me back none. I'm as good as you any day in the week."

"Give me my leg," she said.

He pushed it farther away with his foot. "Come on now, let's begin to have us a good time," he said coaxingly. "We ain't got to know one another good yet."

"Give me my leg!" she screamed and tried to lunge for it but he pushed her down easily.

"What's the matter with you all of a sudden?" he asked, frowning as he screwed the top on the flask and put it quickly back inside the Bible. "You just a while ago said you didn't believe in nothing. I thought you was some girl!"

Her face was almost purple. "You're a Christian!" she hissed. "You're a fine Christian! You're just like them all— say one thing and do another. You're a perfect Christian, you're . . ."

The boy's mouth was set angrily. "I hope you don't think," he said in a lofty indignant tone, "that I believe in that crap! I may sell Bibles but I know which end is up and I wasn't born yesterday and I know where I'm going!"

"Give me my leg!" she screeched. He jumped up so quickly that she barely saw him sweep the cards and the blue box into the Bible and throw the Bible into the valise. She saw him grab the leg and then she saw it for an instant slanted forlornly across the inside of the suitcase with a Bible at either side of its opposite ends. He slammed the lid shut and snatched up the valise and swung it down the hole and then stepped through himself.

When all of him had passed but his head, he turned and regarded her with a look that no longer had any admiration in it. "I've gotten a lot of interesting things," he said. "One time I got a woman's glass eye this way. And you needn't to think you'll catch me because Pointer ain't really my name. I use a different name at every house I call at and don't stay nowhere long. And I'll tell you another thing, Hulga," he said, using the name as if he didn't think much of it, "you ain't so smart. I been believing in nothing ever since I was born!" and then the toast-colored hat disappeared down the hole and the girl was left, sitting on the straw in the dusty sunlight. When she turned her churning face toward the opening, she saw his blue figure struggling successfully over the green speckled lake.

Mrs. Hopewell and Mrs. Freeman, who were in the back pasture, digging up onions, saw him emerge a little later from the woods and head across the meadow toward the highway. "Why, that looks like that nice dull young man that tried to sell me a Bible yesterday," Mrs. Hopewell said, squinting. "He must have been selling them to the Negroes back in there. He was so simple," she said, "but I guess the world would be better off if we were all that simple."

Mrs. Freeman's gaze drove forward and just touched him before he disappeared under the hill. Then she returned her attention to the evil-smelling onion shoot she was lifting from the ground. "Some can't be that simple," she said. "I know I never could."

QUESTIONS

1. What does Mrs. Hopewell mean by "good country people"?

2. Why does Mrs. Freeman sometimes address Mrs. Hopewell's daughter as Hulga?

3. What does Hulga mean when she says to her mother, "Do you ever look inside and see what you are *not*?" (23)

4. Why does Mrs. Hopewell lie to the Bible salesman by telling him that she keeps a Bible by her bedside?

5. What does Hulga mean when she tells the Bible salesman that she is "one of those people who see *through* to nothing"? (36)

6. Why does Hulga feel that the Bible salesman "had touched the truth about her"? (37)

7. Why does the Bible salesman take away Hulga's artificial leg?

FOR FURTHER REFLECTION

1. Is Hulga deserving of her fate?

2. When does the recognition of one's unique qualities turn into excessive pride?

3. What determines whether a quality that distinguishes you from other people functions as a point of strength or a point of vulnerability?

Envy

EDITH WHARTON

Edith Wharton (1862–1937) was born into a wealthy New York City family and educated by private tutors. Proficient in four languages—English, French, German, and Italian—she began writing at a young age and published her first short stories during the 1890s in periodicals including *Scribner's Magazine*. She established her literary reputation with *The House of Mirth* (1905), a novel about upper-crust society and rebellion against its conventions. After 1907 she took up residency in Paris, and six years later divorced her husband, Boston banker Edward Wharton. In 1911, she published *Ethan Frome*. Wharton became the first woman to win a Pulitzer Prize, for her novel *The Age of Innocence* (1920).

Roman Fever

1

From the table at which they had been lunching two American ladies of ripe but well-cared-for middle age moved across the lofty terrace of the Roman restaurant and, leaning on its parapet, looked first at each other, and then down on the outspread glories of the Palatine and the Forum, with the same expression of vague but benevolent approval.

As they leaned there a girlish voice echoed up gaily from the stairs leading to the court below. "Well, come along, then," it cried, not to them but to an invisible companion, "and let's leave the young things to their knitting"; and a voice as fresh laughed back: "Oh, look here, Babs, not actually knitting—" "Well, I mean figuratively," rejoined the first. "After all, we haven't left our poor parents much else to do . . ." and at that point the turn of the stairs engulfed the dialogue.

The two ladies looked at each other again, this time with a tinge of smiling embarrassment, and the smaller and paler one shook her head and colored slightly.

"Barbara!" she murmured, sending an unheard rebuke after the mocking voice in the stairway.

The other lady, who was fuller, and higher in color, with a small determined nose supported by vigorous black eyebrows, gave a good-humored laugh. "That's what our daughters think of us!"

Her companion replied by a deprecating gesture. "Not of us individually. We must remember that. It's just the collective modern idea of Mothers. And you see—" Half guiltily she drew from her handsomely mounted black handbag a twist of crimson silk run through by two fine knitting needles. "One never knows," she murmured. "The new system has certainly given us a good deal of time to kill; and sometimes I get tired just looking—even at this." Her gesture was now addressed to the stupendous scene at their feet.

The dark lady laughed again, and they both relapsed upon the view, contemplating it in silence, with a sort of diffused serenity which might have been borrowed from the spring effulgence of the Roman skies. The luncheon hour was long past, and the two had their end of the vast terrace to themselves. At its opposite extremity a few groups, detained by a lingering look at the outspread city, were gathering up guidebooks and fumbling for tips. The last of them scattered, and the two ladies were alone on the air-washed height.

"Well, I don't see why we shouldn't just stay here," said Mrs. Slade, the lady of the high color and energetic brows. Two derelict basket chairs stood near, and she pushed them into the angle of the parapet, and settled herself in one, her gaze upon the Palatine. "After all, it's still the most beautiful view in the world."

"It always will be, to me," assented her friend Mrs. Ansley, with so slight a stress on the "me" that Mrs. Slade, though she noticed it, wondered if it were not merely accidental, like the random underlinings of old-fashioned letter writers.

"Grace Ansley was always old-fashioned," she thought; and added aloud, with a retrospective smile: "It's a view we've both been familiar with for a good many years. When we first met here we were younger than our girls are now. You remember?"

"Oh, yes, I remember," murmured Mrs. Ansley, with the same undefinable stress.—"There's that headwaiter wondering," she interpolated. She was evidently far less sure than her companion of herself and of her rights in the world.

"I'll cure him of wondering," said Mrs. Slade, stretching her hand toward a bag as discreetly opulent-looking as Mrs. Ansley's. Signing to the headwaiter, she explained that she and her friend were old lovers of Rome, and would like to spend the end of the afternoon looking down on the view—that is, if it did not disturb the service? The headwaiter, bowing over her gratuity, assured her that the ladies were most welcome, and would be still more so if they would condescend to remain for dinner. A full moon night, they would remember . . .

Mrs. Slade's black brows drew together, as though references to the moon were out of place and even unwelcome. But she smiled away her frown as the headwaiter retreated. "Well, why not? We might do worse. There's no knowing, I suppose, when the girls will be back. Do you even know back from *where*? I don't!"

Mrs. Ansley again colored slightly. "I think those young Italian aviators we met at the Embassy invited them to fly to Tarquinia for tea. I suppose they'll want to wait and fly back by moonlight."

"Moonlight—moonlight! What a part it still plays. Do you suppose they're as sentimental as we were?"

"I've come to the conclusion that I don't in the least know what they are," said Mrs. Ansley. "And perhaps we didn't know much more about each other."

"No; perhaps we didn't."

Her friend gave her a shy glance. "I never should have supposed you were sentimental, Alida."

"Well, perhaps I wasn't." Mrs. Slade drew her lids together in retrospect; and for a few moments the two ladies, who had been intimate since childhood, reflected how little they knew each other. Each one, of course, had a label ready to attach to the other's name; Mrs. Delphin Slade, for instance, would have told herself, or anyone who asked her, that Mrs. Horace Ansley, twenty-five years ago, had been exquisitely lovely—no, you wouldn't believe it, would you? . . . though, of course, still charming, distinguished . . . Well, as a girl she had been exquisite; far more beautiful than her daughter Barbara, though certainly Babs, according to the new standards at any rate, was more effective—had more *edge*, as they say. Funny where she got it, with those two nullities as parents. Yes; Horace Ansley was—well, just the duplicate of his wife. Museum specimens of old New York. Good-looking, irreproachable, exemplary. Mrs. Slade and Mrs. Ansley had lived opposite each other—actually as well as figuratively—for years. When the drawing-room curtains in No. 20 East 73rd Street were renewed, No. 23, across the way, was always aware of it. And of all the movings, buyings, travels, anniversaries, illnesses—the tame chronicle of an estimable pair. Little of it escaped Mrs. Slade. But she had grown bored with it by the time her husband made his big coup in Wall Street, and when they bought in upper Park Avenue had already begun to think: "I'd rather live opposite a speakeasy for a change; at least one might see it raided." The idea of seeing Grace raided was so amusing that (before the move) she launched it at a woman's lunch. It made a hit, and went the rounds—she sometimes wondered if it had crossed the street, and reached Mrs. Ansley. She hoped not, but didn't much mind. Those were the days when respectability was at a discount, and it did the irreproachable no harm to laugh at them a little.

A few years later, and not many months apart, both ladies lost their husbands. There was an appropriate exchange of wreaths and condolences, and a brief renewal of intimacy in the half shadow of their mourning; and now, after another interval, they had run across each other in Rome, at the same hotel, each of them the modest appendage of a salient daughter. The similarity of their lot had again drawn them together, lending itself to mild jokes, and the mutual confession that, if in old days it must have been tiring to "keep up" with daughters, it was now, at times, a little dull not to.

No doubt, Mrs. Slade reflected, she felt her unemployment more than poor Grace ever would. It was a big drop from being the wife of Delphin Slade to being his widow. She had always regarded herself (with a certain conjugal pride) as his equal in social gifts, as contributing her full share to the making of the exceptional couple they were; but the difference after his death was irremediable. As the wife of the famous corporation lawyer, always with an international case or two on hand, every day brought its exciting and unexpected obligation: the impromptu entertaining of eminent colleagues from abroad, the hurried dashes on legal business to London, Paris, or Rome, where the entertaining was so handsomely reciprocated; the amusement of hearing in her wake: "What, that handsome woman with the good clothes and the eyes is Mrs. Slade—*the* Slade's wife? Really? Generally the wives of celebrities are such frumps."

Yes, being *the* Slade's widow was a dullish business after that. In living up to such a husband all her faculties had been engaged; now she had only her daughter to live up to, for the son who seemed to have inherited his father's gifts had died suddenly in boyhood. She had fought through that agony because her husband was there, to be helped and to help; now, after the father's death, the thought of the boy had become unbearable. There was nothing left but to mother her daughter; and dear Jenny was such a perfect daughter that she needed no excessive mothering. "Now with Babs Ansley I don't know that I *should* be so quiet," Mrs. Slade sometimes half-enviously reflected; but Jenny, who was younger than her brilliant friend, was that rare accident, an extremely pretty girl who somehow made youth and prettiness seem as safe as their absence. It was all perplexing—and to Mrs. Slade a little boring. She wished that Jenny would fall in love—with the wrong man, even; that she might have to be watched, outmaneuvered, rescued. And instead, it was Jenny who watched her mother, kept her out of draughts, made sure that she had taken her tonic . . .

Mrs. Ansley was much less articulate than her friend, and her mental portrait of Mrs. Slade was slighter, and drawn with fainter touches. "Alida Slade's awfully brilliant; but not as brilliant as she thinks," would have summed it up; though she would have added, for the enlightenment of strangers, that Mrs. Slade had been an extremely dashing girl; much more so than her daughter, who was pretty, of course, and clever in a way, but had none of her mother's— well, "vividness," someone had once called it. Mrs. Ansley would take up current words like this, and cite them in quotation marks, as unheard-of audacities. No, Jenny was not like her mother. Sometimes Mrs. Ansley thought Alida Slade was disappointed; on the whole she had had a sad life. Full of failures and mistakes; Mrs. Ansley had always been rather sorry for her . . .

So these two ladies visualized each other, each through the wrong end of her little telescope.

2

For a long time they continued to sit side by side without speaking. It seemed as though, to both, there was a relief in laying down their somewhat futile activities in the presence of the vast memento mori which faced them. Mrs. Slade sat quite still, her eyes fixed on the golden slope of the Palace of the Caesars, and after a while Mrs. Ansley ceased to fidget with her bag, and she too sank into meditation. Like many intimate friends, the two ladies had never before had occasion to be silent together, and Mrs. Ansley was slightly embarrassed by what seemed, after so many years, a new stage in their intimacy, and one with which she did not yet know how to deal.

Suddenly the air was full of that deep clangor of bells which periodically covers Rome with a roof of silver. Mrs. Slade glanced at her wristwatch. "Five o'clock already," she said, as though surprised.

Mrs. Ansley suggested interrogatively: "There's bridge at the Embassy at five." For a long time Mrs. Slade did not answer. She appeared to be lost in contemplation, and Mrs. Ansley thought the remark had escaped her. But after a while she said, as if speaking out of a dream: "Bridge, did you say? Not unless you want to . . . But I don't think I will, you know."

"Oh, no," Mrs. Ansley hastened to assure her. "I don't care to at all. It's so lovely here; and so full of old memories, as you say." She settled herself in her chair, and almost furtively drew forth her knitting. Mrs. Slade took sideway note of this activity, but her own beautifully cared-for hands remained motionless on her knee.

"I was just thinking," she said slowly, "what different things Rome stands for to each generation of travelers. To our grandmothers, Roman fever; to our mothers, sentimental dangers—how we used to be guarded!—to our daughters, no more dangers than the middle of Main Street. They don't know it—but how much they're missing!"

The long golden light was beginning to pale, and Mrs. Ansley lifted her knitting a little closer to her eyes. "Yes, how we were guarded!"

"I always used to think," Mrs. Slade continued, "that our mothers had a much more difficult job than our grandmothers. When Roman fever stalked the streets it must have been comparatively easy to gather in the girls at the danger hour; but when you and I were young, with such beauty calling us, and the spice of disobedience thrown in, and no worse risk than catching cold during the cool hour after sunset, the mothers used to be put to it to keep us in—didn't they?"

She turned again toward Mrs. Ansley, but the latter had reached a delicate point in her knitting. "One, two, three—

slip two; yes, they must have been," she assented, without looking up.

Mrs. Slade's eyes rested on her with a deepened attention. "She can knit—in the face of *this*! How like her . . ."

Mrs. Slade leaned back, brooding, her eyes ranging from the ruins which faced her to the long green hollow of the Forum, the fading glow of the church fronts beyond it, and the outlying immensity of the Colosseum. Suddenly she thought: "It's all very well to say that our girls have done away with sentiment and moonlight. But if Babs Ansley isn't out to catch that young aviator—the one who's a marchese—then I don't know anything. And Jenny has no chance beside her. I know that too. I wonder if that's why Grace Ansley likes the two girls to go everywhere together? My poor Jenny as a foil—!" Mrs. Slade gave a hardly audible laugh, and at the sound Mrs. Ansley dropped her knitting.

"Yes—?"

"I—oh, nothing. I was only thinking how your Babs carries everything before her. That Campolieri boy is one of the best matches in Rome. Don't look so innocent, my dear—you know he is. And I was wondering, ever so respectfully, you understand . . . wondering how two such exemplary characters as you and Horace had managed to produce anything quite so dynamic." Mrs. Slade laughed again, with a touch of asperity.

Mrs. Ansley's hands lay inert across her needles. She looked straight out at the great accumulated wreckage of passion and splendor at her feet. But her small profile was almost expressionless. At length she said: "I think you overrate Babs, my dear."

Mrs. Slade's tone grew easier. "No, I don't. I appreciate her. And perhaps envy you. Oh, my girl's perfect; if I were a chronic invalid I'd—well, I think I'd rather be in Jenny's hands. There must be times . . . but there! I always wanted a brilliant daughter . . . and never quite understood why I got an angel instead."

Mrs. Ansley echoed her laugh in a faint murmur. "Babs is an angel too."

"Of course—of course! But she's got rainbow wings. Well, they're wandering by the sea with their young men; and here we sit . . . and it all brings back the past a little too acutely."

Mrs. Ansley had resumed her knitting. One might almost have imagined (if one had known her less well, Mrs. Slade reflected) that, for her also, too many memories rose from the lengthening shadows of those august ruins. But no, she was simply absorbed in her work. What was there for her to worry about? She knew that Babs would almost certainly come back engaged to the extremely eligible Campolieri. "And she'll sell the New York house, and settle down near them in Rome, and never be in their way . . . she's much too tactful. But she'll have an excellent cook, and just the right people in for bridge and cocktails . . . and a perfectly peaceful old age among her grandchildren."

Mrs. Slade broke off this prophetic flight with a recoil of self-disgust. There was no one of whom she had less right to think unkindly than of Grace Ansley. Would she never cure herself of envying her? Perhaps she had begun too long ago.

She stood up and leaned against the parapet, filling her troubled eyes with the tranquilizing magic of the hour. But instead of tranquilizing her the sight seemed to increase her exasperation. Her gaze turned toward the Colosseum. Already its golden flank was drowned in purple shadow, and above it the sky curved crystal clear, without light or color. It was the moment when afternoon and evening hang balanced in mid-heaven.

Mrs. Slade turned back and laid her hand on her friend's arm. The gesture was so abrupt that Mrs. Ansley looked up, startled.

"The sun's set. You're not afraid, my dear?"

"Afraid—"

"Of Roman fever or pneumonia? I remember how ill you were that winter. As a girl you had a very delicate throat, hadn't you?"

"Oh, we're all right up here. Down below, in the Forum, it does get deathly cold, all of a sudden . . . but not here."

"Ah, of course you know because you had to be so careful." Mrs. Slade turned back to the parapet. She thought: "I must make one more effort not to hate her." Aloud she said: "Whenever I look at the Forum from up here, I remember that story about a great-aunt of yours, wasn't she? A dreadfully wicked great-aunt?"

"Oh, yes; Great-Aunt Harriet. The one who was supposed to have sent her young sister out to the Forum after sunset to gather a night-blooming flower for her album. All our great-aunts and grandmothers used to have albums of dried flowers."

Mrs. Slade nodded. "But she really sent her because they were in love with the same man—"

"Well, that was the family tradition. They said Aunt Harriet confessed it years afterward. At any rate, the poor little sister caught the fever and died. Mother used to frighten us with the story when we were children."

"And you frightened *me* with it, that winter when you and I were here as girls. The winter I was engaged to Delphin."

Mrs. Ansley gave a faint laugh. "Oh, did I? Really frightened you? I don't believe you're easily frightened."

"Not often, but I was then. I was easily frightened because I was too happy. I wonder if you know what that means?"

"I—yes . . ." Mrs. Ansley faltered.

"Well, I suppose that was why the story of your wicked aunt made such an impression on me. And I thought: 'There's no more Roman fever, but the Forum is deathly cold after sunset—especially after a hot day. And the Colosseum's even colder and damper.'"

"The Colosseum—?"

"Yes. It wasn't easy to get in, after the gates were locked for the night. Far from easy. Still, in those days it could be managed; it *was* managed, often. Lovers met there who couldn't meet elsewhere. You knew that?"

"I—I daresay. I don't remember."

"You don't remember? You don't remember going to visit some ruins or other one evening, just after dark, and catching a bad chill? You were supposed to have gone to see the moon rise. People always said that expedition was what caused your illness."

There was a moment's silence; then Mrs. Ansley rejoined: "Did they? It was all so long ago."

"Yes. And you got well again—so it didn't matter. But I suppose it struck your friends—the reason given for your illness, I mean—because everybody knew you were so prudent on account of your throat, and your mother took such care of you . . . You *had* been out late sightseeing, hadn't you, that night?"

"Perhaps I had. The most prudent girls aren't always prudent. What made you think of it now?"

Mrs. Slade seemed to have no answer ready. But after a moment she broke out: "Because I simply can't bear it any longer—!"

Mrs. Ansley lifted her head quickly. Her eyes were wide and very pale. "Can't bear what?"

"Why—your not knowing that I've always known why you went."

"Why I went—?"

"Yes. You think I'm bluffing, don't you? Well, you went to meet the man I was engaged to—and I can repeat every word of the letter that took you there."

While Mrs. Slade spoke Mrs. Ansley had risen unsteadily to her feet. Her bag, her knitting and gloves, slid in a panic-stricken heap to the ground. She looked at Mrs. Slade as though she were looking at a ghost.

"No, no—don't," she faltered out.

"Why not? Listen, if you don't believe me. 'My one darling, things can't go on like this. I must see you alone. Come to the Colosseum immediately after dark tomorrow. There will be somebody to let you in. No one whom you need fear will suspect'—but perhaps you've forgotten what the letter said?"

Mrs. Ansley met the challenge with an unexpected composure. Steadying herself against the chair she looked at her friend, and replied: "No; I know it by heart too."

"And the signature? 'Only *your* D.S.' Was that it? I'm right, am I? That was the letter that took you out that evening after dark?"

Mrs. Ansley was still looking at her. It seemed to Mrs. Slade that a slow struggle was going on behind the voluntarily controlled mask of her small quiet face. "I shouldn't have thought she had herself so well in hand," Mrs. Slade reflected, almost resentfully. But at this moment Mrs. Ansley spoke. "I don't know how you knew. I burnt that letter at once."

"Yes; you would, naturally—you're so prudent!" The sneer was open now. "And if you burnt the letter you're wondering how on earth I know what was in it. That's it, isn't it?"

Mrs. Slade waited, but Mrs. Ansley did not speak.

"Well, my dear, I know what was in that letter because I wrote it!"

"You wrote it?"

"Yes."

The two women stood for a minute staring at each other in the last golden light. Then Mrs. Ansley dropped back into her chair. "Oh," she murmured, and covered her face with her hands.

Mrs. Slade waited nervously for another word or movement. None came, and at length she broke out: "I horrify you."

Mrs. Ansley's hands dropped to her knee. The face they uncovered was streaked with tears. "I wasn't thinking of you. I was thinking—it was the only letter I ever had from him!"

"And I wrote it. Yes, I wrote it! But I was the girl he was engaged to. Did you happen to remember that?"

Mrs. Ansley's head drooped again. "I'm not trying to excuse myself . . . I remembered . . ."

"And still you went?"

"Still I went."

Mrs. Slade stood looking down on the small bowed figure at her side. The flame of her wrath had already sunk, and she wondered why she had ever thought there would be any satisfaction in inflicting so purposeless a wound on her friend. But she had to justify herself.

"You do understand? I'd found out—and I hated you, hated you. I knew you were in love with Delphin—and I was afraid; afraid of you, of your quiet ways, your sweetness . . . your . . . well, I wanted you out of the way, that's all. Just for a few weeks; just till I was sure of him. So in a blind fury I wrote that letter . . . I don't know why I'm telling you now."

"I suppose," said Mrs. Ansley slowly, "it's because you've always gone on hating me."

"Perhaps. Or because I wanted to get the whole thing off my mind." She paused. "I'm glad you destroyed the letter. Of course I never thought you'd die."

Mrs. Ansley relapsed into silence, and Mrs. Slade, leaning above her, was conscious of a strange sense of isolation, of being cut off from the warm current of human communion. "You think me a monster!"

"I don't know . . . It was the only letter I had, and you say he didn't write it?"

"Ah, how you care for him still!"

"I cared for that memory," said Mrs. Ansley.

Mrs. Slade continued to look down on her. She seemed physically reduced by the blow—as if, when she got up, the wind might scatter her like a puff of dust. Mrs. Slade's jealousy suddenly leapt up again at the sight. All these years the woman had been living on that letter. How she must have loved him, to treasure the mere memory of its ashes! The letter of the man her friend was engaged to. Wasn't it she who was the monster?

"You tried your best to get him away from me, didn't you? But you failed, and I kept him. That's all."

"Yes. That's all."

"I wish now I hadn't told you. I'd no idea you'd feel about it as you do; I thought you'd be amused. It all happened so long ago, as you say; and you must do me the justice to remember that I had no reason to think you'd ever taken it seriously. How could I, when you were married to Horace Ansley two months afterward? As soon as you could get out of bed your mother rushed you off to Florence and married you. People were rather surprised—they wondered at its being done so quickly; but I thought I knew. I had an idea you did it out of pique—to be able to say you'd got ahead of Delphin and me. Girls have such silly reasons for doing the most serious things. And your marrying so soon convinced me that you'd never really cared."

"Yes. I suppose it would," Mrs. Ansley assented.

The clear heaven overhead was emptied of all its gold. Dusk spread over it, abruptly darkening the Seven Hills. Here and there lights began to twinkle through the foliage at their feet. Steps were coming and going on the deserted terrace—waiters looking out of the doorway at the head of the stairs, then reappearing with trays and napkins and flasks of wine. Tables were moved, chairs straightened. A feeble string of electric lights flickered out. Some vases of faded flowers were carried away, and brought back replenished. A stout lady in a dust coat suddenly appeared, asking in broken Italian if anyone had seen the elastic band which held together her tattered Baedeker. She poked with her stick under the table at which she had lunched, the waiters assisting.

The corner where Mrs. Slade and Mrs. Ansley sat was still shadowy and deserted. For a long time neither of them spoke. At length Mrs. Slade began again: "I suppose I did it as a sort of joke—"

"A joke?"

"Well, girls are ferocious sometimes, you know. Girls in love especially. And I remember laughing to myself all that evening at the idea that you were waiting around there in the dark, dodging out of sight, listening for every sound, trying to get in—. Of course I was upset when I heard you were so ill afterward."

Mrs. Ansley had not moved for a long time. But now she turned slowly toward her companion. "But I didn't wait. He'd arranged everything. He was there. We were let in at once," she said.

Mrs. Slade sprang up from her leaning position. "Delphin there? They let you in?— Ah, now you're lying!" She burst out with violence.

Mrs. Ansley's voice grew clearer, and full of surprise. "But of course he was there. Naturally he came—"

"Came? How did he know he'd find you there? You must be raving!"

Mrs. Ansley hesitated, as though reflecting. "But I answered the letter. I told him I'd be there. So he came."

Mrs. Slade flung her hands up to her face. "Oh, God— you answered! I never thought of your answering . . ."

"It's odd you never thought of it, if you wrote the letter."

"Yes. I was blind with rage."

Mrs. Ansley rose, and drew her fur scarf about her. "It is cold here. We'd better go . . . I'm sorry for you," she said, as she clasped the fur about her throat.

The unexpected words sent a pang through Mrs. Slade. "Yes, we'd better go." She gathered up her bag and cloak. "I don't know why you should be sorry for me," she muttered.

Mrs. Ansley stood looking away from her toward the dusky secret mass of the Colosseum. "Well—because I didn't have to wait that night."

Mrs. Slade gave an unquiet laugh. "Yes, I was beaten there. But I oughtn't to begrudge it to you, I suppose. At the end of all these years. After all, I had everything; I had him for twenty-five years. And you had nothing but that one letter that he didn't write."

Mrs. Ansley was again silent. At length she turned toward the door of the terrace. She took a step, and turned back, facing her companion.

"I had Barbara," she said, and began to move ahead of Mrs. Slade toward the stairway.

QUESTIONS

1. How does the meaning of the term "Roman fever" change throughout this story?

2. What does Mrs. Ansley mean by the "collective modern idea of Mothers"? (46) Do the two women think that this idea has changed?

3. In what ways are Mrs. Slade's and Mrs. Ansley's impressions of each other distorted as each visualizes the other "through the wrong end of her little telescope"? (50) Are both women subject to equal amounts of distortion?

4. Why does Mrs. Ansley's knitting irritate Mrs. Slade?

5. Why does Mrs. Slade envy Mrs. Ansley, even though Mrs. Slade seems to consider herself the superior woman?

6. Why does Mrs. Slade tell Mrs. Ansley about the counterfeit letter?

7. How has Mrs. Slade's and Mrs. Ansley's mutual deception affected their relationship over the years?

FOR FURTHER REFLECTION

1. What are the values that Mrs. Slade and Mrs. Ansley most prize? Do they live by different moral values?

2. Is this a story of mutual confession or of competitive combat?

3. Does Barbara's liveliness support the idea that Delphin was worth fighting over?

TOBIAS WOLFF

Tobias Wolff (1945–) was born in Birmingham, Alabama; after his
parents divorced when he was ten, he moved with his mother
to Washington State. There he grew up in a household with an
abusive stepfather, an experience related in his best-known work,
This Boy's Life: A Memoir (1989). He served in the Army
from 1964 to 1968, and recounted his time in Vietnam in
the book *In Pharoah's Army: Memories of the Lost War* (1994).
Upon returning, he earned his bachelor's and master's degrees
from Oxford University, and another master's degree from Stanford
University. He has taught literature and creative writing at Syracuse
and Stanford universities for more than thirty years. His works have
earned the PEN/Faulkner Award, several O. Henry awards, and the
Los Angeles Times Book Prize.

Smokers

I noticed Eugene before I actually met him. There was no way not to notice him. As our train was leaving New York, Eugene, moving from another coach into the one where I sat, managed to get himself jammed in the door between his two enormous suitcases. I watched as he struggled to free himself, fascinated by the hat he wore, a green Alpine hat with feathers stuck in the brim. I wondered if he hoped to reduce the absurdity of his situation by grinning as he did in every direction. Finally something gave and he shot into the coach. I hoped he would not take the seat next to me, but he did.

He started to talk almost the moment he sat down, and he didn't stop until we reached Wallingford. Was I going to Choate? What a coincidence—so was he. My first year? His too. Where was I from? Oregon? No shit? Way the hell and gone up in the boondocks, eh? He was from Indiana— Gary, Indiana. I knew the song, didn't I? I did, but he sang it for me anyway, all the way through, including the tricky ending. There were other boys in the coach, and they were staring at us, and I wished he would shut up.

Did I swim? Too bad, it was a good sport, I ought to go out for it. He had set a freestyle record in the Midwestern

63

conference the year before. What was my favorite subject? He liked math, he guessed, but he was pretty good at all of them. He offered me a cigarette, which I refused.

"I oughta quit myself," he said. "Be the death of me yet."

Eugene was a scholarship boy. One of his teachers told him that he was too smart to be going to a regular high school and gave him a list of prep schools. Eugene applied to all of them—"just for the hell of it"—and all of them accepted him. He finally decided on Choate because only Choate had offered him a travel allowance. His father was dead and his mother, a nurse, had three other kids to support, so Eugene didn't think it would be fair to ask her for anything. As the train came into Wallingford he asked me if I would be his roommate.

I didn't jump at the offer. For one thing, I did not like to look at Eugene. His head was too big for his lanky body, and his skin was oily. He put me in mind of a seal. Then there was the matter of his scholarship. I too was a scholarship boy, and I didn't want to finish myself off before I even got started by rooming with another, the way fat girls hung out together back home. I knew the world Eugene came from. I came from that world myself, and I wanted to leave it behind. To this end I had practiced over the summer an air of secret amusement which I considered to be aristocratic, an association encouraged by English movie actors. I had studied the photographs of the boys in the prep school bulletins, and now my hair looked like their hair and my clothes looked like their clothes.

I wanted to know boys whose fathers ran banks and held Cabinet office and wrote books. I wanted to be their friend and go home with them on vacation and someday marry one of their sisters, and Eugene Miller didn't have much of a place in those plans. I told him that I had a friend at Choate with whom I'd probably be rooming.

"That's okay," he said. "Maybe next year."

I assented vaguely, and Eugene returned to the problem he was having deciding whether to go out for baseball or lacrosse. He was better at baseball, but lacrosse was more fun. He figured maybe he owed it to the school to go out for baseball.

As things worked out, our room assignments were already drawn up. My roommate was a Chilean named Jaime who described himself as a Nazi. He had an enormous poster of Adolph Hitler tacked above his desk until a Jewish boy on our hall complained and the dean made him take it down. Jaime kept a copy of *Mein Kampf* beside his bed like a Gideons Bible and was fond of reading aloud from it in a German accent. He enjoyed practical jokes. Our room overlooked the entrance to the headmaster's house and Jaime always whistled at the headmaster's ancient secretary as she went home from work at night. On Alumni Day he sneaked into the kitchen and spiced up the visitors' mock turtle soup with a number of condoms, unrolled and obscenely knotted. The next day at chapel the headmaster stammered out a sermon about the incident, but he referred to it in terms so coy and oblique that nobody knew what he was talking about. Ultimately the matter was dropped without another word. Just before Christmas Jaime's mother was killed in a plane crash, and he left school and never returned. For the rest of the year I roomed alone.

Eugene drew as his roommate Talbot Nevin. Talbot's family had donated the Andrew Nevin Memorial Hockey Rink and the Andrew Nevin Memorial Library to the school, and endowed the Andrew Nevin Memorial Lecture Series. Talbot Nevin's father had driven his car to second place in the Monaco Grand Prix two years earlier, and celebrity magazines often featured a picture of him with someone like Jill St. John and a caption underneath quoting one of them as saying, "We're just good friends." I wanted to know Talbot Nevin.

So one day I visited their room. Eugene met me at the door and pumped my hand. "Well, what do you know," he said. "Tab, this here's a buddy of mine from Oregon. You don't get any farther up in the boondocks than that."

Talbot Nevin sat on the edge of his bed, threading snow-white laces through the eyes of a pair of dirty sneakers. He nodded without raising his head.

"Tab's father won some big race last year," Eugene went on, to my discomfort. I didn't want Talbot to know that I had heard anything about him. I wanted to come to him fresh, with no possibility of his suspecting that I liked him for anything but himself.

"He didn't win. He came in second." Talbot threw down the sneakers and looked up at me for the first time. He had china-blue eyes under lashes and brows so light you could hardly see them. His hair too was shock-white and lank on his forehead. His face had a molded look, like a doll's face, delicate and unhealthy.

"What kind of race?" I asked.

"Grand Prix," he said, taking off his shoes.

"That's a car race," Eugene said.

Not to have heard of the Grand Prix seemed to me evidence of too great ignorance. "I know. I've heard of it."

"The guys down the hall were talking about it and they said he won." Eugene winked at me as he spoke; he winked continuously as if everything he said was part of a ritual joke and he didn't want a tenderfoot like me to take it too seriously.

"Well, I say he came in second and I damn well ought to know." By now Talbot had changed to his tennis shoes. He stood. "Let's go have a weed."

Smoking at Choate was forbidden. "The use of tobacco in any form," said the student handbook, "carries with it the penalty of immediate expulsion." Up to this moment the rule against smoking had not been a problem for me because I did not smoke. Now it was a problem, because I did not want Eugene to have a bond with Talbot that I did not share. So I followed them downstairs to the music room, where the choir practiced. Behind the conductor's platform was a long, narrow closet where the robes were kept. We huddled in the far end of this closet and Talbot passed out cigarettes. The risk was great and the activity silly, and we started to giggle.

"Welcome to Marlboro Country," I said.

"It's what's up front that counts," Talbot answered. We were smoking Marlboros, not Winstons, and the joke was lame, but I guffawed anyway.

"Better keep it down," Eugene whispered. "Big John might hear us."

Big John was the senior dorm master. He wore three-piece suits and soft-soled shoes and had a way of popping up at awkward moments. He liked to grab boys by the neck, pinching the skin between his forefinger and thumb, squeezing until they cried. "Fuck Big John," I said.

Neither Talbot nor Eugene responded. I fretted in the silence as we finished our cigarettes. I had intended to make Eugene look timid. Had I made myself look frivolous instead?

I saw Talbot several times that week and he barely nodded to me. I had been rash, I decided. I had made a bad impression on him. But on Friday night he came up as we were leaving the dining hall and asked me if I wanted to play tennis the next morning. I doubt that I have ever felt such complete self-satisfaction as I felt that night.

Talbot missed our appointment, however, so I dropped by his room. He was still in bed, reading. "What's going on?" he asked, without looking up from his book.

I sat on Eugene's bed and tried not to sound as disappointed as I was. "I thought we might play a little tennis."

"Tennis?" He continued reading silently for a few moments. "I don't know. I don't feel so hot."

"No big deal. I thought you wanted to play. We could just knock a couple of balls around."

"Hell." He lowered the book onto his chest. "What time is it?"

"Nine o'clock."

"The courts'll be full by now."

"There's always a few empty ones behind the science building."

"They're asphalt, aren't they?"

"Cement." I shrugged. I didn't want to seem pushy. "Like I said, no big deal. We can play some other time." I stood and walked toward the door.

"Wait." Talbot yawned without covering his mouth. "What the hell."

As it happened, the courts were full. Talbot and I sat on the grass and I asked him questions I already knew the answers to, like where was he from and where had he gone to school the year before and who did he have for English. At this question he came to life. "English? Parker, the bald one. I got A's all through school and now Parker tells me I can't write. If he's such a goddamned William Shakespeare what's he teaching here for?"

We sat for a time without speaking. "I'm from Oregon," I said finally. "Near Portland." We didn't live close enough to the city to call it near, I suppose, but in those days I naively assumed everyone had heard of Portland.

"Oregon." He pondered this. "Do you hunt?"

"I've been a few times with my father."

"What kind of weapon do you use?"

"Marlin."

"30–30?"

I nodded.

"Good brush gun," he said. "Useless over a hundred yards. Have you ever killed anything?"

"Deer, you mean?"

"Deer, elk, whatever you hunt in Oregon."

"No."

Talbot had killed a lot of animals, and he named them for me: deer, moose, bear, elk, even an alligator. There were more, many more.

"Maybe you can come out West and go hunting with us sometime."

"Where, to Oregon?" Talbot looked away. "Maybe."

I had not expected to be humiliated on the court. My brother, who played tennis for Oregon State, had coached me through four summers. I had a good hot serve and my brother described my net game as "ruthless." Talbot ran me ragged. He played a kind of tennis different from any I had ever seen. He did not sweat, not the way I did anyway, or pant, or swear when he missed a shot, or get that thin quivering smile that tugged my lips whenever I aced my opponents. He seemed hardly to notice me, gave no sign that he was competing except that twice he called shots out that appeared to me to be well short of the line. I might have been mistaken, though. After he won the second set he walked abruptly off the court and went back to where we had left our sweaters. I followed him.

"Good game," I said.

He pulled impatiently at the sleeve of his sweater. "I can't play on these lousy asphalt courts."

Eugene made himself known around school. You did not wear belted jackets at Choate, or white buck shoes. Certainly you did not wear Alpine hats with feathers stuck in the brim. Eugene wore all three.

Anyone who didn't know who Eugene was found out by mid-November. *Life* magazine ran a series of interviews and pictures showing what it was like to be a student at a typical Eastern prep school. They had based their piece on research done at five schools, of which ours was one. Eugene had been interviewed and one of his remarks appeared in bold face beneath a photograph of students bent morosely over their books in evening study hall. The quotation: "One thing, nobody at Choate ever seems to smile. They think you're weird or something if you smile. You get dumped on all the time."

True enough. We were a joyless lot. Laughter was acceptable only in the sentimental parts of the movies we were shown on alternate Saturday nights. The one category in the yearbook to which everyone aspired was "Most Sarcastic." The arena for these trials of wit was the dining room, and Eugene's statements in *Life* did nothing to ease his load there.

However conspicuous Eugene may have been, he was not unpopular. I never heard anything worse about him than that he was "weird." He did well in his studies, and after the swimming team began to practice, the word went around that Eugene promised to put Choate in the running for the championship. So despite his hat and his eagerness and his determined grin, Eugene escaped the fate I had envisioned for him: the other students dumped on him but they didn't cast him out.

The night before school recessed for Christmas I went up to visit Talbot and found Eugene alone in the room, packing his bags. He made me sit down and poured out a glass of Hawaiian Punch which he laced with some murky substance from a prescription bottle. "Tab rustled up some codeine down at the infirmary," he explained. "This'll get the old yule log burning."

The stuff tasted filthy but I took it, as I did all the other things that made the rounds at school and were supposed to get you off but never did, like aspirin and Coke, after-shave lotion, and BenGay stuffed in the nostrils. "Where's Talbot?"

"I don't know. Maybe over at the library." He reached under his bed and pulled out a trunk-sized suitcase, made of cardboard but tricked up to look like leather, and began filling it with an assortment of pastel shirts with tab collars. Tab collars were another of Eugene's flings at sartorial trailblazing at school. They made me think of what my mother always told my sister when she complained at having to wear Mother's castoff clothes: "You never know, you might start a fashion."

"Where are you going for Christmas?" Eugene asked.

"Baltimore."

"Baltimore? What's in Baltimore?"

"My aunt and uncle live there. How about you?"

"I'm heading on up to Boston."

This surprised me. I had assumed he would return to Indiana for the holidays. "Who do you know in Boston?"

"Nobody. Just Tab is all."

"Talbot? You're going to be staying with Talbot?"

"Yeah. And his family, of course."

"For the whole vacation?"

Eugene gave a sly grin and rolled his eyes from side to side and said in a confidential tone, almost a whisper: "Old Tab's got himself an extra key nobody knows about to his daddy's liquor closet. We aim to do some very big drinking. And I mean very big."

I went to the door. "If I don't see you in the morning, have a Merry Christmas."

"You bet, buddy. Same to you." Eugene grabbed my right hand in both of his. His fingers were soft and damp. "Take it easy on those Baltimore girls. Don't do anything I wouldn't do."

Jaime had been called home the week before by his mother's death. His bed was stripped, the mattress doubled over. All the pictures in the room had gone with him, and the yellow walls glared blankly. I turned out the lights and sat on my bed until the bell rang for dinner.

I had never met my aunt or uncle before. They picked me up at the station in Baltimore with their four children, three girls and a boy. I disliked all of them immediately. During the drive home my aunt asked me if my poor father had ever learned to cope with my mother's moods. One of the girls, Pammy, fell asleep on my lap and drooled on me.

They lived in Sherwood Park, a brick suburb several miles outside the city. My aunt and uncle went out almost every night and left me in charge of the children. This meant turning the television set on and turning it off when they had all passed out in front of it. Putting them to bed any earlier wasn't in the cards. They held on to everything—carpets, electrical cords, the legs of tables and chairs—and when that failed tried to injure themselves by scratching and gouging at their own faces.

One night I broke down. I cried for almost an hour and tried to call Talbot to ask him if I could come up to Boston and stay with him. The Nevins's number was unlisted, however, and after I washed my face and considered the idea again, I thought better of it.

When I returned to school my aunt and uncle wrote my father a letter which he sent on to me. They said that I was selfish and unenterprising. They had welcomed me as a son. They had opened their hearts to me, but I had taken no interest in them or in their children, my cousins, who worshipped the very ground I walked on. They cited an incident when I was in the kitchen reading and the wind blew all my aunt's laundry off the line and I hadn't so much as *asked* if I could help. I just sat there and went right on reading and eating peanuts. Finally, my uncle was missing a set of cuff links that had great sentimental value for him. All things considered, they didn't think my coming to Baltimore had worked out very well. They thought that on future vacations I would be happier somewhere else.

I wrote back to my father, denying all charges and making a few of my own.

After Christmas Talbot and I were often together. Both of us had gone out for basketball, and as neither of us was any good to the team—Talbot because of an ankle injury, me because I couldn't make the ball go through the basket—we sat together on the bench most of the time. He told me Eugene had spoiled his stepmother's Christmas by leaning back in an antique chair and breaking it. Thereafter I thought of Mrs. Nevin as a friend; but I had barely a month to enjoy the alliance because in late January Talbot told me that his father and stepmother had separated.

Eugene was taken up with swimming, and I saw him rarely. Talbot and I had most of our friends among the malcontents in the school: those, like Talbot, to whom every rule gave offense; those who missed their girlfriends or their cars; and those, like me, who knew that something was wrong but didn't know what it was.

Because I was not rich my dissatisfaction could not assume a really combative form. I paddled around on the surface, dabbling in revolt by way of the stories I wrote for *off the record*, the school literary journal. My stories took place at "The Hoatch School" and concerned a student from the West whom I referred to simply as "the boy."

The boy's father came from a distinguished New York family. In his early twenties, he had traveled to Oregon to oversee his family's vast lumber holdings. His family turned on him when he married a beautiful young woman who happened to be part Indian. The Indian blood was noble, but the boy's father was disowned anyway.

The boy's parents prospered in spite of this and raised a large, gifted family. The boy was the most gifted of all, and his father sent him back East to Hoatch, the traditional family school. What he found there saddened him: among the students a preoccupation with money and social position, and among the masters hypocrisy and pettiness. The boy's only friends were a beautiful young dancer who worked as a waitress in a café near the school, and an old tramp. The dancer and tramp were referred to as "the girl" and "the tramp." The boy and girl were forever getting the tramp out of trouble for doing things like painting garbage cans beautiful colors.

I doubt that Talbot ever read my stories—he never mentioned them if he did—but somehow he got the idea I was a writer. One night he came to my room and dropped a notebook on my desk and asked me to read the essay inside. It was on the topic "Why Is Literature Worth Studying?" and it sprawled over four pages, concluding as follows:

I think Literature is worth studying but only in a way. The people of our Country should know how intelligent the people of past history were. They should appreciate what gifts these people had to write such great works of Literature. This is why I think Literature is worth studying.

Talbot had received an F on the essay.

"Parker says he's going to put me in summer school if I flunk again this marking period," Talbot said, lighting a cigarette.

"I didn't know you flunked last time." I stared helplessly at the cigarette. "Maybe you shouldn't smoke. Big John might smell it. "

"I saw Big John going into the library on my way over here." Talbot went to the mirror and examined his profile from the corner of his eye. "I thought maybe you could help me out."

"How?"

"Maybe give me a few ideas. You ought to see the topics he gives us. Like this one." He took some folded papers from his back pocket. "'Describe the most interesting person you know.'" He swore and threw the papers down.

I picked them up. "What's this? Your outline?"

"More like a rough draft, I guess you'd call it."

I read the essay. The writing was awful, but what really shocked me was the absolute lack of interest with which he described the most interesting person he had ever known. This person turned out to be his English teacher from the year before, whose chief virtue seemed to be that he gave a lot of reading periods and didn't expect his students to be William Shakespeare and write him a novel every week.

"I don't think Parker is going to like this very much," I said.

"Why? What's wrong with it?"

"He might get the idea you're trying to criticize him."

"That's his problem."

I folded up the essay and handed it back to Talbot with his notebook.

"You really think he'll give me an F on it?"

"He might."

Talbot crumpled the essay. "Hell."

"When is it due?"

"Tomorrow."

"*Tomorrow*?"

"I'd have come over before this but I've been busy."

We spent the next hour or so talking about other interesting people he had known. There weren't many of them, and the only one who really interested me was a maid named Tina who used to masturbate Talbot when she tucked him in at night and was later arrested for trying to burn the Nevins's house down. Talbot couldn't remember anything about her though, not even her last name. We finally abandoned what promise Tina held of suggesting an essay.

What eventually happened was that I got up at four-thirty next morning and invented a fictional interesting person for Talbot. This person's name was Miles and he was supposed to have been one of Talbot's uncles.

I gave the essay to Talbot outside the dining hall. He read it without expression. "I don't have any Uncle Miles," he said. "I don't have any uncles at all. Just aunts."

"Parker doesn't know that."

"But it was supposed to be about someone interesting." He was frowning at the essay. "I don't see what's so interesting about this guy."

"If you don't want to use it I will."

"That's okay. I'll use it."

I wrote three more essays for Talbot in the following weeks: "Who Is Worse—Macbeth or Lady Macbeth?"; "Is There a God?"; and "Describe a Fountain Pen to a Person Who Has Never Seen One." Mr. Parker read the last essay aloud to Talbot's class as an example of clear expository writing and put a note on the back of the essay saying how pleased he was to see Talbot getting down to work.

In late February the dean put a notice on the bulletin board: those students who wished to room together the following year had to submit their names to him by Friday. There was no time to waste. I went immediately to Talbot's dorm.

Eugene was alone in the room, stuffing dirty clothes into a canvas bag. He came toward me, winking and grinning and snorting. "Hey there, buddy, how they hangin'? Side-by-side for comfort or back-to-back for speed?"

We had sat across from each other at breakfast, lunch, and dinner every day now for three weeks, and each time we met he behaved as if we were brothers torn by Arabs from each other's arms and just now reunited after twenty years.

"Where's Talbot?" I asked.

"He had a phone call. Be back pretty soon."

"Aren't you supposed to be at swimming practice?"

"Not today." He smirked mysteriously.

"Why not?"

"I broke the conference butterfly record yesterday. Against Kent."

"That's great. Congratulations."

"And butterfly isn't even my best stroke. Hey, good thing you came over. I was just about to go see you."

"What about?"

"I was wondering who you were planning on rooming with next year."

"Oh, well, you know, I sort of promised this other guy."

Eugene nodded, still smiling. "Fair enough. I already had someone ask me. I just thought I'd check with you first. Since we didn't have a chance to room together this year." He stood and resumed stuffing the pile of clothes in his bag. "Is it three o'clock yet?"

"Quarter to."

"I guess I better get these duds over to the cleaners before they close. See you later, buddy."

Talbot came back to the room a few minutes afterwards. "Where's Eugene?"

"He was taking some clothes to the cleaners."

"Oh." Talbot drew a cigarette from the pack he kept hidden under the washstand and lit it. "Here," he said, passing it to me.

"Just a drag." I puffed at it and handed it back. I decided to come to the point. "Who are you rooming with next year?"

"Eugene."

"*Eugene?*"

"He has to check with somebody else first but he thinks it'll be all right." Talbot picked up his squash racket and hefted it. "How about you?"

"I don't know. I kind of like rooming alone."

"More privacy," said Talbot, swinging the racket in a broad backhand.

"That's right. More privacy."

"Maybe that South American guy will come back."

"I doubt it."

"You never know. His old man might get better."

"It's his mother. And she's dead."

"Oh." Talbot kept swinging the racket, forehand now.

"By the way, there's something I meant to tell you."

"What's that?"

"I'm not going to be able to help you with those essays any more."

He shrugged. "Okay."

"I've got enough work of my own to do. I can't do my work and yours too."

"I said okay. Parker can't flunk me now anyway. I've got a C+ average. "

"I just thought I'd tell you."

"So you told me." Talbot finished the cigarette and stashed the butt in a tin soap dish. "We'd better go. We're gonna be late for basketball."

"I'm not going to basketball."

"Why not?"

"Because I don't feel like going to basketball, that's why not."

We left the building together and split up at the bottom of the steps without exchanging another word. I went down to the infirmary to get an excuse for not going to basketball. The doctor was out and I had to wait for an hour until he came back and gave me some pills and Kaopectate. When I got back to my room the dorm was in an uproar.

I heard the story from the boys in the room next to mine. Big John had caught Eugene smoking. He had come into Eugene's room and found him there alone and smelled cigarette smoke. Eugene had denied it but Big John tore the room apart and found cigarettes and butts all over the place. Eugene was over at the headmaster's house at this moment.

They told me the story in a mournful way, as though they were really broken up about it, but I could see how excited they were. It was always like that when someone got kicked out of school.

I went to my room and pulled a chair over to the window. Just before the bell rang for dinner a taxi came up the drive. Big John walked out of the dorm with two enormous cardboard suitcases and helped the driver put them in the trunk. He gave the driver some money and said something to him and the driver nodded and got back into the cab. Then the headmaster and the dean came out of the house with Eugene behind them. Eugene was wearing his hat. He shook hands with both of them and then with Big John. Suddenly he bent over and put his hands up to his face. The dean reached out and touched his arm. They stood like that for a long time, the four of them, Eugene's shoulders bucking and heaving. I couldn't watch it. I went to the mirror and combed my hair until I heard the door of the taxi bang shut. When I looked out the window again the cab was gone. The headmaster and the dean were standing in the shadows, but I could see Big John clearly. He was rocking back on his heels and talking, hands on his hips, and something he said made the headmaster laugh; not really a laugh, more like a giggle. The only thing I heard was the word "feathers." I figured they must be talking about Eugene's hat. Then the bell rang and the three of them went into the dining hall.

The next day I walked by the dean's office and almost went in and told him everything. The problem was, if I told the dean about Talbot he would find out about me, too. The rules didn't set forth different punishments according to the amount of smoke consumed. I even considered sending the dean an anonymous note, but I doubted if it would get much attention. They were big on doing the gentlemanly thing at Choate.

On Friday Talbot came up to me at basketball practice and asked if I wanted to room with him next year.

"I'll think about it," I told him.

"The names have to be in by dinnertime tonight."

"I said I'll think about it."

That evening Talbot submitted our names to the dean. There hadn't really been that much to think about. For all I know, Eugene *had* been smoking when Big John came into the room. If you wanted to get technical about it, he was guilty as charged a hundred times over. It wasn't as if some great injustice had been done.

QUESTIONS

1. How much do academic and athletic performance matter at Choate?

2. What do we learn about the narrator from his visit with his relatives in suburban Baltimore?

3. Why does the narrator say he "knew that something was wrong but didn't know what it was"? (73)

4. Why does "the boy" in the narrator's stories so quickly identify his fellow students' problem as one of "preoccupation with money and social position"? (73)

5. In the narrator's stories, why does "the boy" work with the dancer at "forever getting the tramp out of trouble"? (73)

6. What does the narrator mean when he says, "They were big on doing the gentlemanly thing at Choate"? (79)

7. Does the narrator recognize Eugene's integrity?

FOR FURTHER REFLECTION

1. Is the narrator driven more by envy or by shame?

2. Does this story serve as an indictment of the narrator's moral failure? Of the collective moral atmosphere of Choate?

3. Is Eugene responsible for his own cluelessness about how the Choate system works?

Anger

RUDYARD KIPLING

Rudyard Kipling (1865–1936) was born in Bombay (now Mumbai), India, and educated at English boarding schools. He returned to India when he was sixteen, taking a job as assistant editor of the *Civil and Military Gazette* newspaper in Lahore. There he began writing and publishing short stories, and his early collection *Plain Tales from the Hills* (1888) was praised in both India and Great Britain. Kipling, who would be nicknamed "the poet of Empire," received the Nobel Prize in Literature in 1907. Some of his notable works are the story "The Man Who Would Be King" (1888) and the novel *Kim* (1901). "Mary Postgate" was published in the September 1915 issue of *Century* magazine; later that same month, Kipling's eighteen-year-old son, John, was killed in the Battle of Loos.

Mary Postgate

O f Miss Mary Postgate, Lady McCausland wrote that she was "thoroughly conscientious, tidy, companionable, and ladylike. I am very sorry to part with her, and shall always be interested in her welfare."

Miss Fowler engaged her on this recommendation, and to her surprise, for she had had experience of companions, found that it was true. Miss Fowler was nearer sixty than fifty at the time, but though she needed care she did not exhaust her attendant's vitality. On the contrary, she gave out, stimulatingly and with reminiscences. Her father had been a minor Court official in the days when the Great Exhibition of 1851 had just set its seal on Civilisation made perfect. Some of Miss Fowler's tales, nonetheless, were not always for the young. Mary was not young, and though her speech was as colourless as her eyes or her hair, she was never shocked. She listened unflinchingly to every one; said at the end, "How interesting!" or "How shocking!" as the case might be, and never again referred to it, for she prided herself on a trained mind, which "did not dwell on these things." She was, too, a treasure at domestic accounts, for which the village tradesmen, with their weekly books, loved her not. Otherwise she had no enemies; provoked no jealousy even among the plainest; neither gossip nor slander had ever been traced to her; she supplied the odd place at the Rector's or the Doctor's table at half an hour's notice; she was a sort of public aunt to very many small children of the village street, whose parents, while accepting everything, would have been swift to resent what they called "patronage"; she served on the Village Nursing Committee as Miss Fowler's nominee when Miss Fowler was crippled by rheumatoid arthritis, and came out of six months' fortnightly meetings equally respected by all the cliques.

And when Fate threw Miss Fowler's nephew, an unlovely orphan of eleven, on Miss Fowler's hands, Mary Postgate stood to her share of the business of education as practised in private and public schools. She checked printed clothes lists, and unitemised bills of extras; wrote to Head and House masters, matrons, nurses, and doctors, and grieved or rejoiced over half-term reports. Young Wyndham Fowler repaid her in his holidays by calling her "Gatepost," "Postey," or "Packthread," by thumping her between her narrow shoulders, or by chasing her bleating, round the garden, her large mouth open, her large nose high in air, at a stiff-necked shamble very like a camel's. Later on he filled the house with clamour, argument, and harangues as to his personal needs, likes and dislikes, and the limitations of "you women," reducing Mary to tears of physical fatigue, or, when he chose to be humorous, of helpless laughter. At crises, which multiplied as he grew older, she was his ambassadress and his interpretress to Miss Fowler, who had no large sympathy with the young; a vote in his interest at the councils on his future; his sewing woman, strictly accountable for mislaid boots and garments; always his butt and his slave.

And when he decided to become a solicitor, and had entered an office in London; when his greeting had changed from "Hullo, Postey, you old beast," to "Mornin', Packthread," there came a war which, unlike all wars that Mary could remember, did not stay decently outside England and in the newspapers, but intruded on the lives of people whom she knew. As she said to Miss Fowler, it was "most vexatious." It took the Rector's son who was going into business with his elder brother; it took the Colonel's nephew on the eve of fruit farming in Canada; it took Mrs. Grant's son who, his mother said, was devoted to the ministry; and, very early indeed, it took Wynn Fowler, who announced on a postcard that he had joined the Flying Corps and wanted a cardigan waistcoat.

"He must go, and he must have the waistcoat," said Miss Fowler. So Mary got the proper-sized needles and wool, while Miss Fowler told the men of her establishment—two gardeners and an odd man, aged sixty—that those who could join the Army had better do so. The gardeners left. Cheape, the odd man, stayed on, and was promoted to the gardener's cottage. The cook, scorning to be limited in luxuries, also left, after a spirited scene with Miss Fowler, and took the housemaid with her. Miss Fowler gazetted Nellie, Cheape's seventeen-year-old daughter, to the vacant post; Mrs. Cheape to the rank of cook, with occasional cleaning bouts; and the reduced establishment moved forward smoothly.

Wynn demanded an increase in his allowance. Miss Fowler, who always looked facts in the face, said, "He must have it. The chances are he won't live long to draw it, and if three hundred makes him happy—"

Wynn was grateful, and came over, in his tight-buttoned uniform, to say so. His training centre was not thirty miles away, and his talk was so technical that it had to be explained by charts of the various types of machines. He gave Mary such a chart.

"And you'd better study it, Postey," he said. "You'll be seeing a lot of 'em soon." So Mary studied the chart, but when Wynn next arrived to swell and exalt himself before his womenfolk, she failed badly in cross-examination, and he rated her as in the old days.

"You *look* more or less like a human being," he said in his new Service voice. "You *must* have had a brain at some time in your past. What have you done with it? Where d'you keep it? A sheep would know more than you do, Postey. You're lamentable. You are less use than an empty tin can, you dowey old cassowary."

"I suppose that's how your superior officer talks to *you*?" said Miss Fowler from her chair.

"But Postey doesn't mind," Wynn replied. "Do you, Packthread?"

"Why? Was Wynn saying anything? I shall get this right next time you come," she muttered, and knitted her pale brows again over the diagrams of Taubes, Farmans, and Zeppelins.

In a few weeks the mere land and sea battles which she read to Miss Fowler after breakfast passed her like idle breath. Her heart and her interest were high in the air with Wynn, who had finished "rolling" (whatever that might be) and had gone on from a "taxi" to a machine more or less his own. One morning it circled over their very chimneys, alighted on Vegg's Heath, almost outside the garden gate, and Wynn came in, blue with cold, shouting for food. He and she drew Miss Fowler's bath chair, as they had often done, along the Heath footpath to look at the biplane. Mary observed that "it smelt very badly."

"Postey, I believe you think with your nose," said Wynn. "I know you don't with your mind. Now what type's that?"

"I'll go and get the chart," said Mary.

"You're hopeless! You haven't the mental capacity of a white mouse," he cried, and explained the dials and the sockets for bomb-dropping till it was time to mount and ride the wet clouds once more.

"Ah!" said Mary, as the stinking thing flared upward. "Wait till our Flying Corps gets to work! Wynn says it's much safer than in the trenches."

"I wonder," said Miss Fowler. "Tell Cheape to come and tow me home again."

"It's all downhill. I can do it," said Mary, "if you put the brake on." She laid her lean self against the pushing-bar and home they trundled.

"Now, be careful you aren't heated and catch a chill," said overdressed Miss Fowler.

"Nothing makes me perspire," said Mary. As she bumped the chair under the porch she straightened her long back. The exertion had given her a colour, and the wind had loosened a wisp of hair across her forehead. Miss Fowler glanced at her.

"What do you ever think of, Mary?" she demanded suddenly.

"Oh, Wynn says he wants another three pairs of stockings—as thick as we can make them."

"Yes. But I mean the things that women think about. Here you are, more than forty—"

"Forty-four," said truthful Mary.

"Well?"

"Well?" Mary offered Miss Fowler her shoulder as usual.

"And you've been with me ten years now."

"Let's see," said Mary. "Wynn was eleven when he came. He's twenty now, and I came two years before that. It must be eleven."

"Eleven! And you've never told me anything that matters in all that while. Looking back, it seems to me that *I've* done all the talking."

"I'm afraid I'm not much of a conversationalist. As Wynn says, I haven't the mind. Let me take your hat."

Miss Fowler, moving stiffly from the hip, stamped her rubber-tipped stick on the tiled hall floor. "Mary, aren't you *anything* except a companion? Would you *ever* have been anything except a companion?"

Mary hung up the garden hat on its proper peg. "No," she said after consideration. "I don't imagine I ever should. But I've no imagination, I'm afraid."

She fetched Miss Fowler her eleven o'clock glass of Contrexéville.

That was the wet December when it rained six inches to the month, and the women went abroad as little as might be. Wynn's flying chariot visited them several times, and for two mornings (he had warned her by postcard) Mary heard the thresh of his propellers at dawn. The second time she ran to the window, and stared at the whitening sky. A little blur passed overhead. She lifted her lean arms towards it.

That evening at six o'clock there came an announcement in an official envelope that Second Lieutenant W. Fowler had been killed during a trial flight. Death was instantaneous. She read it and carried it to Miss Fowler.

"I never expected anything else," said Miss Fowler; "but I'm sorry it happened before he had done anything."

The room was whirling round Mary Postgate, but she found herself quite steady in the midst of it.

"Yes," she said. "It's a great pity he didn't die in action after he had killed somebody."

"He was killed instantly. That's one comfort," Miss Fowler went on.

"But Wynn says the shock of a fall kills a man at once— whatever happens to the tanks," quoted Mary.

The room was coming to rest now. She heard Miss Fowler say impatiently, "But why can't we cry, Mary?" and herself replying, "There's nothing to cry for. He has done his duty as much as Mrs. Grant's son did."

"And when he died, *she* came and cried all the morning," said Miss Fowler. "'This only makes me feel tired—terribly tired. Will you help me to bed, please, Mary?—And I think I'd like the hot-water bottle."

So Mary helped her and sat beside, talking of Wynn in his riotous youth.

"I believe," said Miss Fowler suddenly, "that old people and young people slip from under a stroke like this. The middle-aged feel it most."

"I expect that's true," said Mary, rising. "I'm going to put away the things in his room now. Shall we wear mourning?"

"Certainly not," said Miss Fowler. "Except, of course, at the funeral. I can't go. You will. I want you to arrange about his being buried here. What a blessing it didn't happen at Salisbury!"

Everyone, from the authorities of the Flying Corps to the Rector, was most kind and sympathetic. Mary found herself for the moment in a world where bodies were in the habit of being despatched by all sorts of conveyances to all sorts of places. And at the funeral two young men in buttoned-up uniforms stood beside the grave and spoke to her afterwards.

"You're Miss Postgate, aren't you?" said one. "Fowler told me about you. He was a good chap—a first-class fellow—a great loss."

"Great loss!" growled his companion. "We're all awfully sorry."

"How high did he fall from?" Mary whispered.

"Pretty nearly four thousand feet, I should think, didn't he? You were up that day, Monkey?"

"All of that," the other child replied. "My bar made three thousand, and I wasn't as high as him by a lot."

"Then *that's* all right," said Mary. "Thank you very much."

They moved away as Mrs. Grant flung herself weeping on Mary's flat chest, under the lych-gate, and cried, "*I* know how it feels! *I* know how it feels!"

"But both his parents are dead," Mary returned, as she fended her off. "Perhaps they've all met by now," she added vaguely as she escaped towards the coach.

"I've thought of that too," wailed Mrs. Grant; "but then he'll be practically a stranger to them. Quite embarrassing!"

Mary faithfully reported every detail of the ceremony to Miss Fowler, who, when she described Mrs. Grant's outburst, laughed aloud.

"Oh, how Wynn would have enjoyed it! He was always utterly unreliable at funerals. D'you remember—" And they talked of him again, each piecing out the other's gaps. "And now," said Miss Fowler, "we'll pull up the blinds and we'll have a general tidy. That always does us good. Have you seen to Wynn's things?"

"Everything—since he first came," said Mary. "He was never destructive—even with his toys."

They faced that neat room.

"It can't be natural not to cry," Mary said at last. "I'm *so* afraid you'll have a reaction."

"As I told you, we old people slip from under the stroke. It's you I'm afraid for. Have you cried yet?"

"I can't. It only makes me angry with the Germans."

"That's sheer waste of vitality," said Miss Fowler. "We must live till the war's finished." She opened a full wardrobe. "Now, I've been thinking things over. This is my plan. All his civilian clothes can be given away—Belgian refugees, and so on."

Mary nodded. "Boots, collars, and gloves?"

"Yes. We don't need to keep anything except his cap and belt."

"They came back yesterday with his Flying Corps clothes"—Mary pointed to a roll on the little iron bed.

"Ah, but keep his Service things. Someone may be glad of them later. Do you remember his sizes?"

"Five feet eight and a half; thirty-six inches round the chest. But he told me he's just put on an inch and a half. I'll mark it on a label and tie it on his sleeping bag."

"So that disposes of *that*," said Miss Fowler, tapping the palm of one hand with the ringed third finger of the other. "What waste it all is! We'll get his old school trunk tomorrow and pack his civilian clothes."

"And the rest?" said Mary. "His books and pictures and the games and the toys—and—and the rest?"

"My plan is to burn every single thing," said Miss Fowler. "Then we shall know where they are and no one can handle them afterwards. What do you think?"

"I think that would be much the best," said Mary. "But there's such a lot of them."

"We'll burn them in the destructor," said Miss Fowler.

This was an open-air furnace for the consumption of refuse; a little circular four-foot tower of pierced brick over an iron grating. Miss Fowler had noticed the design in a gardening journal years ago, and had had it built at the bottom

of the garden. It suited her tidy soul, for it saved unsightly
rubbish heaps, and the ashes lightened the stiff clay soil.

Mary considered for a moment, saw her way clear, and
nodded again. They spent the evening putting away well-
remembered civilian suits, underclothes that Mary had
marked, and the regiments of very gaudy socks and ties. A
second trunk was needed, and, after that, a little packing
case, and it was late next day when Cheape and the local
carrier lifted them to the cart. The Rector luckily knew of
a friend's son, about five feet eight and a half inches high,
to whom a complete Flying Corps outfit would be most
acceptable, and sent his gardener's son down with a barrow
to take delivery of it. The cap was hung up in Miss Fowler's
bedroom, the belt in Miss Postgate's; for, as Miss Fowler
said, they had no desire to make tea-party talk of them.

"That disposes of *that*," said Miss Fowler. "I'll leave
the rest to you, Mary. I can't run up and down the garden.
You'd better take the big clothes basket and get Nellie to
help you."

"I shall take the wheelbarrow and do it myself," said
Mary, and for once in her life closed her mouth.

Miss Fowler, in moments of irritation, had called Mary
deadly methodical. She put on her oldest waterproof and
gardening hat and her ever-slipping goloshes, for the
weather was on the edge of more rain. She gathered fire-
lighters from the kitchen, a half-scuttle of coals, and a faggot
of brushwood. These she wheeled in the barrow down the
mossed paths to the dank little laurel shrubbery where the
destructor stood under the drip of three oaks. She climbed
the wire fence into the Rector's glebe just behind, and from
his tenant's rick pulled two large armfuls of good hay, which
she spread neatly on the fire-bars. Next, journey by journey, passing Miss Fowler's white face at the morning-room
window each time, she brought down in the towel-covered
clothes basket, on the wheelbarrow, thumbed and used
Hentys, Marryats, Levers, Stevensons, Baroness Orczy's,
Garvices, schoolbooks, and atlases, unrelated piles of the

Motor Cyclist, the *Light Car*, and catalogues of Olympia Exhibitions; the remnants of a fleet of sailing ships from ninepenny cutters to a three-guinea yacht; a prep-school dressing gown; bats from three-and-sixpence to twenty-four shillings; cricket and tennis balls; disintegrated steam and clockwork locomotives with their twisted rails; a grey and red tin model of a submarine; a dumb gramophone and cracked records; golf clubs that had to be broken across the knee, like his walking sticks, and an assegai; photographs of private and public school cricket and football elevens, and his O.T.C. on the line of march; kodaks, and film rolls; some pewters, and one real silver cup, for boxing competitions and Junior Hurdles; sheaves of school photographs; Miss Fowler's photograph; her own which he had borne off in fun and (good care she took not to ask!) had never returned; a playbox with a secret drawer; a load of flannels, belts, and jerseys, and a pair of spiked shoes unearthed in the attic; a packet of all the letters that Miss Fowler and she had ever written to him, kept for some absurd reason through all these years; a five-day attempt at a diary; framed pictures of racing motors in full Brooklands career, and load upon load of undistinguishable wreckage of toolboxes, rabbit hutches, electric batteries, tin soldiers, fret-saw outfits, and jigsaw puzzles.

Miss Fowler at the window watched her come and go, and said to herself, "Mary's an old woman. I never realised it before."

After lunch she recommended her to rest.

"I'm not in the least tired," said Mary. "I've got it all arranged. I'm going to the village at two o'clock for some paraffin. Nellie hasn't enough, and the walk will do me good."

She made one last quest round the house before she started, and found that she had overlooked nothing. It began to mist as soon as she had skirted Vegg's Heath, where Wynn used to descend—it seemed to her that she could almost hear the beat of his propellers overhead, but there was nothing to see. She hoisted her umbrella and lunged into the blind wet till she had reached the shelter of the empty village. As she came out of Mr. Kidd's shop with a bottle full of paraffin in her string shopping bag, she met Nurse Eden, the village nurse, and fell into talk with her, as usual, about the village children. They were just parting opposite the "Royal Oak," when a gun, they fancied, was fired immediately behind the house. It was followed by a child's shriek dying into a wail.

"Accident!" said Nurse Eden promptly, and dashed through the empty bar, followed by Mary. They found Mrs. Gerritt, the publican's wife, who could only gasp and point to the yard, where a little cart-lodge was sliding sideways amid a clatter of tiles. Nurse Eden snatched up a sheet drying before the fire, ran out, lifted something from the ground, and flung the sheet round it. The sheet turned scarlet and half her uniform too, as she bore the load into the kitchen. It was little Edna Gerritt, aged nine, whom Mary had known since her perambulator days.

"Am I hurted bad?" Edna asked, and died between Nurse Eden's dripping hands. The sheet fell aside and for an instant, before she could shut her eyes, Mary saw the ripped and shredded body.

"It's a wonder she spoke at all," said Nurse Eden. "What in God's name was it?"

"A bomb," said Mary.

"One o' the Zeppelins?"

"No. An aeroplane. I thought I heard it on the Heath, but I fancied it was one of ours. It must have shut off its engines as it came down. That's why we didn't notice it."

"The filthy pigs!" said Nurse Eden, all white and shaken. "See the pickle I'm in! Go and tell Dr. Hennis, Miss Postgate." Nurse looked at the mother, who had dropped face down on the floor. "She's only in a fit. Turn her over."

Mary heaved Mrs. Gerritt right-side up, and hurried off for the doctor. When she told her tale, he asked her to sit down in the surgery till he got her something.

"But I don't need it, I assure you," said she. "I don't think it would be wise to tell Miss Fowler about it, do you? Her heart is so irritable in this weather."

Dr. Hennis looked at her admiringly as he packed up his bag.

"No. Don't tell anybody till we're sure," he said, and hastened to the "Royal Oak," while Mary went on with the paraffin. The village behind her was as quiet as usual, for the news had not yet spread. She frowned a little to herself, her large nostrils expanded uglily, and from time to time she muttered a phrase which Wynn, who never restrained himself before his womenfolk, had applied to the enemy. "Bloody pagans! They *are* bloody pagans. But," she continued, falling back on the teaching that had made her what she was, "one mustn't let one's mind dwell on these things."

Before she reached the house Dr. Hennis, who was also a special constable, overtook her in his car.

"Oh, Miss Postgate," he said, "I wanted to tell you that that accident at the 'Royal Oak' was due to Gerritt's stable tumbling down. It's been dangerous for a long time. It ought to have been condemned. "

"I thought I heard an explosion too," said Mary.

"You might have been misled by the beams snapping. I've been looking at 'em. They were dry-rotted through and through. Of course, as they broke, they would make a noise just like a gun."

"Yes?" said Mary politely.

"Poor little Edna was playing underneath it," he went on, still holding her with his eyes, "and that and the tiles cut her to pieces, you see?"

"I saw it," said Mary, shaking her head. "I heard it too."

"Well, we cannot be sure." Dr. Hennis changed his tone completely. "I know both you and Nurse Eden (I've been speaking to her) are perfectly trustworthy, and I can rely on you not to say anything—yet at least. It is no good to stir up people unless—"

"Oh, I never do—anyhow," said Mary, and Dr. Hennis went on to the county town.

After all, she told herself, it might, just possibly, have been the collapse of the old stable that had done all those things to poor little Edna. She was sorry she had even hinted at other things, but Nurse Eden was discretion itself. By the time she reached home the affair seemed increasingly remote by its very monstrosity. As she came in, Miss Fowler told her that a couple of aeroplanes had passed half an hour ago.

"I thought I heard them," she replied. "I'm going down to the garden now. I've got the paraffin."

"Yes, but—what *have* you got on your boots'? They're soaking wet. Change them at once."

Not only did Mary obey but she wrapped the boots in a newspaper, and put them into the string bag with the bottle. So, armed with the longest kitchen poker, she left.

"It's raining again," was Miss Fowler's last word, "but—I know you won't be happy till that's disposed of."

"It won't take long. I've got everything down there, and I've put the lid on the destructor to keep the wet out."

The shrubbery was filling with twilight by the time she had completed her arrangements and sprinkled the sacrificial oil. As she lit the match that would burn her heart to ashes, she heard a groan or a grunt behind the dense Portugal laurels.

"Cheape?" she called impatiently, but Cheape, with his ancient lumbago, in his comfortable cottage would be the last man to profane the sanctuary. "Sheep," she concluded, and threw in the fusee. The pyre went up in a roar, and the immediate flame hastened night around her.

"How Wynn would have loved this!" she thought, stepping back from the blaze.

By its light she saw, half-hidden behind a laurel not five paces away, a bareheaded man sitting very stiffly at the foot of one of the oaks. A broken branch lay across his lap—one booted leg protruding from beneath it. His head moved ceaselessly from side to side, but his body was as still as the tree's trunk. He was dressed—she moved sideways to look more closely—in a uniform something like Wynn's, with a flap buttoned across the chest. For an instant, she had some idea that it might be one of the young flying men she had met at the funeral. But their heads were dark and glossy. This man's was as pale as a baby's, and so closely cropped that she could see the disgusting pinky skin beneath. His lips moved.

"What do you say?" Mary moved towards him and stooped.

"Laty! Laty! Laty!" he muttered, while his hands picked at the dead wet leaves. There was no doubt as to his nationality. It made her so angry that she strode back to the destructor, though it was still too hot to use the poker there. Wynn's books seemed to be catching well. She looked up at the oak behind the man; several of the light upper and two or three rotten lower branches had broken and scattered their rubbish on the shrubbery path. On the lowest fork a helmet with dependent strings showed like a bird's nest in the light of a long-tongued flame. Evidently this person had fallen through the tree. Wynn had told her that it was quite possible for people to fall out of aeroplanes. Wynn told her too, that trees were useful things to break an aviator's fall, but in this case the aviator must have been broken or he would have moved from his queer position. He seemed helpless except for his horrible rolling head. On the other hand, she could see a pistol case at his belt—and Mary loathed pistols. Months ago, after reading certain Belgian reports together, she and Miss Fowler had had dealings with one—a huge revolver with flat-nosed bullets, which latter, Wynn said, were forbidden by the rules of war to be used against civilised enemies. "They're good enough for us," Miss Fowler had replied. "Show Mary how it works." And Wynn, laughing at the mere possibility of any such need, had led the craven winking Mary into the Rector's disused quarry, and had shown her how to fire the terrible machine. It lay now in the top-left-hand drawer of her toilet-table—a memento not included in the burning. Wynn would be pleased to see how she was not afraid.

She slipped up to the house to get it. When she came through the rain, the eyes in the head were alive with expectation. The mouth even tried to smile. But at sight of the revolver its corners went down just like Edna Gerritt's. A tear trickled from one eye, and the head rolled from shoulder to shoulder as though trying to point out something.

"Cassée. Tout cassée," it whimpered.

"What do you say?" said Mary disgustedly, keeping well to one side, though only the head moved.

"Cassée," it repeated. "Che me rends. Le médecin! Toctor!"

"Nein!" said she, bringing all her small German to bear with the big pistol. "Ich haben der todt Kinder geschn."

The head was still. Mary's hand dropped. She had been careful to keep her finger off the trigger for fear of accidents. After a few moments' waiting, she returned to the destructor, where the flames were falling, and churned up Wynn's charring books with the poker. Again the head groaned for the doctor.

"Stop that!" said Mary, and stamped her foot. "Stop that, you bloody pagan!"

The words came quite smoothly and naturally. They were Wynn's own words, and Wynn was a gentleman who for no consideration on earth would have torn little Edna into those vividly coloured strips and strings. But this thing hunched under the oak tree had done that thing. It was no question of reading horrors out of newspapers to Miss Fowler. Mary had seen it with her own eyes on the "Royal Oak" kitchen table. She must not allow her mind to dwell upon it. Now Wynn was dead, and everything connected with him was lumping and rustling and tinkling under her busy poker into red black dust and grey leaves of ash. The thing beneath the oak would die too. Mary had seen death more than once. She came of a family that had a knack of dying under, as she told Miss Fowler, "most distressing circumstances." She would stay where she was till she was entirely satisfied that It was dead—dead as dear Papa in the late eighties; Aunt Mary in eighty-nine; Mamma in ninety-one; Cousin Dick in ninety-five; Lady McCausland's housemaid in ninety-nine; Lady McCausland's sister in nineteen hundred and one; Wynn buried five days ago; and Edna Gerritt still waiting for decent earth to hide her. As she thought—her underlip caught up by one faded canine, brows knit and nostrils wide—she wielded the poker with lunges that jarred the grating at the bottom, and careful scrapes round the brickwork above. She looked at her wristwatch. It was getting on to half-past four, and the rain was coming down in earnest. Tea would be at five. If It did not die before that time, she would be soaked and would have to change. Meantime, and this occupied her, Wynn's things were burning well in spite of the hissing wet, though now and again a book-back with a quite distinguishable title would be heaved up out of the mass. The exercise of stoking had given her a glow which seemed to reach to the marrow of her bones. She hummed—Mary never had a voice—to herself. She had never believed in all those advanced views—though Miss Fowler herself leaned a little that way—of woman's work in the world; but now she saw there was much to be said for them. This, for instance, was *her* work—work which no man, least of all Dr. Hennis, would ever have done. A man, at such a crisis, would be what Wynn called a "sportsman"; would leave everything to fetch help, and would certainly bring It into the house. Now a woman's business was to make a happy home for—for a husband and children. Failing these—it was not a thing one should allow one's mind to dwell upon—but—

"Stop it!" Mary cried once more across the shadows. "Nein, I tell you! Ich haben der todt Kinder gesehn."

But it was a fact. A woman who had missed these things could still be useful—more useful than a man in certain respects. She thumped like a pavior through the settling ashes at the secret thrill of it. The rain was damping the fire, but she could feel—it was too dark to see—that her work was done. There was a dull red glow at the bottom of the destructor, not enough to char the wooden lid if she slipped it half over against the driving wet. This arranged, she leaned on the poker and waited, while an increasing rapture laid hold on her. She ceased to think. She gave herself up to feel. Her long pleasure was broken by a sound that she had waited for in agony several times in her life. She leaned forward and listened, smiling. There could be no mistake. She closed her eyes and drank it in. Once it ceased abruptly.

"Go on," she murmured, half-aloud. "That isn't the end."

Then the end came very distinctly in a lull between two rain gusts. Mary Postgate drew her breath short between her teeth and shivered from head to foot. "*That's* all right," said she contentedly, and went up to the house, where she scandalised the whole routine by taking a luxurious hot bath before tea, and came down looking, as Miss Fowler said when she saw her lying all relaxed on the other sofa, "quite handsome!"

QUESTIONS

1. What is the emotional relationship between Wynn Fowler and Mary Postgate?

2. How can Mary's and Miss Fowler's reactions to Wynn's death be characterized?

3. After calling the German soldiers "bloody pagans," in what sense does Mary fall "back on the teaching that had made her what she was"? (96)

4. Why does Dr. Hennis explain to Mary so thoroughly the cause of Edna's death?

5. Why does Mary presume that the German aviator was responsible for Edna's death?

6. What accounts for the "increasing rapture" Mary feels as the German aviator slowly dies? (101)

7. Is Mary more in touch with her emotions at the end of the story than she is at the beginning?

FOR FURTHER REFLECTION

1. What connections are we to draw between Wynn's death and the German aviator's death?

2. In times of war, can an enemy's death provide justifiable catharsis?

3. What is the source of Mary's deep anger?

MARGARET ATWOOD

Margaret Atwood (1939–) is one of Canada's most famous and prolific contemporary writers, with more than seventy books to her name. She was born and raised in Ontario, and studied at the University of Toronto and Radcliffe College. Among her best-known novels are *The Handmaid's Tale* (1985), winner of the Governor General's Literary Award for Fiction, Canada's foremost literary prize, and *The Blind Assassin* (2000), winner of the Booker Prize for Fiction. "Hairball," part of her short story collection *Wilderness Tips* (1991), was originally published in the *New Yorker* in 1990 under the title "Kat."

Hairball

On the thirteenth of November, day of unluck, month of the dead, Kat went into the Toronto General Hospital for an operation. It was for an ovarian cyst, a large one.

Many women had them, the doctor told her. Nobody knew why. There wasn't any way of finding out whether the thing was malignant, whether it contained, already, the spores of death. Not before they went in. He spoke of "going in" the way she'd heard old veterans in TV documentaries speak of assaults on enemy territory. There was the same tensing of the jaw, the same fierce gritting of the teeth, the same grim enjoyment. Except that what he would be going into was her body. Counting down, waiting for the anaesthetic, Kat too gritted her teeth fiercely. She was terrified, but also she was curious. Curiosity has got her through a lot.

She'd made the doctor promise to save the thing for her, whatever it was, so she could have a look. She was intensely interested in her own body, in anything it might choose to do or produce; although when flaky Dania, who did layout at the magazine, told her this growth was a message to her from her body and she ought to sleep with an amethyst under her pillow to calm her vibrations, Kat told her to stuff it.

The cyst turned out to be a benign tumour. Kat liked that use of *benign*, as if the thing had a soul and wished her well. It was big as a grapefruit, the doctor said. "Big as a coconut," said Kat. Other people had grapefruits. "Coconut" was better. It conveyed the hardness of it, and the hairiness, too.

The hair in it was red—long strands of it wound round and round inside, like a ball of wet wool gone berserk or like the guck you pulled out of a clogged bathroom-sink drain. There were little bones in it too, or fragments of bone—bird bones, the bones of a sparrow crushed by a car. There was a scattering of nails, toe or finger. There were five perfectly formed teeth.

"Is this abnormal?" Kat asked the doctor, who smiled. Now that he had gone in and come out again, unscathed, he was less clenched.

"Abnormal? No," he said carefully, as if breaking the news to a mother about a freakish accident to her newborn. "Let's say it's fairly common." Kat was a little disappointed. She would have preferred uniqueness.

She asked for a bottle of formaldehyde, and put the cut-open tumour into it. It was hers, it was benign, it did not deserve to be thrown away. She took it back to her apartment and stuck it on the mantelpiece. She named it Hairball. It isn't that different from having a stuffed bear's head or a preserved ex-pet or anything else with fur and teeth looming over your fireplace; or she pretends it isn't. Anyway, it certainly makes an impression.

Ger doesn't like it. Despite his supposed yen for the new and outré, he is a squeamish man. The first time he comes around (sneaks around, creeps around) after the operation, he tells Kat to throw Hairball out. He calls it "disgusting." Kat refuses point-blank, and says she'd rather have Hairball in a bottle on her mantelpiece than the soppy dead flowers he's brought her, which will anyway rot a lot sooner than Hairball will. As a mantelpiece ornament, Hairball is far superior. Ger says Kat has a tendency to push things to extremes, to go over the edge, merely from a juvenile desire to shock, which is hardly a substitute for wit. One of these days, he says, she will go way too far. Too far for him, is what he means.

"That's why you hired me, isn't it?" she says. "Because I go way too far." But he's in one of his analysing moods. He can see these tendencies of hers reflected in her work on the magazine, he says. All that leather and those grotesque and tortured-looking poses are heading down a track he and others are not at all sure they should continue to follow. Does she see what he means, does she take his point? It's a point that's been made before. She shakes her head slightly, says nothing. She knows how that translates: there have been complaints from the advertisers. *Too bizarre, too kinky.* Tough.

"Want to see my scar?" she says. "Don't make me laugh, though, you'll crack it open." Stuff like that makes him dizzy: anything with a hint of blood, anything gynaecological. He almost threw up in the delivery room when his wife had a baby two years ago. He'd told her that with pride. Kat thinks about sticking a cigarette into the side of her mouth, as in a black-and-white movie of the forties. She thinks about blowing the smoke into his face.

Her insolence used to excite him, during their arguments. Then there would be a grab of her upper arms, a smouldering, violent kiss. He kisses her as if he thinks someone else is watching him, judging the image they make together. Kissing the latest thing, hard and shiny, purple-mouthed, crop-headed; kissing a girl, a woman, a girl, in a little crotch-hugger skirt and skintight leggings. He likes mirrors.

But he isn't excited now. And she can't decoy him into bed; she isn't ready for that yet, she isn't healed. He has a drink, which he doesn't finish, holds her hand as an afterthought, gives her a couple of avuncular pats on the off-white outsized alpaca shoulder, leaves too quickly.

"Goodbye, Gerald," she says. She pronounces the name with mockery. It's a negation of him, an abolishment of him, like ripping a medal off his chest. It's a warning.

He'd been Gerald when they first met. It was she who transformed him, first to Gerry, then to Ger. (Rhymed with *flair*, rhymed with *dare*.) She made him get rid of those sucky pursed-mouth ties, told him what shoes to wear, got him to buy a loose-cut Italian suit, redid his hair. A lot of his current tastes—in food, in drink, in recreational drugs, in women's entertainment underwear—were once hers. In his new phase, with his new, hard, stripped-down name ending on the sharpened note of *r*, he is her creation.

As she is her own. During her childhood she was a romanticized Katherine, dressed by her misty-eyed, fussy mother in dresses that looked like ruffled pillowcases. By high school she'd shed the frills and emerged as a bouncy, round-faced Kathy, with gleaming freshly washed hair and enviable teeth, eager to please and no more interesting than a health-food ad. At university she was Kath, blunt and no-bullshit in her Take-Back-the-Night jeans and checked shirt and her bricklayer-style striped-denim peaked hat. When she ran away to England, she sliced herself down to Kat. It was economical, street-feline, and pointed as a nail. It was also unusual. In England you had to do something to get their attention, especially if you weren't English. Safe in this incarnation, she Ramboed through the eighties.

It was the name, she still thinks, that got her the interview and then the job. The job with an avant-garde magazine, the kind that was printed on matte stock in black and white, with overexposed close-ups of women with hair blowing over their eyes, one nostril prominent: *the razor's edge*, it was called. Haircuts as art, some real art, film reviews, a little stardust, wardrobes of ideas that were clothes and of clothes that were ideas—the metaphysical shoulder pad. She learned her trade well, hands-on. She learned what worked.

She made her way up the ladder, from layout to design, then to the supervision of whole spreads, and then whole issues. It wasn't easy, but it was worth it. She had become a creator; she created total looks. After a while she could walk down the street in Soho or stand in the lobby at openings and witness her handiwork incarnate, strolling around in outfits she'd put together, spouting her warmed-over pronouncements. It was like being God, only God had never got around to off-the-rack lines.

By that time her face had lost its roundness, though the teeth of course remained: there was something to be said for North American dentistry. She'd shaved off most of her hair, worked on the drop-dead stare, perfected a certain turn of the neck that conveyed an aloof inner authority. What you had to make them believe was that you knew something they didn't know yet. What you also had to make them believe was that they too could know this thing, this thing that would give them eminence and power and sexual allure, that would attract envy to them—but for a price. The price of the magazine. What they could never get through their heads was that it was done entirely with cameras. Frozen light, frozen time. Given the angle, she could make any woman look ugly. Any man as well. She could make anyone look beautiful, or at least interesting. It was all photography, it was all iconography. It was all in the choosing eye. This was the thing that could never be bought, no matter how much of your pitiful monthly wage you blew on snakeskin.

Despite the status, *the razor's edge* was fairly low-paying. Kat herself could not afford many of the things she contextualized so well. The grottiness and expense of London began to get to her; she got tired of gorging on the canapés at literary launches in order to scrimp on groceries, tired of the fuggy smell of cigarettes ground into the red-and-maroon carpeting of pubs, tired of the pipes bursting every time it froze in winter, and of the Clarissas and Melissas and Penelopes at the magazine rabbiting on about how they had been literally, absolutely, totally freezing all night, and how it literally, absolutely, totally, usually never got that cold. It always got that cold. The pipes always burst. Nobody thought of putting in real pipes, ones that would not burst next time. Burst pipes were an English tradition, like so many others.

Like, for instance, English men. Charm the knickers off you with their mellow vowels and frivolous verbiage, and then, once they'd got them off, panic and run. Or else stay and whinge. The English called it *whinging* instead of whining. It was better, really. Like a creaking hinge. It was a traditional compliment to be whinged at by an Englishman. It was his way of saying he trusted you, he was conferring upon you the privilege of getting to know the real him. The inner, whinging him. That was how they thought of women, secretly: whinge receptacles. Kat could play it, but that didn't mean she liked it.

She had an advantage over the English women, though: she was of no class. She had no class. She was in a class of her own. She could roll around among the English men, all different kinds of them, secure in the knowledge that she was not being measured against the class yardsticks and accent detectors they carried around in their back pockets, was not subject to the petty snobberies and resentments that lent such richness to their inner lives. The flip side of this freedom was that she was beyond the pale. She was a colonial—how fresh, how vital, how anonymous, how finally of no consequence. Like a hole in the wall, she could be told all secrets and then be abandoned with no guilt.

She was too smart, of course. The English men were very competitive; they liked to win. Several times it hurt. Twice she had abortions, because the men in question were not up for the alternative. She learned to say that she didn't want children anyway, that if she longed for a rug rat she would buy a gerbil. Her life began to seem long. Her adrenaline was running out. Soon she would be thirty, and all she could see ahead was more of the same.

This was how things were when Gerald turned up. "You're terrific," he said, and she was ready to hear it, even from him, even though *terrific* was a word that had probably gone out with fifties crewcuts. She was ready for his voice

by that time too: the flat, metallic nasal tone of the Great
Lakes, with its clear hard *r*'s and its absence of theatricality.
Dull normal. The speech of her people. It came to her sud-
denly that she was an exile.

Gerald was scouting, Gerald was recruiting. He'd heard
about her, looked at her work, sought her out. One of the big
companies back in Toronto was launching a new fashion-
oriented magazine, he said: upmarket, international in its
coverage, of course, but with some Canadian fashion in it
too, and with lists of stores where the items portrayed could
actually be bought. In that respect they felt they'd have it
all over the competition, those American magazines that
assumed you could only get Gucci in New York or Los
Angeles. Heck, times had changed, you could get it in
Edmonton! You could get it in Winnipeg!

Kat had been away too long. There was Canadian fashion now? The English quip would be to say that "Canadian
fashion" was an oxymoron. She refrained from making
it, lit a cigarette with her cyanide-green Covent Garden–
boutique leather-covered lighter (as featured in the May
issue of *the razor's edge*), looked Gerald in the eye. "London
is a lot to give up," she said levelly. She glanced around the
see-me-here Mayfair restaurant where they were finishing
lunch, a restaurant she'd chosen because she'd known he
was paying. She'd never spend that kind of money on food
otherwise. "Where would I eat?"

Gerald assured her that Toronto was now the restaurant
capital of Canada. He himself would be happy to be her
guide. There was a great Chinatown, there was world-class
Italian. Then he paused, took a breath. "I've been meaning to
ask you," he said. "About the name. Is that Kat as in Krazy?"
He thought this was suggestive. She'd heard it before.

"No," she said. "It's Kat as in KitKat. That's a chocolate
bar. Melts in your mouth." She gave him her stare, quirked
her mouth, just a twitch.

Gerald became flustered, but he pushed on. They
wanted her, they needed her, they loved her, he said in

essence. Someone with her fresh, innovative approach and her experience would be worth a lot of money to them, relatively speaking. But there were rewards other than the money. She would be in on the initial concept, she would have a formative influence, she would have a free hand. He named a sum that made her gasp, inaudibly of course. By now she knew better than to betray desire.

So she made the journey back, did her three months of culture shock, tried the world-class Italian and the great Chinese, and seduced Gerald at the first opportunity, right in his junior vice-presidential office. It was the first time Gerald had been seduced in such a location, or perhaps ever. Even though it was after hours, the danger frenzied him. It was the idea of it. The daring. The image of Kat kneeling on the broadloom, in a legendary bra that until now he'd seen only in the lingerie ads of the Sunday *New York Times*, unzipping him in full view of the silver-framed engagement portrait of his wife that complemented the impossible ball-point pen set on his desk. At that time he was so straight he felt compelled to take off his wedding ring and place it carefully in the ashtray first. The next day he brought her a box of David Wood Food Shop chocolate truffles. They were the best, he told her, anxious that she should recognize their quality. She found the gesture banal, but also sweet. The banality, the sweetness, the hunger to impress: that was Gerald.

Gerald was the kind of man she wouldn't have bothered with in London. He was not funny, he was not knowledge-able, he had little verbal charm. But he was eager, he was tractable, he was blank paper. Although he was eight years older than she was, he seemed much younger. She took pleasure from his furtive, boyish delight in his own wickedness. And he was so grateful. "I can hardly believe this is happening," he said, more frequently than was necessary and usually in bed.

His wife, whom Kat encountered (and still encounters) at many tedious company events, helped to explain his gratitude. The wife was a priss. Her name was Cheryl. Her hair looked as if she still used big rollers and embalm-your-hairdo spray; her mind was room-by-room Laura Ashley wallpaper: tiny, unopened pastel buds arranged in straight rows. She probably put on rubber gloves to make love, and checked it off on a list afterwards. One more messy household chore. She looked at Kat as if she'd like to spritz her with air deodorizer. Kat revenged herself by picturing Cheryl's bathrooms: hand towels embroidered with lilies, fuzzy covers on the toilet seats.

The magazine itself got off to a rocky start. Although Kat had lots of lovely money to play with, and although it was a challenge to be working in colour, she did not have the free hand Gerald had promised her. She had to contend with the company board of directors, who were all men, who were all accountants or indistinguishable from them, who were cautious and slow as moles.

"It's simple," Kat told them. "You bombard them with images of what they ought to be, and you make them feel grotty for being the way they are. You're working with the gap between reality and perception. That's why you have to hit them with something new, something they've never seen before, something they aren't. Nothing sells like anxiety."

The board, on the other hand, felt that the readership should simply be offered more of what they already had. More fur, more sumptuous leather, more cashmere. More established names. The board had no sense of improvisation, no wish to take risks, no sporting instincts, no desire to put one over on the readers just for the hell of it. "Fashion is like hunting," Kat told them, hoping to appeal to their male hormones, if any. "It's playful, it's intense, it's predatory. It's blood and guts. It's erotic." But to them it was about good taste. They wanted Dress-for-Success. Kat wanted scattergun ambush.

Everything became a compromise. Kat had wanted to call the magazine *All the Rage*, but the board was put off by the vibrations of anger in the word *rage*. They thought it was too feminist, of all things. "It's a *forties* sound," Kat said. "Forties is *back*. Don't you get it?" But they didn't. They wanted to call it *Or*. French for *gold*, and blatant enough in its values, but without any base note, as Kat told them. They sawed off at *Felice*, which had qualities each side wanted. It was vaguely French-sounding, it meant *happy* (so much less threatening than *rage*), and, although you couldn't expect the others to notice, for Kat it had a feline bouquet which counteracted the laciness. She had it done in hot-pink lipstick-scrawl, which helped some. She could live with it, but it had not been her first love.

This battle has been fought and refought over every innovation in design, every new angle Kat has tried to bring in, every innocuous bit of semi-kink. There was a big row over a spread that did lingerie, half pulled off and with broken glass perfume bottles strewn on the floor. There was an uproar over the two nouveau-stockinged legs, one tied to a chair with a third, different-coloured stocking. They had not understood the man's three-hundred-dollar leather gloves positioned ambiguously around a neck.

And so it has gone on, for five years.

After Gerald has left, Kat paces her living room. Pace, pace. Her stitches pull. She's not looking forward to her solitary dinner of microwaved leftovers. She's not sure now why she came back here, to this flat burg beside the polluted inland sea. Was it Ger? Ludicrous thought but no longer out of the question. Is he the reason she stays, despite her growing impatience with him?

He's no longer fully rewarding. They've learned each other too well, they take shortcuts now; their time together has shrunk from whole stolen rolling and sensuous after-noons to a few hours snatched between work and dinnertime. She no longer knows what she wants from him. She tells herself she's worth more, she should branch out; but she doesn't see other men, she can't, somehow. She's tried once or twice but it didn't work. Sometimes she goes out to dinner or a flick with one of the gay designers. She likes the gossip.

Maybe she misses London. She feels caged, in this country, in this city, in this room. She could start with the room, she could open a window. It's too stuffy in here. There's an undertone of formaldehyde, from Hairball's bottle. The flowers she got for the operation are mostly wilted, all except Gerald's from today. Come to think of it, why didn't he send her any at the hospital? Did he forget, or was it a message?

"Hairball," she says, "I wish you could talk. I could have a more intelligent conversation with you than with most of the losers in this turkey farm." Hairball's baby teeth glint in the light; it looks as if it's about to speak.

Kat feels her own forehead. She wonders if she's running a temperature. Something ominous is going on, behind her back. There haven't been enough phone calls from the magazine; they've been able to muddle on without her, which is bad news. Reigning queens should never go on vacation, or have operations either. Uneasy lies the head. She has a sixth sense about these things, she's been involved in enough palace coups to know the signs, she has sensitive antennae for the footfalls of impending treachery.

The next morning she pulls herself together, downs an espresso from her mini-machine, picks out an aggressive touch-me-if-you-dare suede outfit in armour grey, and drags herself to the office, although she isn't due in till next week. Surprise, surprise. Whispering knots break up in the corridors, greet her with false welcome as she limps past. She settles herself at her minimalist desk, checks her mail. Her head is pounding, her stitches hurt. Ger gets wind of her arrival; he wants to see her ASAP, and not for lunch.

He awaits her in his newly done wheat-on-white office, with the eighteenth-century desk they chose together, the Victorian inkstand, the framed blowups from the magazine, the hands in maroon leather, wrists manacled with pearls, the Hermès scarf twisted into a blindfold, the model's mouth blossoming lusciously beneath it. Some of her best stuff. He's beautifully done up, in a lick-my-neck silk shirt open at the throat, an eat-your-heart-out Italian silk-and-wool loose-knit sweater. Oh, cool insouciance. Oh, eyebrow language. He's a money man who lusted after art, and now he's got some, now he is some. Body art. Her art. She's done her job well; he's finally sexy.

He's smooth as lacquer. "I didn't want to break this to you until next week," he says. He breaks it to her. It's the board of directors. They think she's too bizarre, they think she goes way too far. Nothing he could do about it, although naturally he tried.

Naturally. Betrayal. The monster has turned on its own mad scientist. "I gave you life!" she wants to scream at him.

She isn't in good shape. She can hardly stand. She stands, despite his offer of a chair. She sees now what she's wanted, what she's been missing. Gerald is what she's been missing—the stable, unfashionable, previous, tight-assed Gerald. Not Ger, not the one she's made in her own image. The other one, before he got ruined. The Gerald with a house and a small child and a picture of his wife in a silver frame on his desk. She wants to be in that silver frame. She wants the child. She's been robbed.

"And who is my lucky replacement?" she says. She needs a cigarette, but does not want to reveal her shaking hands.

"Actually, it's me," he says, trying for modesty.

This is too absurd. Gerald couldn't edit a phone book. "You?" she says faintly. She has the good sense not to laugh.

"I've always wanted to get out of the money end of things here," he says, "into the creative area. I knew you'd understand, since it can't be you at any rate. I knew you'd prefer someone who could, well, sort of build on your foundations." Pompous asshole. She looks at his neck. She longs for him, hates herself for it, and is powerless.

The room wavers. He slides towards her across the wheat-coloured broadloom, takes her by the grey suede upper arms. "I'll write you a good reference," he says. "Don't worry about that. Of course, we can still see one another. I'd miss our afternoons."

"Of course," she says. He kisses her, a voluptuous kiss, or it would look like one to a third party, and she lets him. *In a pig's ear.*

She makes it home in a taxi. The driver is rude to her and gets away with it; she doesn't have the energy. In her mailbox is an engraved invitation: Ger and Cheryl are having a drinks party, tomorrow evening. Postmarked five days ago. Cheryl is behind the times.

Kat undresses, runs a shallow bath. There's not much to drink around here, there's nothing to sniff or smoke. What an oversight; she's stuck with herself. There are other jobs. There are other men, or that's the theory. Still, something's been ripped out of her. How could this have happened, to her? When knives were slated for backs, she'd always done the stabbing. Any headed her way she's seen coming in time, and thwarted. Maybe she's losing her edge.

She stares into the bathroom mirror, assesses her face in the misted glass. A face of the eighties, a mask face, a bottom-line face; push the weak to the wall and grab what you can. But now it's the nineties. Is she out of style, so soon? She's only thirty-five, and she's already losing track of what people ten years younger are thinking. That could be fatal. As time goes by she'll have to race faster and faster to keep up, and for what? Part of the life she should have had is just a gap, it isn't there, it's nothing. What can be salvaged from it, what can be redone, what can be done at all?

When she climbs out of the tub after her sponge bath, she almost falls. She has a fever, no doubt about it. Inside her something is leaking, or else festering; she can hear it, like a dripping tap. A running sore, a sore from running so hard. She should go to the emergency ward at some hospital, get herself shot up with antibiotics. Instead she lurches into the living room, takes Hairball down from the mantelpiece in its bottle, places it on the coffee table. She sits cross-legged, listens. Filaments wave. She can hear a kind of buzz, like bees at work.

She'd asked the doctor if it could have started as a child, a fertilized egg that escaped somehow and got into the wrong place. No, said the doctor. Some people thought this kind of tumour was present in seedling form from birth, or before it. It might be the woman's undeveloped twin. What they really were was unknown. They had many kinds of tissue, though. Even brain tissue. Though of course all of these tissues lack structure.

Still, sitting here on the rug looking in at it, she pictures it as a child. lt has come out of her, after all. It is flesh of her flesh. Her child with Gerald, her thwarted child, not allowed to grow normally. Her warped child, taking its revenge.

"Hairball," she says. "You're so ugly. Only a mother could love you." She feels sorry for it. She feels loss. Tears run down her face. Crying is not something she does, not normally, not lately.

Hairball speaks to her, without words. It is irreducible, it has the texture of reality, it is not an image. What it tells her is everything she's never wanted to hear about herself. This is new knowledge, dark and precious and necessary. It cuts.

She shakes her head. What are you doing, sitting on the floor and talking to a hairball? You are sick, she tells herself. Take a Tylenol and go to bed.

The next day she feels a little better. Dania from layout calls her and makes dovelike, sympathetic coos at her, and wants to drop by during lunch hour to take a look at her aura. Kat tells her to come off it. Dania gets huffy, and says that Kat's losing her job is a price for immoral behaviour in a previous life. Kat tells her to stuff it; anyway, she's done enough immoral behaviour in this life to account for the whole thing. "Why are you so full of hate?" asks Dania. She doesn't say it like a point she's making, she sounds truly baffled.

"I don't know," says Kat. It's a straight answer.

After she hangs up she paces the floor. She's crackling inside, like hot fat under the broiler. What she's thinking about is Cheryl, bustling about her cosy house, preparing for the party. Cheryl fiddles with her freeze-framed hair, positions an overloaded vase of flowers, fusses about the caterers. Gerald comes in, kisses her lightly on the cheek. A connubial scene. His conscience is nicely washed. The witch is dead, his foot is on the body, the trophy; he's had his dirty fling, he's ready now for the rest of his life.

Kat takes a taxi to the David Wood Food Shop and buys two dozen chocolate truffles. She has them put into an oversized box, then into an oversized bag with the store logo on it. Then she goes home and takes Hairball out of its bottle. She drains it in the kitchen strainer and pats it damp-dry, tenderly, with paper towels. She sprinkles it with powdered cocoa, which forms a brown pasty crust. It still smells like formaldehyde, so she wraps it in Saran Wrap and then in tinfoil, and then in pink tissue paper, which she ties with a mauve bow. She places it in the David Wood box in a bed of shredded tissue, with the truffles nestled around. She closes the box, tapes it, puts it into the bag, stuffs several sheets of pink paper on top. It's her gift, valuable and dangerous. It's her messenger, but the message it will deliver is its own. It will tell the truth, to whoever asks. It's right that Gerald should have it; after all, it's his child too.

She prints on the card, "Gerald, Sorry I couldn't be with you. This is all the rage. Love, K."

When evening has fallen and the party must be in full swing, she calls a delivery taxi. Cheryl will not distrust anything that arrives in such an expensive bag. She will open it in public, in front of everyone. There will be distress, there will be questions. Secrets will be unearthed. There will be pain. After that, everything will go way too far.

She is not well; her heart is pounding, space is wavering once more. But outside the window it's snowing, the soft, damp, windless flakes of her childhood. She puts on her coat and goes out, foolishly. She intends to walk just to the corner, but when she reaches the corner she goes on. The snow melts against her face like small fingers touching. She has done an outrageous thing, but she doesn't feel guilty. She feels light and peaceful and filled with charity, and temporarily without a name.

QUESTIONS

1. Why does Kat decide to keep the tumor in a transparent jar of formaldehyde on her mantelpiece?

2. What lies behind Kat's changing her name—and Gerald's? What does each of these names suggest?

3. What is Kat referring to when she speaks of "this thing that would give them eminence and power and sexual allure, that would attract envy to them"? (109)

4. Why is Kat fired from the magazine?

5. What is "the truth" that Hairball will deliver to its recipient? (119)

6. In what sense is Hairball Gerald's "child too"? (119)

7. Why does Kat feel "temporarily without a name" at the end of the story? (120)

FOR FURTHER REFLECTION

1. Does Kat's envy of Gerald and Cheryl's conventional married life indicate that she, too, is at heart conventional?

2. Do you think Kat should feel "guilty" about the "outrageous thing" she has done?

3. Is the ending of this story hopeful?

Sloth

ANTON CHEKHOV

Born in Taganrog, Russia, Anton Chekhov (1860–1904) moved to Moscow in 1879, where he attended medical school and began writing to help support his family. After graduating, he practiced throughout his life, but, as he famously remarked, though medicine was his lawful wife, literature was his mistress. "The Lady with the Little Dog" (1899) is the best known of his short-story masterpieces. Late in his short life—ended by the tuberculosis from which he suffered for many years—he became an equally brilliant playwright. Among his greatest plays are *Three Sisters* (1901) and *The Cherry Orchard* (1904). Many of his stories and plays are deceptively simple explorations of the scarcely apprehended motivations that eventually give shape to an individual life.

The House with the Mezzanine

AN ARTIST'S STORY

1

This was six or seven years ago, when I was living in one of the districts of T—— province, on the estate of the landowner Belokurov, a young man who got up very early, went about in a vest, drank beer in the evenings, and kept complaining to me that he met with no sympathy anywhere or from anyone. He lived in a cottage in the garden, and I in the old mansion, in a huge hall with columns, where there was no furniture except a wide sofa on which I slept and a table on which I played patience. Here, even in calm weather, something always howled in the old Amosov stoves, but during a thunderstorm the whole house trembled and seemed to crack to pieces, and it was a little frightening, especially at night, when all ten big windows were suddenly lit up by lightning.

Condemned by fate to permanent idleness, I was doing decidedly nothing. I spent whole hours looking out my windows at the sky, the birds, the avenues, read everything that came in the mail, slept. Sometimes I left the house and wandered about somewhere till late in the evening.

Once, returning home, I accidentally wandered onto an unfamiliar estate. The sun was already hiding, and evening shadows stretched across the flowering rye. Two rows of old, closely planted, very tall fir trees stood like two solid walls, forming a beautiful, gloomy avenue. I easily climbed the fence and went down this avenue, slipping on the fir needles that lay inches-thick on the ground. It was quiet, dark, and only high in the treetops did a bright golden light tremble here and there and play iridescently on the spider webs. There was a strong, almost stifling, smell of fir needles. Then I turned down a long linden avenue. Here, too, there was old age and desolation; last year's leaves rustled sorrowfully under my feet, and shadows hid in the twilight between the trees. To the right, in an old orchard, an oriole sang reluctantly, in a weak voice—it must have been a little old lady, too. But now the lindens also ended; I passed a white house with a terrace and a mezzanine, and before me there unexpectedly opened up a view of the manor yard and a wide pond with a bathing house, a stand of green willows, a village on the other side, with a tall, slender belfry, the cross of which blazed, reflecting the setting sun. For a moment I felt the enchantment of something dear and very familiar, as if I had already seen this same panorama sometime in my childhood.

And by the white stone gateway that led from the yard into the fields, by the sturdy old gates with their lions, stood two girls. One of them, the elder, slender, pale, very beautiful, with a whole mass of chestnut hair on her head, with a small, stubborn mouth, had a stern expression and barely paid any attention to me; the other, still very young—she was seventeen or eighteen years old, not more—also slender and pale, with a big mouth and big eyes, looked at me in surprise as I passed by, said something in English, and became embarrassed, and it seemed to me that these two sweet faces had also been long familiar to me. And I returned home feeling as if I had had a good dream.

Soon after that, around noon one day, as Belokurov and I were strolling near the house, a spring carriage, swishing through the grass, unexpectedly drove into the yard, with one of those girls sitting in it. It was the older one. She had come with a subscription list, seeking aid for the victims of a fire. Without looking at us, she told us very seriously and in detail how many houses had burned down in the village of Siyanovo, how many men, women, and children had been left without a roof, and what the committee for the victims, of which she was now a member, intended to undertake as a first step. After having us sign it, she put the list away and at once began taking her leave.

"You've quite forgotten us, Pyotr Petrovich," she said to Belokurov, giving him her hand. "Come over, and if Monsieur X" (she said my name) "wishes to have a look at how some admirers of his talent live, and is so good as to visit us, Mama and I will be very glad."

I bowed.

When she left, Pyotr Petrovich told me the story. This girl, in his words, was from a good family, her name was Lydia Volchaninova, and the estate she lived on with her mother and sister was called Shelkovka, the same as the one across the pond. Her father had once occupied a prominent position in Moscow and had died with the rank of privy councilor. Although they were well off, the Volchaninovs lived permanently in the country, summer and winter, and Lydia was a teacher in a zemstvo school in her own Shelkovka and earned twenty-five rubles a month. She spent only this money on herself and was proud to be living at her own expense.

"An interesting family," said Belokurov. "We might go and see them sometime. They'd be very glad to have you."

After dinner once, on a feast day, we remembered the Volchaninovs and went to visit them in Shelkovka. They, the mother and both daughters, were at home. The mother, Ekaterina Pavlovna, evidently beautiful once but now flabby beyond her years, suffering from shortness of breath, sad, distracted, tried to engage me in a conversation about painting. Having learned from her daughter that I might visit Shelkovka, she had hastily recalled two or three landscapes of mine that she had seen at exhibitions in Moscow, and now asked me what I had meant to express in them. Lydia, or Lida, as they called her at home, talked more with Belokurov than with me. Serious, unsmiling, she asked him why he did not serve in the zemstvo and why he had never yet come to a single zemstvo meeting.

"It's not good, Pyotr Petrovich," she said reproachfully. "It's not good. It's a shame."

"True, Lida, true," her mother agreed. "It's not good."

"Our whole district is in the hands of Balagin," Lida went on, turning to me. "He himself is the chairman of the board, and he's given all the posts in the district to his nephews and sons-in-law and does whatever he likes. We must fight. The young people should form a strong party, but you see what kind of young people we have. It's a shame, Pyotr Petrovich!"

While we talked about the zemstvo, the younger sister, Zhenya, was silent. She did not take part in serious conversations, the family did not consider her grown up yet, and called her Missyus, like a little girl, because that was what she had called Miss, her governess, as a child. She kept looking at me with curiosity, and when I glanced through the photograph album, she explained to me: "That's my uncle . . . That's my godfather," and moved her little finger over the portraits, and at that moment she touched me childishly with her shoulder, and I could see close-up her weak, undeveloped breast, her slender shoulders, her braid, and her thin body, tightly bound with a sash.

We played croquet and lawn tennis, strolled about the garden, had tea, and then a long supper. After the enormous, empty hall with columns, I felt somehow ill at ease in this small, cozy house in which there were no oleographs on the walls and the servants were addressed formally, and everything seemed young and pure to me, owing to the presence of Lida and Missyus, and everything breathed respectability. Over supper Lida again talked with Belokurov about the zemstvo, about Balagin, about the school libraries.

She was a lively, sincere girl, with deep convictions, and it was interesting to listen to her, though she talked a lot and loudly—perhaps because she was used to talking at school. On the other hand, my Pyotr Petrovich, who from his student days had kept the manner of turning every conversation into an argument, spoke dully, listlessly, and at length, with the obvious wish of appearing to be an intelligent and progressive man. Gesticulating, he overturned the sauceboat with his sleeve, and a big puddle formed on the tablecloth, but, except for me, no one seemed to notice it.

When we returned home, it was dark and still.

"Good manners doesn't mean not spilling sauce on the tablecloth, but not noticing when someone else does," said Belokurov, and he sighed. "Yes, a wonderful, intellectual family. I've lost touch with good people, indeed I have! I'm always busy, busy, busy!"

He talked of how much one had to work if one wanted to be a model farmer. And I thought: what a sluggish and lazy fellow he is! When he talked about something serious, he drawled and strained, "E-e-eh," and he worked the same way as he talked—slow, always late, missing all deadlines. I had little faith in his business abilities, if only because when I asked him to mail some letters for me, he carried them around in his pockets for weeks.

"The hardest thing of all," he muttered, walking beside me, "the hardest thing of all is to work and get no sympathy from anybody. No sympathy at all!"

2

I began to visit the Volchaninovs. Usually I sat on the bottom step of the terrace; dissatisfaction with myself oppressed me, I felt sorry for my life, which was passing so quickly and uninterestingly, and I kept thinking how good it would be to tear this heart, which had grown so heavy, out of my breast. And all the while there would be talking on the terrace; one could hear the rustling of dresses and the leafing-through of books. I soon became accustomed to Lida's receiving sick people in the afternoon, handing out books, and often leaving for the village, bareheaded under her parasol, and in the evening talking loudly about the zemstvo and schools. This slender, beautiful, invariably severe girl, with her small, gracefully outlined mouth, would turn to me whenever a practical conversation began, and say drily:

"This is of no interest to you."

She did not find me sympathetic. She disliked me because I was a landscape painter and did not portray the needs of the people in my pictures, and because I was, as it seemed to her, indifferent to what she so strongly believed in. I remember once riding along the shore of Baikal and meeting a Buryat girl in a shirt and blue dungaree trousers, on horseback; I asked her if she would sell me her pipe, and as we spoke, she looked scornfully at my European face and my hat, and after a minute got sick of talking to me, whooped, and galloped off. In the same way, Lida scorned the alien in me. She did not express her indisposition toward me in any external way, but I sensed it and, sitting on the bottom step of the terrace, felt annoyed and said that to treat peasants without being a doctor was to deceive them and that it was easy to be philanthropic when one owned five thousand acres.

But her sister, Missyus, had no cares and spent her life in total idleness, as I did. When she got up in the morning, she at once took a book and started reading, sitting on the terrace in a deep armchair, so that her little feet barely touched the ground, or she hid herself with a book in the linden avenue, or went out the gates into the fields. She read for the whole day, peering greedily into her book, and only because her eyes sometimes became tired, dazed, and her face very pale, could you guess that this reading wearied her brain. When I came, she would blush slightly on seeing me, put her book down, and, looking into my face with her big eyes, tell me excitedly about things that had happened for instance, that there had been a chimney fire in the servants' quarters or that some worker had caught a big fish in the pond. On weekdays she usually went about in a pale blouse and a dark blue skirt. We took walks together, picked cherries for preserves, went for boat rides, and when she jumped up to reach a cherry, or handled the oars, her thin, weak arms showed through her loose sleeves. Or else I would paint a study, and she would stand beside me and watch with admiration.

One Sunday at the end of July, I came to the Volchaninovs' in the morning, around nine o'clock. I walked through the park, keeping away from the house, and looked for mushrooms, which were very numerous that summer, and marked the places, in order to pick them later with Zhenya. A warm breeze was blowing. I saw Zhenya and her mother, both in pale festive dresses, walking from church to the house, and Zhenya keeping her hat from blowing off in the wind. Then I heard them having tea on the terrace.

For a carefree man like me, seeking to justify his constant idleness, these festive summer mornings on our country estates have always been extremely attractive. When a green garden, still moist with dew, shines all over in the sun and looks happy, when there is a smell of mignonette and oleander around the house, the young people have just come back from church and are having tea in the garden, and when everyone is so nicely dressed and cheerful, and when you know that all these healthy, well-fed, handsome people will do nothing all day long, then you want all of life to be like that. And now I was thinking the same thing and walking in the garden, ready to walk that way, idly and aimlessly, all day, all summer.

Zhenya came with a basket; she looked as if she knew or anticipated that she would find me in the garden. We picked mushrooms and talked, and when she asked about something, she went ahead so as to see my face.

"Yesterday a miracle took place in our village," she said. "Lame Pelageya was sick for a whole year, no doctors or medicines helped her, but yesterday an old woman whispered something and it went away."

"That's no matter," I said. "We shouldn't look for miracles only around sick people and old women. Isn't health a miracle? And life itself? Whatever is incomprehensible is a miracle."

"Aren't you afraid of what's incomprehensible?"

"No. I approach phenomena that I don't understand with good cheer and don't give in to them. I'm above them. Man should be aware that he is above lions, tigers, stars, above everything in nature, even above what is incomprehensible and seems miraculous, otherwise he's not a man but a mouse afraid of everything."

Zhenya thought that, being an artist, I knew a lot and could make right guesses about what I did not know. She would have liked me to lead her into the region of the eternal and the beautiful, that higher world where, in her opinion, I was at home, and she talked to me about God, about eternal life, about the miraculous. And, unable to conceive that I and my imagination would perish forever after death, I replied: "Yes, people are immortal," "Yes, eternal life awaits us." And she listened, believed, and did not ask for proof.

As we walked toward the house, she suddenly stopped and said:

"Our Lida is a remarkable person. Isn't it so? I love her dearly and could sacrifice my life for her at any moment. But tell me," Zhenya touched my sleeve with her finger, "tell me, why do you argue with her all the time? Why are you annoyed?"

"Because she's wrong."

Zhenya shook her head, and tears came to her eyes.

"It's so incomprehensible!" she said.

At that moment Lida had just returned from somewhere and, standing by the porch with a whip in her hand, trim, beautiful, lit by the sun, was giving orders to a workman. Hurrying and talking loudly, she received two or three patients, then, with a busy, preoccupied air, she went through the rooms, opening first one cupboard, then another, and went up to the mezzanine; they spent a long time looking for her and calling her to dinner, and she came when we had already finished the soup. For some reason I remember and love all these little details, and I remember that whole day vividly, though nothing special happened. After dinner Zhenya read, lying in a deep armchair, and I sat on the bottom step of the terrace. We were silent. The whole sky clouded over, and a fine, light rain began to drizzle. It was hot, the wind had died down long ago, and it seemed the day would never end. Ekaterina Pavlovna came out to us on the terrace, sleepy, holding a fan.

"Oh, Mama," said Zhenya, kissing her hand, "it's not good for you to sleep in the afternoon."

They adored each other. Whenever one went to the garden, the other would stand on the terrace and, looking at the trees, call: "Hello-o-o, Zhenya!" or "Mamochka, where are you?" They always prayed together, and both had the same beliefs and understood each other very well even when they were silent. And their attitude toward people was the same. Ekaterina Pavlovna, too, soon became accustomed and attached to me, and when I did not appear for two or three days, she would send to find out if I was well. She, too, looked at my studies with admiration, and, as loquaciously and candidly as Missyus, told me about things that had happened and often entrusted me with her domestic secrets.

She stood in awe of her elder daughter. Lida was never tender, she spoke only about serious things; she lived her own separate life and for her mother and sister was as sacred and slightly mysterious a personage as an admiral who always remains in his cabin is for his sailors.

"Our Lida is a remarkable person," the mother often said. "Isn't it so?"

And now, as the rain drizzled, we talked of Lida.

"She's a remarkable person," the mother said and added in a conspiratorial half-whisper, looking around tearfully:

"It would be hard to find the like of her anywhere, though, you know, I'm beginning to worry a little. School, first-aid kits, books—it's all very good, but why go to extremes? She's nearly twenty-four; it's time she thought seriously about herself. With all these books and first-aid kits, she won't see how life is passing by . . . She should marry."

Zhenya, pale from reading, her hair disheveled, raised her head and, looking at her mother, said as if to herself:

"Mamochka, it all depends on God's will!"

And again she immersed herself in reading.

Belokurov came in a vest and an embroidered shirt. We played croquet and lawn tennis, then, when it grew dark, had a long supper, and Lida again talked about schools and about Balagin, who had the whole district in his hands. Leaving the Volchaninovs' that evening, I went away with the impression of a very long, idle day, and the sad awareness that everything in this world, however long, comes to an end. Zhenya accompanied us to the gate, and perhaps because she had spent the whole day with me from morning till evening, I felt that without her I was somehow dull and that this whole dear family was close to me; and for the first time all summer I wanted to paint.

"Tell me, why is your life so dull, so colorless?" I asked Belokurov, walking home with him. "My life is dull, heavy, monotonous, because I'm an artist, a strange man, from my youth I've been chafed by jealousy, dissatisfaction with myself, lack of faith in what I'm doing, I'm always poor, I'm a vagabond, but you, you're a healthy, normal person, a landowner, a squire—why do you live so uninterestingly, why do you take so little from life? Why, for instance, haven't you fallen in love with Lida or Zhenya yet?"

"You forget that I love another woman," Belokurov replied.

He was speaking of his friend, Lyubov Ivanovna, who lived with him in the cottage. Every day I saw this lady, very stout, plump, imposing, like a well-fed goose, strolling in the garden, in a Russian costume with beads, always under a parasol, and a serving girl kept calling her, now to eat, now to have tea. Some three years before she had rented one of the cottages as a dacha and had simply gone on living at Belokurov's, apparently forever. She was a good ten years older than he and ruled him so strictly that, whenever he went away from the house, he had to ask her permission. She sobbed frequently in a male voice, and then I would send word that unless she stopped I would give up my lodgings, and she would stop.

When we came home, Belokurov sat on the sofa and frowned pensively, and I began pacing the hall, feeling a quiet excitement, as if I were in love. I wanted to talk about the Volchaninovs.

"Lida can only fall in love with a zemstvo activist, whose passions are the same as hers—hospitals and schools," I said. "Oh, for the sake of such a girl you could not only join the zemstvo, but even wear out a pair of iron shoes, as in the old tale. And Missyus? How lovely this Missyus is!"

Belokurov, with his drawn out "E-e-eh," began talking at length about the disease of the age—pessimism. He spoke confidently and in such a tone as if I were arguing with him. Hundreds of miles of deserted, monotonous, scorched steppe cannot produce such gloom as one man when he sits and talks and nobody knows when he will leave.

"The point isn't pessimism or optimism," I said irritably, "but that ninety-nine people out of a hundred are witless."

Belokurov took it personally, became offended, and left.

3

"The prince is visiting in Malozyomovo and sends you his greetings," Lida was saying to her mother, having returned from somewhere and taking off her gloves. "He tells many interesting things . . . He promises to raise the question of a dispensary in Malozyomovo again in the provincial assem bly, but he says there's little hope." And turning to me, she said: "Excuse me, I keep forgetting that this cannot be of interest to you."

I felt annoyed.

"Why not?" I asked and shrugged my shoulders. "You have no wish to know my opinion, but I assure you the question is of lively interest to me."

"It is?"

"Yes, it is. In my opinion there's no need at all for a dispensary in Malozyomovo."

My annoyance communicated itself to her; she looked at me, narrowing her eyes, and asked:

"What do they need? Landscapes?"

"No need for landscapes either. They don't need anything."

She finished taking off her gloves and opened a newspaper that had just been brought from the post office; after a minute she said softly, obviously restraining herself:

"Last week Anna died in childbirth. If there had been a dispensary nearby, she would still be alive. And it seems to me that gentleman landscape painters ought to have some sort of convictions in that regard."

"I have very definite convictions in that regard, I assure you," I replied, but she shielded herself from me with the newspaper as if she did not wish to listen. "In my opinion, dispensaries, schools, libraries, first-aid kits, under the existing conditions, only serve enslavement. The people are fettered with a great chain, and you don't cut the chain, you merely add new links to it—there's my conviction for you."

She raised her eyes to me and smiled derisively, while I went on trying to grasp my main thought:

"What matters is not that Anna died in childbirth, but that all these Annas, Mavras, Pelageyas bend their backs from early morning till dark, get sick from overwork, tremble all their lives for their hungry and sick children, fear death and sickness all their lives, get treated all their lives, fade early, age early, and die in dirt and stench; their children grow up and start the same tune, and so hundreds of years go by, and billions of people live worse than animals—only for the sake of a crust of bread, knowing constant fear. The whole horror of their situation is that they have no time to think of their souls, no time to remember their image and likeness; hunger, cold, animal fear, a mass of work, like a snowslide, bar all the paths to spiritual activity, to what precisely distinguishes man from animal and is the only thing worth living for. You come to their aid with hospitals and schools, but that doesn't free them from bondage, but, on the contrary, enslaves them still more, because, by introducing new prejudices in their life, you increase the number of their needs, not to mention that they must pay the zemstvo for their little pills and primers, and that means bending their backs even more."

"I won't argue with you," said Lida, lowering the newspaper. "I've already heard it all. I'll tell you just one thing: it's impossible to sit with folded arms. True, we're not saving mankind, and maybe we're mistaken in many ways, but we do what we can, and we're right. The highest and holiest task for a cultured person is to serve his neighbor, and we try to serve as we can. You don't like it, but one can't please everyone."

"True, Lida, true," said the mother.

She was always timid in Lida's presence, and kept glancing at her anxiously when she spoke, afraid of saying something unnecessary or inappropriate, and she never contradicted her, but always agreed—true, Lida, true.

"Dispensaries, peasant literacy, books with pathetic precepts and jokes cannot diminish either ignorance or mortality, any more than the light from your windows can illuminate this huge garden," I said. "You give nothing with your interference in these people's lives, you only create new needs, new pretexts for work."

"Ah, my God, but something must be done!" Lida said with vexation, and from her tone it was clear that she considered my arguments worthless and despised them.

"The people must be freed from heavy physical labor," I said. "Their yoke must be lightened, they must be given a respite, so that they don't spend their whole lives at the stove, the washtub, and in the fields, but also have time to think about their souls, about God, to give wider scope to their spiritual capacities. Every man's calling lies in spiritual activity—in a constant search for truth and the meaning of life. Make it so that crude, brutish labor is not necessary for them, let them feel themselves free, and then you'll see what a mockery these books and first-aid kits essentially are. Once a man is conscious of his true calling, he can be satisfied only by religion, the sciences, the arts, and not these trifles."

"Free them from labor!" Lida grinned. "Is that really possible?"

"Yes. Take a share of their work on yourself. If all of us, city and country dwellers, all of us without exception, agreed to divide up the work expended by mankind in general to satisfy its physical needs, the portion for each of us might be no more than two or three hours a day. Imagine that all of us, rich and poor, work only three hours a day, and the rest of our time is left free. Imagine, too, that in order to depend still less on our bodies and to work less, we invent machines to work for us, and try to reduce the number of our needs to the minimum. We train ourselves and our children not to fear hunger and cold, so that we don't constantly tremble for their health as Anna, Mavra, and Pelageya do. Imagine that we don't get treated, don't keep pharmacies, tobacco factories, distilleries—what a lot of free time we'd have in the end! All of us together would devote this leisure to the arts and sciences. As peasants sometimes get together to mend a road, so all of us together would seek truth and the meaning of life, and—I'm certain of it—the truth would be discovered very soon, man would be delivered from this constant, tormenting, oppressive fear, and even from death itself."

"You contradict yourself, however," said Lida. "You say science, science, yet you reject literacy."

"Literacy, when a man can only use it to read pothouse signboards and occasional books that he doesn't understand—such literacy has been with us since the time of Rurik; Gogol's Petrushka has been reading for a long time, and yet the village remains to this day what it was under Rurik. What we need is not literacy, but the freedom to give wide scope to our spiritual capacities. We need not schools but universities."

"You reject medicine as well."

"Yes. It would be needed only for the study of illnesses as phenomena of nature, not for their treatment. If we're to treat something, it should be not illnesses but their causes. Remove the main cause—physical work—and there will be no illnesses. I don't recognize the science of treatment," I went on excitedly. "The arts and sciences, when genuine, aspire not to temporary, not to specific purposes, but to the eternal and the general—they seek truth and the meaning of life, they seek God, the soul, and when they're harnessed to the needs and evils of the day, to first-aid kits and libraries, they only complicate and clutter life. We have lots of doctors, pharmacists, lawyers, there are lots of literate people, but no biologists, mathematicians, philosophers, poets. All our intelligence, all our inner energies have gone to satisfying temporary, passing needs . . . Among scientists, writers, and artists, work is at the boil, the comforts of life increase every day thanks to them, bodily needs multiply, and yet the truth is still far off, and man still remains the most predatory and slovenly of animals, and the tendency in the majority of mankind is towards degeneration and the permanent loss of all vitality. In such conditions an artist's life has no meaning, and the more talented he is, the more strange and incomprehensible his role, since it turns out that, in reality, he is working for the amusement of a predatory, slovenly animal and supporting the existing order of things. But I don't want to work and will not . . . Nothing's any use, let the earth go to hell and gone!"

"Missyuska, leave us," Lida said to her sister, obviously finding my words harmful for such a young girl.

Zhenya looked sadly at her sister and mother and left.

"Such nice things are commonly said when one wants to justify one's indifference," said Lida. "To reject hospitals and schools is easier than to treat or teach people."

"True, Lida, true," the mother agreed.

"You threaten to stop working," Lida went on. "Obviously you value your works highly. But let's stop arguing; we'll never see eye to eye, because I place the least perfect of all little libraries and first-aid kits, which you've just spoken of with such scorn, above all the landscape paintings in the world." And straightaway, turning to her mother, she began in a completely different tone: "The prince has lost a lot of weight and is greatly changed since he visited us. They sent him to Vichy."

She told her mother about the prince, so as not to speak with me. Her face was burning, and to conceal her agitation, she bent low to the table, as if she were nearsighted, pretending to read the newspaper. My presence was disagreeable. I said good night and went home.

4

Outside it was quiet; the village on the other side of the pond was already asleep, there was not a single light to be seen, and only the pale reflections of stars shone faintly on the pond. By the gate with the lions Zhenya stood motionless, waiting to see me off.

"Everyone's asleep in the village," I said to her, trying to make out her face in the darkness, and I saw her dark, sorrowful eyes directed at me. "The tavern keeper and the horse thieves are sleeping peacefully, and we respectable people annoy each other and argue."

It was a sad August night—sad because autumn was already in the air; covered by a purple cloud, the moon was rising, barely lighting up the road and the dark fields of winter wheat on either side. There were lots of falling stars. Zhenya walked down the road beside me, trying not to look at the sky, so as not to see the falling stars, which for some reason frightened her.

"I think you're right," she said, shivering from the night's dampness. "If all people together could give themselves to spiritual activity, they would soon know everything."

"Of course. We are higher beings, and if we were really conscious of the whole power of human genius and lived only for higher purposes, then in the end we would become like gods. But that will never be—mankind will degenerate, and there won't be any trace of genius left."

When the gates could no longer be seen, Zhenya stopped and hastily pressed my hand.

"Good night," she said, shivering; her shoulders were covered only by a little blouse, and she hunched up from the cold. "Come tomorrow."

The thought that I would be left alone, annoyed, dissatisfied with myself and with other people, gave me an eerie feeling; and now I myself tried not to look at the falling stars.

"Spend another moment with me," I said. "I beg you."

I loved Zhenya. It must be that I loved her for meeting me and seeing me off, for looking at me tenderly and with admiration. How touchingly beautiful her pale face was, her slender neck, her slender arms, her frailty, her idleness, her books! And her intelligence? I suspected that she was of uncommon intelligence; I admired the breadth of her views, perhaps because she thought differently from the severe and beautiful Lida, who did not like me. Zhenya liked me as an artist, I had won her heart with my talent, I passionately wanted to paint for her alone, and I dreamed of her as my little queen who, together with me, would one day possess these trees, fields, mists, the dawn, this nature, wonderful, enchanting, but in the midst of which I had till then felt myself hopelessly lonely and useless.

"Stay another moment," I asked. "I implore you."

I took off my coat and covered her chilled shoulders; she, afraid of looking ridiculous and unattractive in a man's coat, laughed and threw it off, and at that moment I embraced her and began to shower kisses on her face, shoulders, hands.

"Till tomorrow!" she whispered, and cautiously, as if afraid of breaking the silence of the night, embraced me. "We have no secrets from each other; I must tell Mama and my sister everything at once . . . It's so scary! Mama's nothing, Mama likes you, but Lida!"

She ran towards the gates.

"Goodbye!" she called.

And then for about two minutes I listened to her running. I had no wish to go home, nor any reason to go there. I stood for a while in thought and quietly trudged back, to look again at the house where she lived, a dear, naive old house, which seemed to look at me with the windows of its mezzanine as if with eyes, and to understand everything. I went past the terrace, sat down on a bench by the tennis court, in the darkness under an old elm, and looked at the house from there. In the windows of the mezzanine, where Missyus lived, there was a flash of bright light, then a peaceful green—the lamp had been covered with a shade. Shadows moved about . . . I was filled with tenderness, quietude, and satisfaction with myself—satisfaction that I could be carried away and fall in love—and at the same time I felt discomfort at the thought that just then, a few steps away from me, in one of the rooms of that house, lived Lida, who did not like, and perhaps hated, me. I sat and kept waiting, in case Zhenya came out, listening, and it seemed to me that there was talking in the mezzanine.

About an hour passed. The green light went out, and the shadows could no longer be seen. The moon had risen high over the house, lighting up the sleeping garden, the paths; the dahlias and roses in the flower garden in front of the house were clearly visible and seemed to be all of the same color. It was getting very cold. I left the garden, picked up my coat on the road, and unhurriedly plodded home.

When I came to the Volchaninovs' the next day after dinner, the glass door to the garden was wide open. I sat on the terrace, expecting that Zhenya would appear at any moment on the tennis court beyond the flower garden, or on one of the paths, or that her voice would come from inside; then I went to the drawing room, the dining room. There was not a soul. From the dining room I walked down the long corridor to the front hall, then back. There were several doors in the corridor, and behind one of them Lida's voice rang out.

"To a crow somewhere . . . God . . ." she said loudly and slowly, probably dictating. "God sent a piece of cheese . . . To a crow . . . somewhere. . . Who's there?" she suddenly called out, hearing my footsteps.

"It's me."

"Ah! Excuse me, I can't come right now; I'm busy with Dasha."

"Is Ekaterina Pavlovna in the garden?"

"No, she and my sister left this morning to visit our aunt in Penza province. And in the winter they will probably go abroad . . ." she added after a pause. "To a crow somewhere . . . God sent a pie-e-ece of che-e-ese . . . Have you written that?"

I went out to the front hall and, not thinking of anything, stood and looked from there at the pond and the village, and the words came to me:

"A piece of cheese . . . To a crow somewhere God sent a piece of cheese . . ."

And I left the estate by the same road I had come there on the first time, only in reverse: from the yard to the garden, past the house, then down the linden avenue . . . There a boy caught up with me and gave me a note. "I told my sister everything, and she demands that I part with you," I read. "It is beyond me to upset her by my disobedience. Forgive me, and God grant you happiness. If you only knew how bitterly Mama and I are weeping!"

Then the dark avenue of firs, the collapsed fence . . . In the field where rye was flowering then and quail were calling, cows and hobbled horses now wandered. Here and there on the hills the winter wheat showed bright green. A sober, everyday mood came over me, and I felt ashamed of everything I had said at the Volchaninovs, and bored with life, as before. I went home, packed, and left that evening for Petersburg.

I never saw the Volchaninovs again. Recently, going to the Crimea, I met Belokurov on the train. As usual, he was wearing his vest and embroidered shirt, and when I asked how he was getting along, he said: "By your prayers." We got to talking. He had sold his estate and bought another, a smaller one, in Lyubov Ivanovna's name. Of the Volchaninovs he said little. Lida, according to him, was still living at Shelkovka and teaching children in the school; she had gradually succeeded in gathering a circle of people sympathetic to her, who had formed themselves into a strong party and, at the last zemstvo elections, had "ousted" Balagin, who till then had had the whole district in his hands. Of Zhenya, Belokurov told me only that she was not living at home and he did not know where she was.

I am beginning to forget about the house with the mezzanine, and only rarely, while painting or reading, will I suddenly recall, as if at random, now the green light in the window, now the sound of my own footsteps in the fields at night, as I, in love, made my way home, rubbing my hands from the cold. And still more rarely, at moments when solitude weighs on me and I feel sad, I dimly remember, and for some reason I am gradually beginning to think that I, too, am remembered, waited for, and that we will meet . . .

Missyus, where are you?

QUESTIONS

1. Why does Zhenya find it "incomprehensible" that Lida's beliefs are wrong? (132)

2. Why does spending time with the Volchaninovs make the narrator want to paint?

3. Are the narrator's arguments against the usefulness of Lida's endeavors an attempt, as she says, "to justify one's indifference"? (140)

4. Are we meant to see the narrator's and Lida's points of view regarding work and sloth as equally valid?

5. To what extent is the end of the narrator's relationship with Zhenya a kind of resolution of his arguments with Lida?

6. Why does the narrator come to feel ashamed of everything he said at the Volchaninovs' house?

7. What does the Volchaninovs' house represent to the narrator?

FOR FURTHER REFLECTION

1. Would everyone be better off if, as the narrator proposes, each of us worked only two or three hours a day to meet all our material needs?

2. What is the relationship, if any, between physical labor and spiritual well-being?

3. Do you agree with Lida that "the least perfect of all little libraries and first-aid kits" should be placed above all the landscape paintings in the world?

BOBBIE ANN MASON

Bobbie Ann Mason (1940–) was born and raised on a dairy farm in rural Kentucky. After college she wrote for movie magazines in New York City and earned a PhD in literature, but by her late thirties she had turned to literary writing full-time; her breakthrough work, *Shiloh and Other Stories* (1982), won the 1983 Ernest Hemingway Award for best first fiction. Mason's stories and novels, including *In Country* (1985) and *Spence + Lila* (1988), depict the lives of rural and small-town Kentuckians as they cope with economic and social change. Mason's stories have appeared in the *Atlantic Monthly*, the *New Yorker*, and the *Paris Review*, and she has received both a Guggenheim and a National Endowment for the Arts fellowship.

Shiloh

Leroy Moffitt's wife, Norma Jean, is working on her pectorals. She lifts three-pound dumbbells to warm up, then progresses to a twenty-pound barbell. Standing with her legs apart, she reminds Leroy of Wonder Woman.

"I'd give anything if I could just get these muscles to where they're real hard," says Norma Jean. "Feel this arm. It's not as hard as the other one."

"That's 'cause you're right-handed," says Leroy, dodging as she swings the barbell in an arc.

"Do you think so?"

"Sure."

Leroy is a truck driver. He injured his leg in a highway accident four months ago, and his physical therapy, which involves weights and a pulley, prompted Norma Jean to try building herself up. Now she is attending a bodybuilding class. Leroy has been collecting temporary disability since his tractor-trailer jackknifed in Missouri, badly twisting his left leg in its socket. He has a steel pin in his hip. He will probably not be able to drive his rig again. It sits in the backyard, like a gigantic bird that has flown home to roost. Leroy has been home in Kentucky for three months, and his leg is almost healed, but the accident frightened him and he does not want to drive any more long hauls. He is not sure what to do next. In the meantime, he makes things from craft kits. He started by building a miniature log cabin from notched Popsicle sticks. He varnished it and placed it on the TV set, where it remains. It reminds him of a rustic Nativity scene. Then he tried string art (sailing ships on black velvet), a macramé owl kit, a snap-together B-17 Flying Fortress, and a lamp made out of a model truck, with a light fixture screwed in the top of the cab. At first the kits were diversions, something to kill time, but now he is thinking about building a full-scale log house from a kit. It would be considerably cheaper than building a regular house, and besides, Leroy has grown to appreciate how things are put together. He has begun to realize that in all the years he was on the road he never took time to examine anything. He was always flying past scenery.

"They won't let you build a log cabin in any of the new subdivisions," Norma Jean tells him.

"They will if I tell them it's for you," he says, teasing her. Ever since they were married, he has promised Norma Jean he would build her a new home one day. They have always rented, and the house they live in is small and nondescript. It does not even feel like a home, Leroy realizes now.

Norma Jean works at the Rexall drugstore, and she has acquired an amazing amount of information about cosmetics. When she explains to Leroy the three stages of complexion care, involving creams, toners, and moisturizers, he thinks happily of other petroleum products—axle grease, diesel fuel. This is a connection between him and Norma Jean. Since he has been home, he has felt unusually tender about his wife and guilty over his long absences. But he can't tell what she feels about him. Norma Jean has never complained about his traveling; she has never made hurt remarks, like calling his truck a "widow-maker." He is reasonably certain she has been faithful to him, but he wishes she would celebrate his permanent homecoming more happily. Norma Jean is often startled to find Leroy at home, and he thinks she seems a little disappointed about it. Perhaps he reminds her too much of the early days of their marriage, before he went on the road. They had a child who died as an infant, years ago. They never speak about their memories of Randy, which have almost faded, but now that Leroy is home all the time, they sometimes feel awkward around each other, and Leroy wonders if one of them should mention the child. He has the feeling that they are waking up out of a dream together—that they must create a new marriage, start afresh. They are lucky they are still married. Leroy has read that for most people losing a child destroys the marriage—or else he heard this on *Donahue*. He can't always remember where he learns things anymore.

At Christmas, Leroy bought an electric organ for Norma Jean. She used to play the piano when she was in high school. "It don't leave you," she told him once. "It's like riding a bicycle."

The new instrument had so many keys and buttons that she was bewildered by it at first. She touched the keys tentatively, pushed some buttons, then pecked out "Chopsticks." It came out in an amplified fox-trot rhythm, with marimba sounds.

"It's an orchestra!" she cried.

The organ had a pecan-look finish and eighteen preset chords, with optional flute, violin, trumpet, clarinet, and banjo accompaniments. Norma Jean mastered the organ almost immediately. At first she played Christmas songs. Then she bought *The Sixties Songbook* and learned every tune in it, adding variations to each with the rows of brightly colored buttons.

"I didn't like these old songs back then," she said. "But I have this crazy feeling I missed something."

"You didn't miss a thing," said Leroy.

Leroy likes to lie on the couch and smoke a joint and listen to Norma Jean play "Can't Take My Eyes Off You" and "I'll Be Back." He is back again. After fifteen years on the road, he is finally settling down with the woman he loves. She is still pretty. Her skin is flawless. Her frosted curls resemble pencil trimmings.

Now that Leroy has come home to stay, he notices how much the town has changed. Subdivisions are spreading across western Kentucky like an oil slick. The sign at the edge of town says "Pop: 11,500"—only seven hundred more than it said twenty years before. Leroy can't figure out who is living in all the new houses. The farmers who used to gather around the courthouse square on Saturday afternoons to play checkers and spit tobacco juice have gone. It has been years since Leroy has thought about the farmers, and they have disappeared without his noticing.

Leroy meets a kid named Stevie Hamilton in the parking lot at the new shopping center. While they pretend to be strangers meeting over a stalled car, Stevie tosses an ounce of marijuana under the front seat of Leroy's car. Stevie is wearing orange jogging shoes and a T-shirt that says CHATTAHOOCHEE SUPER-RAT. His father is a prominent doctor who lives in one of the expensive subdivisions in a new white-columned brick house that looks like a funeral parlor. In the phone book under his name there is a separate number, with the listing "Teenagers."

"Where do you get this stuff?" asks Leroy. "From your pappy?"

"That's for me to know and you to find out." Stevie says. He is slit-eyed and skinny.

"What else you got?"

"What you interested in?"

"Nothing special. Just wondered."

Leroy used to take speed on the road. Now he has to go slowly. He needs to be mellow. He leans back against the car and says, "I'm aiming to build me a log house, soon as I get time. My wife, though, I don't think she likes the idea."

"Well, let me know when you want me again," Stevie says. He has a cigarette in his cupped palm, as though sheltering it from the wind. He takes a long drag, then stomps it on the asphalt and slouches away.

Stevie's father was two years ahead of Leroy in high school. Leroy is thirty-four. He married Norma Jean when they were both eighteen, and their child Randy was born a few months later, but he died at the age of four months and three days. He would be about Stevie's age now. Norma Jean and Leroy were at the drive-in, watching a double feature (*Dr. Strangelove* and *Lover Come Back*), and the baby was sleeping in the back seat. When the first movie ended, the baby was dead. It was the sudden infant death syndrome. Leroy remembers handing Randy to a nurse at the emergency room, as though he were offering her a large doll as a present. A dead baby feels like a sack of flour. "It just happens sometimes," said the doctor, in what Leroy always recalls as a nonchalant tone. Leroy can hardly remember the child anymore, but he still sees vividly a scene from *Dr. Strangelove* in which the president of the United States was talking in a folksy voice on the hotline to the Soviet premier about the bomber accidentally headed toward Russia. He was in the war room, and the world map was lit up. Leroy remembers Norma Jean standing catatonically beside him in the hospital and himself thinking: Who is this strange girl? He had forgotten who she was. Now scientists are saying that crib death is caused by a virus. Nobody knows anything, Leroy thinks. The answers are always changing.

When Leroy gets home from the shopping center, Norma Jean's mother, Mabel Beasley, is there. Until this year, Leroy has not realized how much time she spends with Norma Jean. When she visits, she inspects the closets and then the plants, informing Norma Jean when a plant is droopy or yellow. Mabel calls the plants "flowers," although there are never any blooms. She always notices if Norma Jean's laundry is piling up. Mabel is a short, overweight woman whose tight, brown-dyed curls look more like a wig than the actual wig she sometimes wears. Today she has brought Norma Jean an off-white dust ruffle she made for the bed; Mabel works in a custom-upholstery shop.

"This is the tenth one I made this year," Mabel says. "I got started and couldn't stop."

"It's real pretty," says Norma Jean.

"Now we can hide things under the bed," says Leroy, who gets along with his mother-in-law primarily by joking with her. Mabel has never really forgiven him for disgracing her by getting Norma Jean pregnant. When the baby died, she said that fate was mocking her.

"What's that thing?" Mabel says to Leroy in a loud voice, pointing to a tangle of yarn on a piece of canvas.

Leroy holds it up for Mabel to see. "It's my needlepoint," he explains. "This is a *Star Trek* pillow cover."

"That's what a woman would do," says Mabel. "Great day in the morning!"

"All the big football players on TV do it," he says.

"Why, Leroy, you're always trying to fool me. I don't believe you for one minute. You don't know what to do with yourself—that's the whole trouble. Sewing!"

"I'm aiming to build us a log house," says Leroy. "Soon as my plans come."

"Like *heck* you are," says Norma Jean. She takes Leroy's needlepoint and shoves it into a drawer. "You have to find a job first. Nobody can afford to build now anyway."

Mabel straightens her girdle and says, "I still think before you get tied down y'all ought to take a little run to Shiloh."

"One of these days, Mama," Norma Jean says impatiently.

Mabel is talking about Shiloh, Tennessee. For the past few years, she has been urging Leroy and Norma Jean to visit the Civil War battleground there. Mabel went there on her honeymoon—the only real trip she ever took. Her husband died of a perforated ulcer when Norma Jean was ten, but Mabel, who was accepted into the United Daughters of the Confederacy in 1975, is still preoccupied with going back to Shiloh.

"I've been to kingdom come and back in that truck out yonder," Leroy says to Mabel, "but we never yet set foot in that battleground. Ain't that something? How did I miss it?"

"It's not even that far," Mabel says.

After Mabel leaves, Norma Jean reads to Leroy from a list she has made. "Things you could do," she announces. "You could get a job as a guard at Union Carbide, where they'd let you set on a stool. You could get on at the lumberyard. You could do a little carpenter work, if you want to build so bad. You could—"

"I can't do something where I'd have to stand up all day."

"You ought to try standing up all day behind a cosmetics counter. It's amazing that I have strong feet, coming from two parents that never had strong feet at all." At the moment Norma Jean is holding on to the kitchen counter, raising her knees one at a time as she talks. She is wearing two-pound ankle weights.

"Don't worry," says Leroy. "I'll do something."

"You could truck calves to slaughter for somebody. You wouldn't have to drive any big old truck for that."

"I'm going to build you this house," says Leroy. "I want to make you a real home."

"I don't want to live in any log cabin."

"It's not a cabin. It's a house."

"I don't care. It looks like a cabin."

"You and me together could lift those logs. It's just like lifting weights."

Norma Jean doesn't answer. Under her breath, she is counting. Now she is marching through the kitchen. She is doing goose steps.

Before his accident, when Leroy came home he used to stay in the house with Norma Jean, watching TV in bed and playing cards. She would cook fried chicken, picnic ham, chocolate pie—all his favorites. Now he is home alone much of the time. In the mornings, Norma Jean disappears, leaving a cooling place in the bed. She eats a cereal called

Body Buddies, and she leaves the bowl on the table, with the soggy tan balls floating in a milk puddle. He sees things about Norma Jean that he never realized before. When she chops onions, she stares off into a corner, as if she can't bear to look. She puts on her house slippers almost precisely at nine o'clock every evening and nudges her jogging shoes under the couch. She saves bread heels for the birds. Leroy watches the birds at the feeder. He notices the peculiar way goldfinches fly past the window. They close their wings, then fall, then spread their wings to catch and lift themselves. He wonders if they close their eyes when they fall. Norma Jean closes her eyes when they are in bed. She wants the lights turned out. Even then, he is sure she closes her eyes.

He goes for long drives around town. He tends to drive a car rather carelessly. Power steering and an automatic shift make a car feel so small and inconsequential that his body is hardly involved in the driving process. His injured leg stretches out comfortably. Once or twice he has almost hit something, but even the prospect of an accident seems minor in a car. He cruises the new subdivisions, feeling like a criminal rehearsing for a robbery. Norma Jean is probably right about a log house being inappropriate here in the new subdivisions. All the houses look grand and complicated. They depress him.

One day when Leroy comes home from a drive he finds Norma Jean in tears. She is in the kitchen making a potato and mushroom-soup casserole, with grated-cheese topping. She is crying because her mother caught her smoking.

"I didn't hear her coming. I was standing here puffing away pretty as you please," Norma Jean says, wiping her eyes.

"I knew it would happen sooner or later," says Leroy, putting his arm around her.

"She don't know the meaning of the word 'knock,'" says Norma Jean. "It's a wonder she hadn't caught me years ago."

"Think of it this way," Leroy says. "What if she caught me with a joint?"

"You better not let her!" Norma Jean shrieks. "I'm warning you, Leroy Moffitt!"

"I'm just kidding. Here, play me a tune. That'll help you relax."

Norma Jean puts the casserole in the oven and sets the timer. Then she plays a ragtime tune, with horns and banjo, as Leroy lights up a joint and lies on the couch, laughing to himself about Mabel's catching him at it. He thinks of Stevie Hamilton—a doctor's son pushing grass. Everything is funny. The whole town seems crazy and small. He is reminded of Virgil Mathis, a boastful policeman Leroy used to shoot pool with. Virgil recently led a drug bust in a back room at a bowling alley, where he seized ten thousand dollars' worth of marijuana. The newspaper had a picture of him holding up the bags of grass and grinning widely. Right now, Leroy can imagine Virgil breaking down the door and arresting him with a lungful of smoke. Virgil would probably have been alerted to the scene because of all the racket Norma Jean is making. Now she sounds like a hard-rock band. Norma Jean is terrific. When she switches to a Latin-rhythm version of "Sunshine Superman," Leroy hums along. Norma Jean's foot goes up and down, up and down.

"Well, what do you think?" Leroy says, when Norma Jean pauses to search through her music.

"What do I think about what?"

His mind has gone blank. Then he says, "I'll sell my rig and build us a house." That wasn't what he wanted to say. He wanted to know what she thought—what she *really* thought—about them.

"Don't start in on that again," says Norma Jean. She begins playing "Who'll Be the Next in Line?"

Leroy used to tell hitchhikers his whole life story— about his travels, his hometown, the baby. He would end with a question: "Well, what do you think?" It was just a rhetorical question. In time, he had the feeling that he'd been telling the same story over and over to the same hitch- hikers. He quit talking to hitchhikers when he realized how his voice sounded—whining and self-pitying, like some teenage-tragedy song. Now Leroy has the sudden impulse to tell Norma Jean about himself, as if he had just met her. They have known each other so long they have forgotten a lot about each other. They could become reacquainted. But when the oven timer goes off and she runs to the kitchen, he forgets why he wants to do this.

The next day, Mabel drops by. It is Saturday and Norma Jean is cleaning. Leroy is studying the plans of his log house, which have finally come in the mail. He has them spread out on the table—big sheets of stiff blue paper, with diagrams and numbers printed in white. While Norma Jean runs the vacuum, Mabel drinks coffee. She sets her coffee cup on a blueprint.

"I'm just waiting for time to pass," she says to Leroy, drumming her fingers on the table.

As soon as Norma Jean switches off the vacuum, Mabel says in a loud voice, "Did you hear about the datsun dog that killed the baby?"

Norma Jean says, "The word is 'dachshund.'"

"They put the dog on trial. It chewed the baby's legs off. The mother was in the next room all the time." She raises her voice. "They thought it was neglect."

Norma Jean is holding her ears. Leroy manages to open the refrigerator and get some Diet Pepsi to offer Mabel. Mabel still has some coffee and she waves away the Pepsi.

"Datsuns are like that," Mabel says. "They're jealous dogs. They'll tear a place to pieces if you don't keep an eye on them."

"You better watch out what you're saying, Mabel," says Leroy.

"Well, facts is facts."

Leroy looks out the window at his rig. It is like a huge piece of furniture gathering dust in the backyard. Pretty soon it will be an antique. He hears the vacuum cleaner. Norma Jean seems to be cleaning the living room rug again.

Later, she says to Leroy, "She just said that about the baby because she caught me smoking. She's trying to pay me back."

"What are you talking about?" Leroy says, nervously shuffling blueprints.

"You know good and well," Norma Jean says. She is sitting in a kitchen chair with her feet up and her arms wrapped around her knees. She looks small and helpless. She says, "The very idea, her bringing up a subject like that! Saying it was neglect."

"She didn't mean that," Leroy says.

"She might not have *thought* she meant it. She always says things like that. You don't know how she goes on."

"But she didn't really mean it. She was just talking."

Leroy opens a king-sized bottle of beer and pours it into two glasses, dividing it carefully. He hands a glass to Norma Jean and she takes it from him mechanically. For a long time, they sit by the kitchen window watching the birds at the feeder.

Something is happening. Norma Jean is going to night school. She has graduated from her six-week bodybuilding course and now she is taking an adult-education course in composition at Paducah Community College. She spends her evenings outlining paragraphs.

"First you have a topic sentence," she explains to Leroy. "Then you divide it up. Your secondary topic has to be connected to your primary topic."

To Leroy, this sounds intimidating. "I never was any good in English," he says.

"It makes a lot of sense."

"What are you doing this for, anyhow?"

She shrugs. "It's something to do." She stands up and lifts her dumbbells a few times.

"Driving a rig, nobody cared about my English."

"I'm not criticizing your English."

Norma Jean used to say, "If I lose ten minutes' sleep, I just drag all day." Now she stays up late, writing compositions. She got a B on her first paper—a how-to theme on soup-based casseroles. Recently Norma Jean has been cooking unusual foods—tacos, lasagna, Bombay chicken. She doesn't play the organ anymore, though her second paper was called "Why Music Is Important to Me." She sits at the kitchen table, concentrating on her outlines, while Leroy plays with his log house plans, practicing with a set of Lincoln Logs. The thought of getting a truckload of notched, numbered logs scares him, and he wants to be prepared. As he and Norma Jean work together at the kitchen table, Leroy has the hopeful thought that they are sharing something, but he knows he is a fool to think this. Norma Jean is miles away. He knows he is going to lose her. Like Mabel, he is just waiting for time to pass.

One day, Mabel is there before Norma Jean gets home from work, and Leroy finds himself confiding in her. Mabel, he realizes, must know Norma Jean better than he does.

"I don't know what's got into that girl," Mabel says. "She used to go to bed with the chickens. Now you say she's up all hours. Plus her a-smoking. I like to died."

"I want to make her this beautiful home," Leroy says, indicating the Lincoln Logs. "I don't think she even wants it. Maybe she was happier with me gone."

"She don't know what to make of you, coming home like this."

"Is that it?"

Mabel takes the roof off his Lincoln Log cabin. "You couldn't get *me* in a log cabin," she says. "I was raised in one. It's no picnic, let me tell you."

"They're different now," says Leroy.

"I tell you what," Mabel says, smiling oddly at Leroy.

"What?"

"Take her on down to Shiloh. Y'all need to get out together, stir a little. Her brain's all balled up over them books."

Leroy can see traces of Norma Jean's features in her mother's face. Mabel's worn face has the texture of crinkled cotton, but suddenly she looks pretty. It occurs to Leroy that Mabel has been hinting all along that she wants them to take her with them to Shiloh.

"Let's all go to Shiloh," he says. "You and me and her. Come Sunday."

Mabel throws up her hands in protest. "Oh, no, not me. Young folks want to be by theirselves."

When Norma Jean comes in with groceries, Leroy says excitedly, "Your mama here's been dying to go to Shiloh for thirty-five years. It's about time we went, don't you think?"

"I'm not going to butt in on anybody's second honeymoon," Mabel says.

"Who's going on a honeymoon, for Christ's sake?" Norma Jean says loudly.

"I never raised no daughter of mine to talk thataway," Mabel says.

"You ain't seen nothing yet," says Norma Jean. She starts putting away boxes and cans, slamming cabinet doors.

"There's a log cabin at Shiloh," Mabel says. "It was there during the battle. There's bullet holes in it."

"When are you going to *shut up* about Shiloh, Mama?" asks Norma Jean.

"I always thought Shiloh was the prettiest place, so full of history," Mabel goes on. "I just hoped y'all could see it once before I die, so you could tell me about it." Later, she whispers to Leroy, "You do what I said. A little change is what she needs."

"Your name means 'the king,'" Norma Jean says to Leroy that evening. He is trying to get her to go to Shiloh, and she is reading a book about another century.

"Well, I reckon I ought to be right proud."

"I guess so."

"Am I still king around here?"

Norma Jean flexes her biceps and feels them for hardness. "I'm not fooling around with anybody, if that's what you mean," she says.

"Would you tell me if you were?"

"I don't know."

"What does *your* name mean?"

"It was Marilyn Monroe's real name."

"No kidding!"

"Norma comes from the Normans. They were invaders," she says. She closes her book and looks hard at Leroy. "I'll go to Shiloh with you if you'll stop staring at me."

On Sunday, Norma Jean packs a picnic and they go to Shiloh. To Leroy's relief, Mabel says she does not want to come with them. Norma Jean drives, and Leroy, sitting beside her, feels like some boring hitchhiker she has picked up. He tries some conversation, but she answers him in monosyllables. At Shiloh, she drives aimlessly through the park, past bluffs and trails and steep ravines. Shiloh is an immense place, and Leroy cannot see it as a battleground. It is not what he expected. He thought it would look like a golf course. Monuments are everywhere, showing through the thick clusters of trees. Norma Jean passes the log cabin Mabel mentioned. It is surrounded by tourists looking for bullet holes.

"That's not the kind of log house I've got in mind," says Leroy apologetically.

"I know *that*."

"This is a pretty place. Your mama was right."

"It's O.K.," says Norma Jean. "Well, we've seen it. I hope she's satisfied."

They burst out laughing together.

At the park museum, a movie on Shiloh is shown every half hour, but they decide that they don't want to see it.

They buy a souvenir Confederate flag for Mabel, and then they find a picnic spot near the cemetery, Norma Jean has brought a picnic cooler, with pimiento sandwiches, soft drinks, and Yodels. Leroy eats a sandwich and then smokes a joint, hiding it behind the picnic cooler. Norma Jean has quit smoking altogether. She is picking cake crumbs from the cellophane wrapper, like a fussy bird.

Leroy says, "So the boys in gray ended up in Corinth. The Union soldiers zapped 'em finally. April 7, 1862."

They both know that he doesn't know any history. He is just talking about some of the historical plaques they have read. He feels awkward, like a boy on a date with an older girl. They are still just making conversation.

"Corinth is where Mama eloped to," says Norma Jean.

They sit in silence and stare at the cemetery for the Union dead and, beyond, at a tall cluster of trees. Campers are parked nearby, bumper to bumper, and small children in bright clothing are cavorting and squealing. Norma Jean wads up the cake wrapper and squeezes it tightly in her hand. Without looking at Leroy, she says, "I want to leave you."

Leroy takes a bottle of Coke out of the cooler and flips off the cap. He holds the bottle poised near his mouth but cannot remember to take a drink. Finally he says. "No, you don't."

"Yes, I do."

"I won't let you."

"You can't stop me."

"Don't do me that way."

Leroy knows Norma Jean will have her own way. "Didn't I promise to be home from now on?" he says.

"In some ways, a woman prefers a man who wanders," says Norma Jean. "That sounds crazy, I know."

"You're not crazy."

Leroy remembers to drink from his Coke. Then he says, "Yes, you *are* crazy. You and me could start all over again. Right back at the beginning."

"We *have* started all over again," says Norma Jean. "And this is how it turned out."

"What did I do wrong?"

"Nothing."

"Is this one of those women's lib things?" Leroy asks.

"Don't be funny."

The cemetery, a green slope dotted with white markers, looks like a subdivision site. Leroy is trying to comprehend that his marriage is breaking up, but for some reason he is wondering about white slabs in a graveyard.

"Everything was fine till Mama caught me smoking," says Norma Jean, standing up. "That set something off."

"What are you talking about?"

"She won't leave me alone—*you* won't leave me alone." Norma Jean seems to be crying, but she is looking away from him. "I feel eighteen again. I can't face that all over again." She starts walking away. "No, it *wasn't* fine. I don't know what I'm saying. Forget it."

Leroy takes a lungful of smoke and closes his eyes as Norma Jean's words sink in. He tries to focus on the fact that thirty-five hundred soldiers died on the grounds around him. He can only think of that war as a board game with plastic soldiers. Leroy almost smiles, as he compares the Confederates' daring attack on the Union camps and Virgil Mathis's raid on the bowling alley. General Grant, drunk and furious, shoved the Southerners back to Corinth, where Mabel and Jet Beasley were married years later, when Mabel was still thin and good-looking. The next day, Mabel and Jet visited the battleground, and then Norma Jean was born, and then she married Leroy and they had a baby, which they lost, and now Leroy and Norma Jean are here at the same battleground. Leroy knows he is leaving out a lot. He is leaving out the insides of history. History was always just names and dates to him. It occurs to him that building a house out of logs is similarly empty—too simple. And the real inner workings of a marriage, like most of history, have escaped him. Now he sees that building a log house is the dumbest idea he could have had. It was clumsy of him to think Norma Jean would want a log house. It was a crazy idea. He'll have to think of something else, quickly. He will wad the blueprints into tight balls and fling them into the lake. Then he'll get moving again. He opens his eyes. Norma Jean has moved away and is walking through the cemetery, following a serpentine brick path.

Leroy gets up to follow his wife, but his good leg is asleep and his bad leg still hurts him. Norma Jean is far away, walking rapidly toward the bluff by the river, and he tries to hobble toward her. Some children run past him, screaming noisily. Norma Jean has reached the bluff, and she is looking out over the Tennessee River. Now she turns toward Leroy and waves her arms. Is she beckoning to him? She seems to be doing an exercise for her chest muscles. The sky is unusually pale—the color of the dust ruffle Mabel made for their bed.

QUESTIONS

1. Why does Leroy spend his time making plans to build a log house instead of selling his rig and finding a new job?

2. Why do the "grand and complicated" houses in the new subdivisions depress Leroy? (154)

3. Why does Norma Jean take bodybuilding and writing courses and cook unusual foods after Leroy has returned home to stay?

4. Why does Norma Jean finally agree to make the trip to Shiloh?

5. What does Norma Jean mean when she says, "You ain't seen nothing yet"? (159)

6. When Norma Jean tries to explain to Leroy why she wants to leave him, why does she finally tell him, "I don't know what I'm saying. Forget it"? (162)

7. What makes Leroy realize that "building a log house is the dumbest idea he could have had"? (162–163)

FOR FURTHER REFLECTION

1. What significance does Mason give to Shiloh, both as the title of the story and as the setting of the final scene?

2. At the end of the story, do either Leroy or Norma Jean know what they want to make of their lives?

3. Can excessive activity be as much a sign of sloth as not enough activity?

Greed

D. H. LAWRENCE

David Herbert Lawrence (1885–1930) was raised in Nottinghamshire, England, where his father was a coal miner; his mother, a teacher and poet, introduced her son to literature. From his late twenties on, Lawrence led a restless existence, living in Europe, the United States, and Mexico. His intense and contentious relations with other writers, his German wife, Frieda, and other women (including his mother) are reflected in many of his novels, including *Sons and Lovers* (1913), *The Rainbow* (1915), and *Women in Love* (1920). He often explores how the constraints of modern civilization distort sexual relationships between men and women, a theme central to his most notorious novel, *Lady Chatterley's Lover* (1928), which was banned in the United States and Great Britain for many years. In spite of poor health, Lawrence was prolific, producing numerous novels, short stories, travel books, essays, poems, and letters.

The Rocking-Horse Winner

There was a woman who was beautiful, who started with all the advantages, yet she had no luck. She married for love, and the love turned to dust. She had bonny children, yet she felt they had been thrust upon her, and she could not love them. They looked at her coldly, as if they were finding fault with her. And hurriedly she felt she must cover up some fault in herself. Yet what it was that she must cover up she never knew. Nevertheless, when her children were present, she always felt the centre of her heart go hard. This troubled her, and in her manner she was all the more gentle and anxious for her children, as if she loved them very much. Only she herself knew that at the centre of her heart was a hard little place that could not feel love, no, not for anybody. Everybody else said of her: "She is such a good mother. She adores her children." Only she herself, and her children themselves, knew it was not so. They read it in each other's eyes.

There were a boy and two little girls. They lived in a pleasant house, with a garden, and they had discreet servants, and felt themselves superior to anyone in the neighbourhood.

Although they lived in style, they felt always an anxiety in the house. There was never enough money. The mother had a small income, and the father had a small income, but not nearly enough for the social position which they had to keep up. The father went into town to some office. But though he had good prospects, these prospects never materialised. There was always the grinding sense of the shortage of money, though the style was always kept up.

At last the mother said: "I will see if *I* can't make something." But she did not know where to begin. She racked her brains, and tried this thing and the other, but could not find anything successful. The failure made deep lines come into her face. Her children were growing up, they would have to go to school. There must be more money, there must be more money. The father, who was always very handsome and expensive in his tastes, seemed as if he never *would* be able to do anything worth doing. And the mother, who had a great belief in herself, did not succeed any better, and her tastes were just as expensive.

And so the house came to be haunted by the unspoken phrase: *There must be more money! There must be more money!* The children could hear it all the time, though nobody said it aloud. They heard it at Christmas, when the expensive and splendid toys filled the nursery. Behind the shining modern rocking horse, behind the smart doll's house, a voice would start whispering: "There *must* be more money! There *must* be more money!" And the children would stop playing, to listen for a moment. They would look into each other's eyes, to see if they had all heard. And each one saw in the eyes of the other two that they too had heard. "There *must* be more money! There *must* be more money!"

It came whispering from the springs of the still-swaying rocking horse, and even the horse, bending his wooden, champing head, heard it. The big doll, sitting so pink and smirking in her new pram, could hear it quite plainly, and seemed to be smirking all the more self-consciously because of it. The foolish puppy, too, that took the place of the teddy bear, he was looking so extraordinarily foolish for no other reason but that he heard the secret whisper all over the house: "There *must* be more money!"

Yet nobody ever said it aloud. The whisper was everywhere, and therefore no one spoke it. Just as no one ever says: "We are breathing!" in spite of the fact that breath is coming and going all the time.

"Mother," said the boy Paul one day, "why don't we keep a car of our own? Why do we always use uncle's, or else a taxi?"

"Because we're the poor members of the family," said the mother.

"But why *are* we, mother?"

"Well—I suppose," she said slowly and bitterly, "it's because your father has no luck."

The boy was silent for some time.

"Is luck money, mother?" he asked, rather timidly.

"No, Paul. Not quite. It's what causes you to have money."

"Oh!" said Paul vaguely. "I thought when Uncle Oscar said *filthy lucker*, it meant money."

"*Filthy lucre* does mean money," said the mother. "But it's lucre, not luck."

"Oh!" said the boy. "Then what *is* luck, mother?"

"It's what causes you to have money. If you're lucky you have money. That's why it's better to be born lucky than rich. If you're rich, you may lose your money. But if you're lucky, you will always get more money."

"Oh! Will you? And is father not lucky?"

"Very unlucky, I should say," she said bitterly.

The boy watched her with unsure eyes.

"Why?" he asked.

"I don't know. Nobody ever knows why one person is lucky and another unlucky."

"Don't they? Nobody at all? Does *nobody* know?"

"Perhaps God. But he never tells."

"He ought to, then. And aren't you lucky either, mother?"

"I can't be, if I married an unlucky husband."

"But by yourself, aren't you?"

"I used to think I was, before I married. Now I think I am very unlucky indeed."

"Why?"

"Well—never mind! Perhaps I'm not really," she said.

The child looked at her to see if she meant it. But he saw, by the lines of her mouth, that she was only trying to hide something from him.

"Well, anyhow," he said stoutly, "I'm a lucky person."

"Why?" said his mother, with a sudden laugh.

He stared at her. He didn't even know why he had said it.

"God told me," he asserted, brazening it out.

"I hope he did, dear!" she said, again with a laugh, but rather bitter.

"He did, mother!"

"Excellent!" said the mother, using one of her husband's exclamations.

The boy saw she did not believe him; or rather, that she paid no attention to his assertion. This angered him somewhere, and made him want to compel her attention.

He went off by himself, vaguely, in a childish way, seeking for the clue to "luck." Absorbed, taking no heed of other people, he went about with a sort of stealth, seeking inwardly for luck. He wanted luck, he wanted it, he wanted it. When the two girls were playing dolls in the nursery, he would sit on his big rocking horse, charging madly into space, with a frenzy that made the little girls peer at him uneasily. Wildly the horse careered, the waving dark hair of the boy tossed, his eyes had a strange glare in them. The little girls dared not speak to him.

When he had ridden to the end of his mad little journey, he climbed down and stood in front of his rocking horse, staring fixedly into its lowered face. Its red mouth was slightly open, its big eye was wide and glassy-bright.

"Now!" he would silently command the snorting steed. "Now, take me to where there is luck! Now take me!"

And he would slash the horse on the neck with the little whip he had asked Uncle Oscar for. He *knew* the horse could take him to where there was luck, if only he forced it. So he would mount again and start on his furious ride, hoping at last to get there. He knew he could get there.

"You'll break your horse, Paul!" said the nurse.

"He's always riding like that! I wish he'd leave off!" said his elder sister Joan.

But he only glared down on them in silence. Nurse gave him up. She could make nothing of him. Anyhow, he was growing beyond her.

One day his mother and his Uncle Oscar came in when he was on one of his furious rides. He did not speak to them.

"Hallo, you young jockey! Riding a winner?" said his uncle.

"Aren't you growing too big for a rocking horse? You're not a very little boy any longer, you know," said his mother.

But Paul only gave a blue glare from his big, rather close-set eyes. He would speak to nobody when he was in full tilt. His mother watched him with an anxious expression on her face.

At last he suddenly stopped forcing his horse into the mechanical gallop and slid down.

"Well, I got there!" he announced fiercely, his blue eyes still flaring, and his sturdy long legs straddling apart.

"Where did you get to?" asked his mother.

"Where I wanted to go," he flared back at her.

"That's right, son!" said Uncle Oscar. "Don't you stop till you get there. What's the horse's name?"

"He doesn't have a name," said the boy.

"Gets on without all right?" asked the uncle.

"Well, he has different names. He was called Sansovino last week."

"Sansovino, eh? Won the Ascot. How did you know this name?"

"He always talks about horseraces with Bassett," said Joan.

The uncle was delighted to find that his small nephew was posted with all the racing news. Bassett, the young gardener, who had been wounded in the left foot in the war and had got his present job through Oscar Cresswell, whose batman he had been, was a perfect blade of the "turf." He lived in the racing events, and the small boy lived with him.

Oscar Cresswell got it all from Bassett.

"Master Paul comes and asks me, so I can't do more than tell him, sir," said Bassett, his face terribly serious, as if he were speaking of religious matters.

"And does he ever put anything on a horse he fancies?"

"Well—I don't want to give him away—he's a young sport, a fine sport, sir. Would you mind asking him himself? He sort of takes a pleasure in it, and perhaps he'd feel I was giving him away, sir, if you don't mind."

Bassett was serious as a church.

The uncle went back to his nephew and took him off for a ride in the car.

"Say, Paul, old man, do you ever put anything on a horse?" the uncle asked.

The boy watched the handsome man closely.

"Why, do you think I oughtn't to?" he parried.

"Not a bit of it! I thought perhaps you might give me a tip for the Lincoln."

The car sped on into the country, going down to Uncle Oscar's place in Hampshire.

"Honour bright?" said the nephew.

"Honour bright, son!" said the uncle.

"Well, then, Daffodil."

"Daffodil! I doubt it, sonny. What about Mirza?"

"I only know the winner:' said the boy. "That's Daffodil."

"Daffodil, eh?"

There was a pause. Daffodil was an obscure horse comparatively.

"Uncle!"

"Yes, son?"

"You won't let it go any further, will you? I promised Bassett."

"Bassett be damned, old man! What's he got to do with it?"

"We're partners. We've been partners from the first. Uncle, he lent me my first five shillings, which I lost. I promised him, honour bright, it was only between me and him; only you gave me that ten-shilling note I started winning with, so I thought you were lucky. You won't let it go any further, will you?"

The boy gazed at his uncle from those big, hot, blue eyes, set rather close together. The uncle stirred and laughed uneasily.

"Right you are, son! I'll keep your tip private. Daffodil, eh? How much are you putting on him?"

"All except twenty pounds," said the boy. "I keep that in reserve."

The uncle thought it a good joke.

"You keep twenty pounds in reserve, do you, you young romancer? What are you betting, then?"

"I'm betting three hundred," said the boy gravely. "But it's between you and me, Uncle Oscar! Honour bright?"

The uncle burst into a roar of laughter.

"It's between you and me all right, you young Nat Gould," he said, laughing. "But where's your three hundred?"

"Bassett keeps it for me. We're partners."

"You are, are you! And what is Bassett putting on Daffodil?"

"He won't go quite as high as I do, I expect. Perhaps he'll go a hundred and fifty."

"What, pennies?" laughed the uncle.

"Pounds," said the child, with a surprised look at his uncle. "Bassett keeps a bigger reserve than I do."

Between wonder and amusement Uncle Oscar was silent. He pursued the matter no further, but he determined to take his nephew with him to the Lincoln races.

"Now, son," he said, "I'm putting twenty on Mirza, and I'll put five on for you on any horse you fancy. What's your pick?"

"Daffodil, uncle."

"No, not the fiver on Daffodil!"

"I should if it was my own fiver," said the child.

"Good! Good! Right you are! A fiver for me and a fiver for you on Daffodil."

The child had never been to a race meeting before, and his eyes were blue fire. He pursed his mouth tight and watched. A Frenchman just in front had put his money on Lancelot. Wild with excitement, he flayed his arms up and down, yelling "*Lancelot! Lancelot!*" in his French accent.

Daffodil came in first, Lancelot second, Mirza third. The child, flushed and with eyes blazing, was curiously serene. His uncle brought him four five-pound notes, four to one.

"What am I to do with these?" he cried, waving them before the boy's eyes.

"I suppose we'll talk to Bassett," said the boy. "I expect I have fifteen hundred now; and twenty in reserve; and this twenty."

His uncle studied him for some moments.

"Look here, son!" he said. "You're not serious about Bassett and that fifteen hundred, are you?"

"Yes, I am. But it's between you and me, uncle. Honour bright?"

"Honour bright all right, son! But I must talk to Bassett."

"If you'd like to be a partner, uncle, with Bassett and me, we could all be partners. Only, you'd have to promise, honour bright, uncle, not to let it go beyond us three. Bassett and I are lucky, and you must be lucky, because it was your ten shillings I started winning with. . . ."

Uncle Oscar took both Bassett and Paul into Richmond Park for an afternoon, and there they talked.

"It's like this, you see, sir," Bassett said. "Master Paul would get me talking about racing events, spinning yarns, you know, sir. And he was always keen on knowing if I'd made or if I'd lost. It's about a year since, now, that I put five shillings on Blush of Dawn for him—and we lost. Then the luck turned, with that ten shillings he had from you, that we put on Singhalese. And since that time, it's been pretty steady, all things considering. What do you say, Master Paul?"

"We're all right when we're sure," said Paul. "It's when we're not quite sure that we go down."

"Oh, but we're careful then," said Bassett.

"But when are you *sure*?" smiled Uncle Oscar.

"It's Master Paul, sir," said Bassett in a secret, religious voice. "It's as if he had it from heaven. Like Daffodil, now, for the Lincoln. That was as sure as eggs."

"Did you put anything on Daffodil?" asked Oscar Cresswell.

"Yes, sir. I made my bit."

"And my nephew?"

Bassett was obstinately silent, looking at Paul.

"I made twelve hundred, didn't I, Bassett? I told uncle I was putting three hundred on Daffodil."

"That's right," said Bassett, nodding.

"But where's the money?" asked the uncle.

"I keep it safe locked up, sir. Master Paul he can have it any minute he likes to ask for it."

"What, fifteen hundred pounds?"

"And twenty! And *forty*, that is, with the twenty he made on the course.

"It's amazing!" said the uncle.

"If Master Paul offers you to be partners, sir, I would, if I were you, if you'll excuse me," said Bassett.

Oscar Cresswell thought about it.

"I'll see the money," he said.

They drove home again, and, sure enough, Bassett came round to the garden house with fifteen hundred pounds in notes. The twenty pounds reserve was left with Joe Glee, in the Turf Commission deposit.

"You see, it's all right, uncle, when I'm *sure*! Then we go strong, for all we're worth. Don't we, Bassett?"

"We do that, Master Paul."

"And when are you sure?" said the uncle, laughing.

"Oh, well, sometimes I'm *absolutely* sure, like about Daffodil," said the boy; "and sometimes I have an idea; and sometimes I haven't even an idea, have I, Bassett? Then we're careful, because we mostly go down."

"You do, do you! And when you're sure, like about Daffodil, what makes you sure, sonny?"

"Oh, well, I don't know," said the boy uneasily. "I'm sure, you know, uncle; that's all."

"It's as if he had it from heaven, sir," Bassett reiterated.

"I should say so!" said the uncle.

But he became a partner. And when the Leger was coming on Paul was "sure" about Lively Spark, which was a quite inconsiderable horse. The boy insisted on putting a thousand on the horse, Bassett went for five hundred, and Oscar Cresswell two hundred. Lively Spark came in first, and the betting had been ten to one against him. Paul had made ten thousand.

"You see," he said, "I was absolutely sure of him."

Even Oscar Cresswell had cleared two thousand.

"Look here, son," he said, "this sort of thing makes me nervous."

"It needn't, uncle! Perhaps I shan't be sure again for a long time."

"But what are you going to do with your money?" asked the uncle.

"Of course," said the boy, "I started it for mother. She said she had no luck, because father is unlucky, so I thought if *I* was lucky, it might stop whispering."

"What might stop whispering?"

"Our house. I *hate* our house for whispering."

"What does it whisper?"

"Why—why"—the boy fidgeted—"why, I don't know But it's always short of money, you know, uncle."

"I know it, son, I know it."

"You know people send mother writs, don't you, uncle?"

"I'm afraid I do," said the uncle.

"And then the house whispers, like people laughing at you behind your back. It's awful, that is! I thought if I was lucky——"

"You might stop it," added the uncle.

The boy watched him with big blue eyes, that had an uncanny cold fire in them, and he said never a word.

"Well, then!" said the uncle. "What are we doing?"

"I shouldn't like mother to know I was lucky," said the boy.

"Why not, son?"

"She'd stop me."

"I don't think she would."

"Oh!"—and the boy writhed in an odd way—"I *don't* want her to know, uncle."

"All right, son! We'll manage it without her knowing."

They managed it very easily. Paul, at the other's suggestion, handed over five thousand pounds to his uncle, who deposited it with the family lawyer, who was then to inform Paul's mother that a relative had put five thousand pounds into his hands, which sum was to be paid out a thousand pounds at a time, on the mother's birthday, for the next five years.

"So she'll have a birthday present of a thousand pounds for five successive years," said Uncle Oscar. "I hope it won't make it all the harder for her later."

Paul's mother had her birthday in November. The house had been "whispering" worse than ever lately, and, even in spite of his luck, Paul could not bear up against it. He was very anxious to see the effect of the birthday letter, telling his mother about the thousand pounds.

When there were no visitors, Paul now took his meals with his parents, as he was beyond the nursery control. His

mother went into town nearly every day. She had discovered that she had an odd knack of sketching furs and dress
materials, so she worked secretly in the studio of a friend
who was the chief "artist" for the leading drapers. She drew
the figures of ladies in furs and ladies in silk and sequins for
the newspaper advertisements. This young woman artist
earned several thousand pounds a year, but Paul's mother
only made several hundreds, and she was again dissatisfied.
She so wanted to be first in something, and she did not succeed, even in making sketches for drapery advertisements.

She was down to breakfast on the morning of her birthday. Paul watched her face as she read her letters. He knew
the lawyer's letter. As his mother read it, her face hardened
and became more expressionless. Then a cold, determined
look came on her mouth. She hid the letter under the pile of
others, and said not a word about it.

"Didn't you have anything nice in the post for your
birthday, mother?" said Paul.

"Quite moderately nice," she said, her voice cold and
absent.

She went away to town without saying more.

But in the afternoon Uncle Oscar appeared. He said
Paul's mother had had a long interview with the lawyer,
asking if the whole five thousand could not be advanced at
once, as she was in debt.

"What do you think, uncle?" said the boy.

"I leave it to you, son."

"Oh, let her have it, then! We can get some more with
the other," said the boy.

"A bird in the hand is worth two in the bush, laddie!"
said Uncle Oscar.

"But I'm sure to *know* for the Grand National, or the
Lincolnshire, or else the Derby. I'm sure to know for *one* of
them," said Paul.

So Uncle Oscar signed the agreement, and Paul's mother
touched the whole five thousand. Then something very
curious happened. The voices in the house suddenly went

mad, like a chorus of frogs on a spring evening. There were certain new furnishings, and Paul had a tutor. He was *really* going to Eton, his father's school, in the following autumn. There were flowers in the winter, and a blossoming of the luxury Paul's mother had been used to. And yet the voices in the house, behind the sprays of mimosa and almond blossom, and from under the piles of iridescent cushions, simply trilled and screamed in a sort of ecstasy: "There *must* be more money! Oh-h-h; there *must* be more money. Oh, now, now-w! Now-w-w—there *must* be more money!—more than ever! More than ever!"

It frightened Paul terribly. He studied away at his Latin and Greek with his tutor. But his intense hours were spent with Bassett. The Grand National had gone by; he had not "known," and had lost a hundred pounds. Summer was at hand. He was in agony for the Lincoln. But even for the Lincoln he didn't "know," and he lost fifty pounds. He became wild-eyed and strange, as if something were going to explode in him.

"Let it alone, son! Don't you bother about it!" urged Uncle Oscar. But it was as if the boy couldn't really hear what his uncle was saying.

"I've got to know for the Derby! I've got to know for the Derby!" the child reiterated, his big blue eyes blazing with a sort of madness.

His mother noticed how overwrought he was.

"You'd better go to the seaside. Wouldn't you like to go now to the seaside, instead of waiting? I think you'd better," she said, looking down at him anxiously, her heart curiously heavy because of him.

But the child lifted his uncanny blue eyes.

"I couldn't possibly go before the Derby, mother!" he said. "I couldn't possibly!"

"Why not?" she said, her voice becoming heavy when she was opposed. "Why not? You can still go from the seaside to see the Derby with your Uncle Oscar, if that's what you wish. No need for you to wait here. Besides, I think you care too much about these races. It's a bad sign. My family has been a gambling family, and you won't know till you grow up how much damage it has done. But it has done damage. I shall have to send Bassett away, and ask Uncle Oscar not to talk racing to you, unless you promise to be reasonable about it; go away to the seaside and forget it. "You're all nerves!"

"I'll do what you like, mother, so long as you don't send me away till after the Derby," the boy said.

"Send you away from where? Just from this house?"

"Yes," he said, gazing at her.

"Why, you curious child, what makes you care about this house so much, suddenly? I never knew you loved it."

He gazed at her without speaking. He had a secret within a secret, something he had not divulged, even to Bassett or to his Uncle Oscar.

But his mother, after standing undecided and a little bit sullen for some moments, said:

"Very well, then! Don't go to the seaside till after the Derby, if you don't wish it. But promise me you won't let your nerves go to pieces. Promise you won't think so much about horseracing and *events*, as you call them!"

"Oh no," said the boy casually. "I won't think much about them, mother. You needn't worry. I wouldn't worry, mother, if I were you."

"If you were me and I were you," said his mother, "I wonder what we *should* do!"

"But you know you needn't worry, mother, don't you?" the boy repeated.

"I should be awfully glad to know it," she said wearily.

"Oh, well, you *can*, you know. I mean, you *ought* to know you needn't worry," he insisted.

"Ought I? Then I'll see about it," she said.

Paul's secret of secrets was his wooden horse, that which had no name. Since he was emancipated from a nurse and a nursery governess, he had had his rocking horse removed to his own bedroom at the top of the house.

"Surely you're too big for a rocking horse!" his mother had remonstrated.

"Well, you see, mother, till I can have a *real* horse, I like to have *some* sort of animal about," had been his quaint answer.

"Do you feel he keeps you company?" she laughed.

"Oh yes! He's very good, he always keeps me company, when I'm there," said Paul.

So the horse, rather shabby, stood in an arrested prance in the boy's bedroom.

The Derby was drawing near, and the boy grew more and more tense. He hardly heard what was spoken to him, he was very frail, and his eyes were really uncanny. His mother had sudden strange seizures of uneasiness about him. Sometimes, for half an hour, she would feel a sudden anxiety about him that was almost anguish. She wanted to rush to him at once, and know he was safe.

Two nights before the Derby, she was at a big party in town, when one of her rushes of anxiety about her boy, her firstborn, gripped her heart till she could hardly speak. She fought with the feeling, might and main, for she believed in common sense. But it was too strong. She had to leave the dance and go downstairs to telephone to the country. The children's nursery governess was terribly surprised and startled at being rung up in the night.

"Are the children all right, Miss Wilmot?"

"Oh yes, they are quite all right."

"Master Paul? Is he all right?"

"He went to bed as right as a trivet. Shall I run up and look at him?"

"No," said Paul's mother reluctantly. "No! Don't trouble. It's all right. Don't sit up. We shall be home fairly soon." She did not want her son's privacy intruded upon.

"Very good," said the governess.

It was about one o'clock when Paul's mother and father drove up to their house. All was still. Paul's mother went to her room and slipped off her white fur cloak. She had told her maid not to wait up for her. She heard her husband downstairs, mixing a whisky and soda.

And then, because of the strange anxiety at her heart, she stole upstairs to her son's room. Noiselessly she went along the upper corridor. Was there a faint noise? What was it?

She stood, with arrested muscles, outside his door, listening. There was a strange, heavy, and yet not loud noise. Her heart stood still. It was a soundless noise, yet rushing and powerful. Something huge, in violent, hushed motion. What was it? What in God's name was it? She ought to know. She felt that she knew the noise. She knew what it was.

Yet she could not place it. She couldn't say what it was. And on and on it went, like a madness.

Softly, frozen with anxiety and fear, she turned the door handle.

The room was dark. Yet in the space near the window, she heard and saw something plunging to and fro. She gazed in fear and amazement.

Then suddenly she switched on the light, and saw her son, in his green pyjamas, madly surging on the rocking horse. The blaze of light suddenly lit him up, as he urged the wooden horse, and lit her up, as she stood, blond, in her dress of pale green and crystal, in the doorway.

"Paul!" she cried. "Whatever are you doing?"

"It's Malabar!" he screamed in a powerful, strange voice. "It's Malabar!"

His eyes blazed at her for one strange and senseless second, as he ceased urging his wooden horse. Then he fell with a crash to the ground, and she, all her tormented motherhood flooding upon her, rushed to gather him up.

But he was unconscious, and unconscious he remained, with some brain fever. He talked and tossed, and his mother sat stonily by his side.

"Malabar! It's Malabar! Bassett, Bassett, I *know*! It's Malabar!"

So the child cried, trying to get up and urge the rocking horse that gave him his inspiration.

"What does he mean by Malabar?" asked the heart-frozen mother.

"I don't know," said the father stonily.

"What does he mean by Malabar?" she asked her brother Oscar.

"It's one of the horses running for the Derby," was the answer.

And, in spite of himself, Oscar Cresswell spoke to Bassett, and himself put a thousand on Malabar—at fourteen to one.

The third day of the illness was critical: they were waiting for a change. The boy, with his rather long, curly hair, was tossing ceaselessly on the pillow. He neither slept nor regained consciousness, and his eyes were like blue stones. His mother sat, feeling her heart had gone, turned actually into a stone.

In the evening, Oscar Cresswell did not come, but Bassett sent a message, saying could he come up for one moment, just one moment? Paul's mother was very angry at the intrusion, but on second thoughts she agreed. The boy was the same. Perhaps Bassett might bring him to consciousness.

The gardener, a shortish fellow with a little brown moustache and sharp little brown eyes, tiptoed into the room, touched his imaginary cap to Paul's mother, and stole to the bedside, staring with glittering, smallish eyes at the tossing, dying child.

"Master Paul!" he whispered. "Master Paul! Malabar came in first all right, a clean win. I did as you told me. You've made over seventy thousand pounds, you have; you've got over eighty thousand. Malabar came in all right, Master Paul."

"Malabar! Malabar! Did I say Malabar, mother? Did I say Malabar? Do you think I'm lucky, mother? I knew Malabar, didn't I? Over eighty thousand pounds! I call that lucky, don't you, mother? Over eighty thousand pounds! I knew, didn't I know I knew? Malabar came in all right. If I ride my horse till I'm sure, then I tell you, Bassett, you can go as high as you like. Did you go for all you were worth, Bassett?"

"I went a thousand on it, Master Paul."

"I never told you, mother, that if I can ride my horse, and *get there*, then I'm absolutely sure—oh, absolutely! Mother, did I ever tell you? I *am* lucky!"

"No, you never did," said his mother.

But the boy died in the night.

And even as he lay dead, his mother heard her brother's voice saying to her: "My God, Hester, you're eighty-odd thousand to the good, and a poor devil of a son to the bad. But, poor devil, poor devil, he's best gone out of a life where he rides his rocking horse to find a winner."

QUESTIONS

1. Why does Paul's mother tell him that the family has financial problems "because your father has no luck"? (171)

2. What makes Paul think that he can become lucky through his own efforts? Why does he seek luck by furiously riding his rocking horse?

3. Why doesn't Paul want his mother to know that he is lucky? Why does Paul say that his mother would stop him, even though he is accumulating money for her?

4. Why does Paul have so much trouble being sure of a winner after he lets his mother have the five thousand pounds?

5. Why doesn't Paul divulge his "secret of secrets" about the rocking horse to Bassett or to Uncle Oscar? (182)

6. When Paul is dying, why does his mother feel that "her heart had gone, turned actually into a stone"? (185)

7. What does Uncle Oscar mean in saying that Paul is "best gone out of a life where he rides his rocking horse to find a winner"? (186)

FOR FURTHER REFLECTION

1. Who is responsible for Paul's obsession with winning money? Who is responsible for his death?

2. Why does riding the rocking horse allow Paul to know which horses will win the races?

3. Why do some people who have plenty of money want even more?

ELIZABETH BOWEN

Elizabeth Bowen (1899–1973) was born into an Anglo-Irish family in Dublin, but moved to England as a child. Her early life was unstable—her father suffered a mental breakdown when Bowen was seven and her mother died when Bowen was twelve—and she often depicts with psychological subtlety the plight of isolated individuals, notably in her novel *The Death of the Heart* (1938). The characters in Bowen's short stories and novels, such as *The Last September* (1929) and *The House in Paris* (1935), are typically members of the educated upper-middle class, and her portrayal of them, hovering between comedy and tragedy, has been compared to Henry James blended with Jane Austen. Bowen worked for the British Ministry of Information during World War II. For her many literary achievements she received honorary doctorates from Trinity College in Dublin and Oxford University, as well as the title Commander of the Order of the British Empire.

The Inherited Clock

Yes, I can see you now," said Aunt Addie, "skipping about the terrace at Sandyhill in your little scarlet highwayman coat. I think I had never seen you in such high spirits. It was such a beautiful March day, hazy, but warm and sunny, and Cousin Rosanna and your mother and I were in the winter garden with the door open. Each time you came dancing down our end of the terrace you would toss your curls and go dancing away again. Your mother feared you were overexcited; I said, 'It's the spring, perhaps,' but Cousin Rosanna said, 'Not at all: it's the clock.' We three had come down for the day; Paul was staying with her. I don't remember where *he* was at the time: I'm afraid probably sulking somewhere about the place."

"I remember my coat," said her niece Clara, "but I don't remember the day. What has made you think of it?"

"As you know, I was at Sandyhill yesterday: they are taking two more of Cousin Rosanna's servants, so she has decided to close some more of the house, including that little anteroom through to the library. She had been hesitating whether to move the clock: before I left, after tea, she had made up her mind not to—that might have meant some unnecessary jolt or jar. 'How it is to travel to Clara's, ultimately,' she said, 'is not my affair. I am taking no risks with it during my own lifetime.'"

Clara, surprised, said: "Travel to me?"

"That will have to be thought of, of course, dear."

"But what clock are you talking about?"

Miss Detter began to say something, tripped up, glanced askance at her niece, then turned an unhappy red, as though Clara had said something irreligious. "Why, yours—the one she is leaving to you," she said. "You know she refers to that constantly, in your presence. That skeleton clock that you like so much. How can you look so blank? Cousin Rosanna would be quite hurt if she thought it meant as little as that to you. It was the discussion yesterday, whether or not to move it, that brought back that day when you wore—"

"My scarlet coat. Yes, but why?"

"As we watched you through the door of the winter garden, Cousin Rosanna turned and said to your mother, 'I have been telling Clara that, ultimately, she is to have the clock.' Your mother, knowing what a part the clock had played in Rosanna's life, was much touched. There was a good deal of bustle, I remember, about getting us off to the train, it being discovered, just before we started, that you had hurt the poor little forefinger of your right hand. It was really rather a shocking sight: black and blue with several small ugly cuts. You were loyally mum about what had happened, but we all suspected that Master Paul had been up to some more cruel tricks. This, naturally, made you a little nervous in the train. So your mother, hoping to cheer you up, said, 'So, Clara, when Cousin Rosanna goes to heaven she is going to send you her lovely skeleton clock.' I don't know whether it was the idea of Cousin Rosanna going away to heaven, or whether the word 'skeleton' frightened you, but you burst into tears and became almost hysterical. Not liking to see you cry in a railway carriage, I said, 'You know the reason Cousin Rosanna loves it? It has not stopped ticking for more than a hundred years!' But that only seemed to unsettle you still more."

"Well, if you say this happened, Aunt Addie, of course it did," Clara said—with a somehow encaged and rebellious feeling. "I know I was six the winter I had that coat: I am thirty now—one cannot expect to remember everything."

"Yes, I remember you before you remember your-self," said Aunt Addie, looking at her affectionately. "Of course, I have always taken an interest in you—but then, you have always taken an interest in yourself. I don't mean that unkindly: why shouldn't you? You have an exceptional character."

"Only to you, I think."

"At least," Aunt Addie said, in a brisker tone, "you will make a point, won't you, next time you're at Sandyhill, of saying something enthusiastic about the clock? Let her see how much you are looking forward to it."

"Might that not seem—?"

"Why, Clara? You know Cousin Rosanna likes you and Paul to be perfectly natural about the money, and if about money why not about the clock, when she so much connects it with you in her own mind?"

There was, it was true, a singular lack of nonsense about Rosanna Detter's relations with her two young heirs. She had named them as such early on in their infancy, made a point of having them frequently at her house, and insisted that their expectations should be discussed and defined. The contents of her will had long ago been made known, and she proposed, she said, in ordinary fairness to make no changes in it without warning. Apart from bequests to charities, legacies to old servants, and £5000 for Addie Detter (who had declared fervently this was much too much), Rosanna's fortune was to be divided equally between Paul Ardeen and Clara Detter, respectively son and daughter of two of her first cousins, and thus, second cousins to one another. Clara lived, as a child, with her widowed mother in a small house in Ealing; Paul with his not prosperous doctor father on the

outskirts of an industrial town: the two young people's surroundings, as well as their temperaments, could not fail to
attach them to their auspicious future. Meanwhile, Cousin
Rosanna made them no allowances and few presents—
though there were times when the watchful Clara suspected
that Rosanna paid the more pressing of Paul's debts.

It gratified Cousin Rosanna, herself an only child, to
watch these two high-spirited only children quarrel. Their
co-heirship had not created a happy tie. Dark bullet-headed
Paul, at once cool and bragging, and blond fine-strung
Clara, with her fairylike affectations, seldom relaxed, during
visits to Sandyhill, their resourceful campaign against one
another. Cousin Rosanna, in packing them off to play (for
she could tolerate neither for very long at a time) could assure
herself that they were equally tough. The children worked
on each other like two indestructible pieces of sandpaper.
It might have been thought that Rosanna, in selecting heirs
near in age and of opposite sexes, entertained some romantic
spinsterish project that they should marry, and that their
declared hostility pleased her as being, admittedly, the first
phase of love. This cannot have been so, for Paul's marriage,
at twenty-two, was, by all showing, not adversely seen. It
was Clara, surprisingly, who was piqued. She perceived, if
Rosanna chose to ignore, a touch of Paul's usual insolence
in the choice. The fortunate Edmée—blond like Clara, but
of how different a type—was to be recognized, at the first
glance, as being just one more in the succession of fancies
with whom Paul by habit went round town: nor did she
show any reason why she should be the last. Summoned for
the occasion to Sandyhill, Clara stood by at the presenta-
tion of the heavy-lidded bride. She was able to watch Paul
fold, with expressionless satisfaction, preparatory to slipping into his wallet, Rosanna's five-hundred-pound cheque
for the honeymoon.

It had been two years later, when she was twenty-one,
that Clara met her fate in the person of Henry Harley; who,
already a married man, was forced to tell her that he saw

little prospect of changing his way of life. He was not well off; his wife had been irreproachable; the payment of alimony would cripple him, and he was not disposed to let scandal prejudice his career. She chose to continue obstinate in her feeling, and in her hopes of things taking a better turn. Her poverty, to which one dared set no term, meanwhile made everything more difficult: the circumstances under which their affair was conducted constantly alarmed Henry and oppressed her. This had gone on now for nine years, and provided the reason why Clara at thirty was unmarried. As the years went by, she became increasingly grateful to Cousin Rosanna for either her resolute ignorance or her tolerance, and she had reproached herself, before the war started, for not going down more often to Sandyhill. Since the war, she was tied to exacting work; also, the closing of that coastal area interdicted visits from London—except, of course, on the plea of family business that could from time to time be produced. Cousin Rosanna's influence in her neighbourhood was more considerable than one ought, these days, to admit. The officially dangerous position of Sandyhill disqualified the house as a hospital or a repository for children; but also, so far no soldiers had been billeted there. And she had kept intact, until very lately, her staff of middle-aged servants.

Sandyhill itself was to go to Paul, who did not conceal his intention of selling it. It might do well, he expected, for a private asylum, when peace should bring back happier days. The house *had*, it is true, already in some ways the look of an institution, though of an expensive kind: it stood among pleasure grounds dark with ilex, girt by a high flint wall. The avenue ran downhill between ramparts of evergreen, to debouch into the main street of an unassuming seaside resort. Sandyhill had been built by Rosanna's great-uncle, from whom (fairly late in her own life) she had inherited it, with substantial wealth: cleverly sheltered by trees from the sea winds, it faced south and enjoyed a good deal of sunshine. From the terrace, from the adjoining winter garden, and from the plate-glass windows upstairs and down, you also enjoyed, if this were your pleasure, a view of the Channel above the ilex groves. Indoors, the rooms were powerfully heated, brocade-papered, and so planned that you looked through an enfilade of pine-framed doorways. They composed a museum of discredited objets d'art which, up to now, had been always specklessly kept.

In one of the hollows about the grounds had been placed a small lake, sunless most of the day and overlooked by a kiosk. Into this lake had dropped, since Clara's last visit, what had so far been Sandyhill's only bomb; the blast had wrenched the shutters off the kiosk, and, by a freak of travel, obliterated the glass winter garden projecting west of the house . . . This day of Clara's return, not long after the conversation with Aunt Addie, was an almost eerie extension of her aunt's memory: it was in March, "hazy, but warm and sunny." Clara and Cousin Rosanna lunched in the morning room. "As Addie no doubt will have told you, they've taken Preeps and Marchant, so I have closed the dining room and the library." Nodding towards a door on her left hand, Cousin Rosanna added: "Therefore the house stops there."

"May I look, later?"

Cousin Rosanna stared. "By all means, if you are interested in dust sheets." Her eyes, always prominent, were today more so: about her face and her manner appeared the something you less at the time observe than afterwards recollect—*then*, you say you saw the beginning of the end. At sixty-five, the big woman was to be felt contracting, withdrawing from life with the same heavy indifference with which she withdrew her life from room after room. Clara did notice that her dictatorial "ultimatelys" were fewer. Though lunch was served with most of its old formality the dried-egg omelette was rubbery: the contempt with which Cousin Rosanna ate it had been, more, a contempt for her own palate, that with impunity one could now insult.

She now, by abruptly turning her chair to the fire, implied she had left the table: her guest could do as she liked. Clara, accordingly, rose and went frankly straight to the door where the house had been forced by war to stop. This led to the anteroom which, in its turn, led to the library. At once, she could hear a clock expectantly ticking. The anteroom french window was shuttered up: only cracks of light from the terrace fell on the shrouded sofa and on the sheet tucked bibwise over the bookcase on which the clock stood. The gleam of the glass of the dome inside which the ticking proceeded was just, but only just, to be seen.

"What are you up to in there?" called out Cousin Rosanna. "Looking at your clock?"

"I can't see it, yet."

"Well, you ought to know what it looks like, goodness knows!" Clara did not reply. Her cousin, restless, repeated: "What are you doing *now*?"

"Opening a shutter—may I?"

"If you shut it again. You haven't got Preeps and Marchant to dance round clearing up after you now, you know."

The skeleton clock, in daylight, was threatening to a degree its oddness could not explain. Looking through the glass at its wheels, cogs, springs, and tensions, and at its upraised striker, awaiting with a sensible quiver the finish of the hour that was in force, Clara tried to tell herself that it was, only, shocking to see the anatomy of time. The clock was without a face, its twelve numerals being welded on to a just-visible wire ring. As she watched, the minute hand against its background of nothing made one, then another, spectral advance. This was enough: if she did not yet feel she could anticipate feeling her sanity being demolished, by one degree more, as every sixtieth second brought round this unheard click. Retreating, she looked round the walls of the anteroom: she saw the dark-patterned oblongs where the pictures had hung. She could remember which picture used to hang in each oblong; she remembered the names of the books in the bookcase under the sheet.

But as far as she knew she had not seen the clock before.

"None the worse, you see," vouchsafed Cousin Rosanna, as Clara returned to the morning room.

"You mean," Clara said with an effort, "the same as ever?"

"No, I don't; I mean none the worse for the bomb. As it stood up to that, it should see *you* out, we may hope. So you can take it for granted, as I have done, instead of rushing to look for it every time you come here." Cousin Rosanna, however, did not seem wholly displeased.

"Do I really?" said Clara, trying to smile this off.

"Unless you walk in your sleep, and sleep in daytime, in which case you had better go to the doctor.—Have you seen the winter garden?"

"Not yet: I—"

"It isn't there.—By the way, you will have to see that that clock's attended to. I have had the same man, out from Southstone, to wind it for twenty-four years: he took on when that previous poor fellow—shocking affair that was!—And another thing: keep a careful eye on Paul, or he'll get his hands on it before you can say knife. However, you don't need me to tell you *that*!"

"No, no, of course not, Cousin Rosanna . . . He wants it so much," Clara added, as though musingly.

"For the reason we know," said Rosanna, with a protuberant meaning stare. "You know really, Clara, in view of all, you ought not to begrudge Paul that one bit of fun. Dear me, a cat would have laughed, and I must say I did. I can see you now—"

"I was wearing my scarlet coat?"

"Scarlet? Good heavens no; at least, I should hope not: you were fat to be wearing scarlet at fourteen. Not that, with you standing there with that glass thing over your head, one looked twice at whatever else you had on. However—'Now then, Paul,' I said, 'that's enough. She can't breathe in there: take it off her.'—However," concluded Cousin Rosanna, who for the first time today showed genuine pleasure, "easier said than done." Her mood changed; she looked at

Clara with moody boredom. "Did you say you wanted to go for a turn?" she said. "Because if that's what you want you had better go."

Clara was fat no longer: that growing phase had been brief. Today her step on the terrace, if more assertive, was not much heavier than it had been as a child's. Her height and her feverish fair good looks were set off by clothes that showed an expensive taste—taste that she could not fully indulge, yet. She glanced, without shock as without feeling, at the site of the winter garden—here some exotic creepers had already perished against the exposed wall. Then she slanted downwards across the lawn, into one of the paths that entered the woods of ilex. These sombre pleasure grounds, unchanging as might have been a photograph of themselves, were charged for her with a past that, though discontinuous, maintained a continuous atmosphere of its own. To these she had sometimes escaped; they had equally been the scene of those inescapable games with Paul. She could have thought she heard what war had suspended— still dead leaves being brushed from hard paths with stiff brooms. To each cut-out of a branch against the diluted sky attached some calculation or fear or unhopeful triumph. Every glade, every seat, every vista at the turn of a path only drew out the story. To be coming, for instance, into view of the lake, and of the kiosk reflected in its apathetic water, was to breathe the original horror of Paul's telling her that "they" kept the headless ladies locked up in there. He had looked in, he told her, between the slats of the shutters, but could not advise her to do the same. Now, with the shutters gone, she saw mildewed inside walls: as she stared at the kiosk, like someone performing an exercise, even lungfuls of horror seemed salutary. No, there was nothing, no single thing, in the history of Clara at Sandyhill that she could not remember.—Yet, was there?

With regard to no place other than Sandyhill could this opening and splitting wider of a crevasse in her memory have alarmed her more. At its deepness, she dared not attempt to guess; its extent, if it ever did stop, must simply wait to be seen.

That, as things turned out, was to be Clara's last visit to Sandyhill, except for the day of Cousin Rosanna's funeral. Neither Clara nor Paul received any deathbed summons: their cousin's loss of interest must have been so entire that she could not be bothered putting them through the last hoop. The funeral was correct but for one detail—Paul failed to be there. Stationed far up north, he had (his telegram told them) missed the necessary train. Clara returned to London that same evening, leaving Aunt Addie at Sandyhill to console the servants and to receive Paul whenever he should arrive. A week later, fairly late in the evening, Aunt Addie came staggering into Clara's St. John's Wood flat with the clock embraced inside her exhausted arms. It was not packed—in a packing case it might have got knocked about, in which case it might have stopped. As it was, it had gone on ticking, and had struck twice in the train, to the interest of everyone, and once again in the lift, coming up here to Clara's flat.

"I took the precaution of travelling first class," Aunt Addie said. "I knew you would want to have it as soon as possible. Look, I am putting it *here*, for the time being"—(that meant, the only table the size of the room allowed)—"but when I get my breath back, we'll put it where you intend. You must often have seen it here, in your mind's eye.—Not, I hope, on anything it could fall off?"

"In that case, I can only think of the floor."

"Oh," said Aunt Addie, preoccupied, "I seem to have left fingerprints on the dome." She breathed on the glass and began to polish them off. "Naturally, you have had a good deal to think about. In fact, I should not be surprised if this changed the course of your life."

"A clock—how could it?" said Clara wildly.

"No, I was referring to Cousin Rosanna's death, dear. I could already see some little changes in Paul."

". . . By the way, did Paul say anything when you took the clock?"

"Er, no," said Aunt Addie, colouring faintly. "He was not about, as it happened; he was so busy."

Clara's life, ever since she had been told of the will (which was practically as far back as she could remember) had, of course, hinged on the prospect of this immense change. Not unreasonably, she expected everything to go better. She perceived that her nature was of the kind that is only able to flower in clement air: either wealth or reciprocal love, ideally both, were necessary. To begin with, she intended to buy herself surroundings that suited her, that would set her off. But chiefly, as her obsessive love for Henry became, in the course of nine years, the centre of everything, she had quite simply looked to her coming money for the one consummation of this, marriage. The humiliating uncertainties of their relationship, and, still more, the thought of him living there with his wife, were more of a torment than she had dared to allow. Humble about herself with regard to him, and humbly bare of illusions regarding Henry, she believed that her, Clara's, coming into her money would be the one thing needed to make him break with his wife. Should his career show damage from the divorce proceedings, he could afford to abandon it: she could compensate him. She could buy open some other door for his ambition. As for love—so far Henry had only loved her, as you might say, on trust. She had yet to gain him wholly by showing what she could, in the whole, be. Now she could feel the current of her nature stirring strongly under the thinning ice. Had it been the strength of the current that thinned the ice? Or had the ice had to be thinned by the breath of financial summer before the current, however strong, could be felt?

When Aunt Addie had gone, Clara tried again to realize all that was now, since last week, within her reach. She went across to the mirror and stood and stared at herself imperiously. But the current, without warning, ceased to be felt: no kind of exultation was possible. The newly arrived clock, chopping off each second to fall and perish, recalled how many seconds had gone to make up her years, how many of these had been either null or bitter, how many had been void before the void claimed them. She had been subject to waiting as to an illness; the tissues of her being had been consumed by it. Was it impossible that the past should be able to injure the future irreparably? Turning away from the mirror, she made herself face the clock; she looked through into the nothing behind its hands. Turning away from the clock, she went to the telephone.

Henry's reply, at the same time cautious and social, warned her that, as so often at this hour, he was not alone.— All the same: "What do you think? My clock has arrived," she said. "Aunt Addie has just brought it, from Sandyhill."

"Indeed. Which is that?"

"Which clock? Surely you know, Henry. The one I must have so often told you about . . . Didn't I? Well, it's with me now, in this room. Can you hear it ticking?"

"No, I'm afraid not."

She got up, pulling the telephone with her as far as the cord would go, then stretched the receiver at arm's length towards the glass dome. After some seconds she went on: "You heard it *that* time? I like to think we are hearing the same thing. They say it has never stopped for more than a hundred years: don't you think it sounds like that? Cousin Rosanna insisted I was to have this clock."

"Thrown in," Henry said, "with the pound of tea." But his voice, besides being ironical, was distrait: all the time, he was thinking up some story that could account for his end of the conversation, and was being careful to make, in his wife's hearing, no remark that would not fit in with that.

"Yes," said Clara, quivering, "with, with my pound of tea. Do you think that could mean she did really care for me? I wish I could think so. There is something frightening about the death of someone who always kept one so near her, without love. Still, there it is: she's dead. And because of that—Henry, tell me again that you're glad?"

"Of course."

"For both our sakes—yours and mine?"

"Of course . . . Well, this has been nice, but I fear I must say good night. We were thinking of listening to the European news."

"Stop, wait, don't go for a minute! I can't bear this clock! I dread it; I can't stay with it in the room! What am I to do this evening? Where can I go?"

"I'm afraid I can't think, really."

"There's no *possible* chance you . . . ?"

"No, I'm afraid not."

"But you do love me?"

"Of course."

So Clara, to stop herself thinking, rang up two or three friends, but not one of them answered: their telephones went on ringing. Therefore she put on her overcoat, found her torch, dropped down in the lift, and went for a walk in the blackout. It was late enough for the streets to be almost empty. Clara, walking at high speed into the solid darkness, was surprised all over her body to feel no impact: she seemed to pass like a ghost through an endless wall. No segment of moon peered at her, no stars guided. Brought to a halt for breath, she began to spy with her torch at the things round her—a postbox, a corner with no railing, the white plate of a street name. Nothing told her anything, except one thing—unless she had lost her memory, she had lost her way. She dived into a wardens' post to ask where this was, or where she was, and in the glare in there they all stared at her. "Where did you want to get back to?" someone said, and for either a second or an eternity she fancied she might be unable to tell him . . . When Clara once again found herself at the portico of the block of flats where she lived, tomorrow had begun to curdle the sky. Having hesitated with her key in her own door she let herself in and went quickly through to her bedroom. But the wall between herself and the clock was thin. Getting up, lying down, getting up, she continued, until her telephone called her, her search for the earplugs that Aunt Addie had given her when first the raids began.

When Aunt Addie rang up, two mornings later, it was to announce that, after a search of London, she *had* succeeded in finding an old man to wind the clock. "I knew you'd be anxious; I know I was! Providentially, however, I am in time."

"In time for what?"

"For the day it is always wound. So you will know when to expect the man," said Aunt Addie.

Therefore Clara, who started for work at cockcrow, not to return till some time on in the evening, told the porter to admit, on whichever day he should come, an old man to wind the clock in her flat. The day must have been Friday, for that evening she came home to find a door ajar. There was somebody, besides the clock, in possession—this turned out to be Paul. Having arranged the blackout and turned the lights on, he was comfortably sitting on her sofa, smoking one of his superior cigarettes. He was, of course, in khaki. "Really, what hours you keep!" he said. "However, I've had my dinner. I trust you have?" At this point, as though recollecting himself, Paul sprang up and smote Clara matily on the shoulder. He then stood back to inspect her. "Radiant—and can one wonder?" he added. "By the way, I was sorry to miss you the other day. I hope I wasn't missed?"

"At the funeral? Everyone thought that looked pretty queer; and Cousin Rosanna, of course, would have been furious."

"If so, most unfairly. I missed my train that morning because I had made a night of it, and I made a night of it because I felt like hell. You might not think so, and I was surprised myself. After all, she had never wanted anything."

"Never wanted us to love her?"

"Well, if you put it that way—never gave us a chance. However, I snapped out of that. I feel fine now."

"How nice . . . How is Edmée?"

"I thought her looking wonderfully herself. And how is Henry? As nice as ever?"

Clara said frigidly: "How did you get in?"

"A civil old burglar, or somebody, let me in. He said nothing to me, so I said nothing to him. He put the glass back on the clock and went away quietly, so I decided to wait."

Paul, whose way of standing about was characteristic, did not seem disposed to sit down again. Having flicked ash into a shell not meant for an ashtray, he remained with his back to the mantelpiece, fixing on nothing particular his tolerant, narrow-eyed, level look. His uniform fitted and suited him just a degree too well, and gave him the air of being on excellent terms with war. He had thickened slightly: otherwise, little change appeared in the dark bullet-head, rather Mongolian features, and compact, tactile hands that had made him by turns agreeably disagreeable and disagreeably agreeable as a little boy. "Tick-tock, tick-tock," he said, out of the blue. "Sounds louder than ever, in here; though as nice as ever, of course. You don't think it's a little large for the room?"

"I shall be moving soon, I expect," said Clara, who had not only sat down but put her feet up on her sofa, to show that Paul's presence affected her in no sort of way.

"Oh, shall you really? How right." Paul glanced down at the toe of one shoe, lifted his eyebrows and went on: "This isn't, of course, a point I should ever bother to raise, but you do of course realize that nothing should have left Sandyhill until the valuation had been made for probate?"

"I don't suppose Aunt Addie understood that. You could always have stopped her!"

"On the contrary: the devoted creature nipped off to the train with the clock while my back was turned. When I thought of your face at this end, I must say I had to smile."

"Really," said Clara touchily, "why?"

Paul not only looked at his cousin but, somehow, gave the impression that only indolence kept him from looking harder. "It is just as well, as we both see now," he observed, "that the point of that joke *is* known only to you and me. That you have never enjoyed it seems unfair. Still, I suppose it is partly in view of that that I've come round this evening to do the handsome thing—"

"Yes, I wondered what you had come about."

"I make you an offer, Clara. I'll buy you out of the clock. Cash down—as soon as I touch the cash.'

Clara, not so much as raising her eyes from her rather too delicate ringless hands, said: "Cousin Rosanna warned me this might happen."

"What you mean—and how stupid of me, and how right you are—is that cash is no longer an object with you, either? Look, I'll go one better: I'll take the clock away for nothing. And better still, I'll take it away tonight."

Clara went rigid immediately: her cheeks flamed and her voice shot into the particular note for so long familiar to her and Paul.

"Why should you take it simply because you want it?"

"Why should you keep it when you don't want it, simply because I do?" Even Paul's imperturbability showed, as of old, a crack. "Well, we both know why—and better leave it at that. All the same, Clara, have some sense. It's one thing to cut your nose off to spite my face. But is it really worth going crackers?"

"Crackers—what do you mean?"

"Well, look at yourself in the glass."

The mirror being exactly opposite the sofa, Clara had looked before she could stop herself. As quickly, she said: "I don't see anything wrong. And didn't you say I was looking radiant?"

"Because, frankly, my one thought was, 'We must keep her calm.'" Paul, having ground out his cigarette with an air at once resigned and concerned, came to sit down on the sofa beside Clara. He pushed her feet off gently to make room for himself. Leaning a little towards her, he placed one hand, like a hostage, or like an invitation to read his entire motive, palm upwards on the brocade between them. His nearness enveloped Clara in a sense of complicity, frightening because it was acutely familiar, more frightening because she could not guess at its source. While his eyes expressed no more than good-natured fondness, and his manner regretful conciliation, both conveyed a threat for which no memory could account. "I hate," he said, "to see you all shot up. Doesn't Henry?"

"Why should he? I haven't asked him."

Her cousin, at once quickly and darkly, said: "Possibly better not. I'm all, if we can, for keeping this in the family."

"The clock?"

"No, I mean its effect on you. When you think it's only three days since Aunt Addie imported it.—And to think how well she meant, the old dear!"

Rearing up among the cushions at her end of the sofa, Clara exclaimed: "You think that will work? Cousin Rosanna intended the clock for me. So this is just one thing you must do without. I would sooner drop it out of the window . . ."

"I am sure you would," said Paul. "In fact, I expect you've tried?"

He was right. Once in the small hours of a sleepless night, once on the occasion of an unnerving return home, that solution had already offered itself. Clara had turned the lights out, opened her eighth-floor window, found her way to the clock by the noise it made in the dark, and gone so far as to balance it on the windowsill. In her fingertips, as they supported it, could be felt its confident vibration—through the dome, through the stand projecting some inches into the night. She had awaited in vain some infinitesimal check, some involuntary metallic shudder with which the clock should anticipate its last second, the first it would not consume for a hundred years. Annihilation waited—the concrete roadway under the block of flats. By the concrete roadway the clock would be struck, not to strike again. Towards the dawn of the coming, unthreatened day, some early goer to work would halt, step back, and bend his torch on the cogs, uncoiled springs, and incomprehensible splinters that had startled him by crunching under his boot.—But, suppose not. Suppose gravity failed? Or suppose the tick stayed up here without the clock, or the nothing that had shown through its skeleton form continued to bear its skeleton shadow? If what she purposed to do could *be* done, how was it it had never been done before? . . . Clara, quailing, hoped that she only did so before the conventionality of her own nature. She was not the woman, it seemed (if there were indeed such a woman) who could drop a clock from the window of a St. John's Wood flat. The chance of somebody passing at the decisive second, the immediate alarm to be raised by what would sound like a bomb, the likelihood of the affair being traced to her, the attention already drawn to the clock by its sentimental arrival with Aunt Addie, and her own talk about it with the flats porter—all these Clara, too gladly, let weigh with her. She reprieved not so much the clock as her own will. She had returned the clock to its place on the table—twice.

"However," Paul said, "if that's how you feel . . . I let you see that I want it—apparently, that's enough." He shrugged his shoulders, and slowly withdrew his hand: the interlude of frankness could be taken as over. Getting up, he strolled across to the clock, and, taking up his stand between it and Clara, could be felt to hold communication with it. Intently stooping, he squinted into its works. "Yes," he said remotely, "I am stuck on this clock. Always have been, and I suppose always shall."

"Why?"

"Why should there be any why?" said Paul, without turning round. "I am simply stuck on this clock. One is bound to be stuck on something: what is wrong with a clock? *Your* trouble seems to be that you are stuck on the past."

Clara, eyes indecisively on Paul's khaki back, licked her lips once or twice before she actually spoke. Then she cried:

"Have you *no* idea that I've no idea what you mean? Or Cousin Rosanna, or Aunt Addie either? Unless you three are combining to send me mad, someone had better tell me what this is all about. As far as I know, the first time I saw that clock was the last day I spent with Rosanna at Sandyhill. I detest it, and should be glad if you'd tell me why. Every time I am told I remember something I don't remember, it turns out to be something about that clock; and there's such high feeling about it I don't know which way to turn.—Did you, for instance, once put the clock glass over my head, and did I get stuck inside it?"

This engaged Paul's attention: he turned round slowly, gained time by soundlessly whistling, then said: "You're not serious?" He considered her. "But what a thing to forget! We damn' nearly chipped your face off. Besides, that came quite late on."

"But late on in what?"

"In our story. If you'll tell me how much you've forgotten, I'll tell you where we begin. If you *have* forgotten, you must have some rather too good reason—in which case, don't I err in bringing the whole thing up? . . . Very well. Yes, I popped that thing over your head because it was time to stop you, and I thought that might do it. Stop you what? Stop you blackmailing me. We were by then no longer in the Garden of Eden, and I observed Rosanna showing the red light."—At this point, Paul gave Clara a final suspicious look; what he saw appeared to convince him, for he went on: "Since the day we did that with the clock you had almost never let up. It was, 'Oh, Paul, I feel so wicked; we've been so wicked: I have simply got to confess to Cousin Rosanna!' Then, 'Very well, kiss me, then perhaps I'll feel better, then perhaps I won't have to tell Cousin Rosanna *this* time.' And this year in, year out, my sweet, every holiday you and I were at Sandyhill. Castor oil got to be lovely compared to your upturned face. Your particular mise en scène was the anteroom: you used to put your ear to the clock glass and say, 'You know, it *still* doesn't sound the same.' That meant your feeling bad and my having to come across. To make things more interesting, one could never be certain that Rosanna might not pop in at one or the other door, not to speak of her passing the terrace window. You and me on such close terms (she wasn't to know the reason) and, of all places, right there by her precious clock—that *would* have finally torn it, for you and me."

"You don't mean, she'd have cut us out of the will?"

"Well, Clara, ask yourself—would she not? Given, I mean, that peculiar obsession *she* had."

"If Rosanna had an obsession, I don't remember that, either." She attempted a wintry smile, and added: "This seems to be like a whole continent that's submerged, you know."

"Poetic idea," Paul conceded, with a glance to the left of his cousin's ear. "To return to Cousin Rosanna—you know how when you are waiting you have to look back and back again at the clock? Now our friend, as it happened, had been Rosanna's from girlhood, so it was this clock she connected with her particular habit—a habit she'd had every reason to form. There was nothing Rosanna did not know about waiting. Great-Uncle, from whom she got Sandyhill and the money, did not quit the stage till she was well on in life. Therefore Rosanna waited, throughout what are called one's best years—not only for money, exactly like you and me, but for a young man, like, if may say so, you. The young man—not a nice character, unlike Henry—wasn't moving till Rosanna could declare the bank open. Great-Uncle, unfriendly to romance, lived just too long: by the time the money came to Rosanna the man had lost heart and married somebody else. And in those days, if you remember, that was considered final. So Rosanna, like the great girl she was, in her way, cut her losses in the romance direction and went all out to make the money her big thing. She felt free, all things considered, to buy what she liked with it; she jingled her new purse and looked around for her fun. You and I were her fun. Can't you see how the thing worked out? The younger the heirs you name, the longer they have to wait, and the more the waiting can do to them. Again, *she'd* expected both love and money, and got money only: can you blame her if she was damned if she'd contemplate you and me, or you or me, having both? So my marriage—than which I'm sure there are many worse—and your, er, stalemate with regard to Henry, suited her book ideally—couldn't have suited better. As for you and me, biting bits out of each other all over Sandyhill—how her dear old good face used to light up! The better we loathed each other, the better she liked us. But then came what looked like our interlude—that *that* was no more than a new and more subtle manifestation of mutual hate was, I suppose unavoidably, lost on her. Therefore that, as I tell you, did damn' nearly cook our goose."

"How ironical," supplied Clara, "that would have been, we well know.—All the same, what made her so set on my having to have the clock?"

"I can only think, because you were a fellow woman. It was Rosanna's way of saying, 'Over to you!'"

"But, so equally set on the clock never being yours?"

"*That* couldn't be clearer. I'd more than shown that I liked it; I'd asked her for it point-blank. I was a man, so she liked my going without. Yes, I did get those cheques, I know—as you also noted. She liked me to make a fool of myself qua man. I wanted the clock, so you were to have it—could the mental process be more straightforward? . . . Yes, I tell you, I asked for it. I was a fool, at nine, and that clock was the only thing in that god-awful house I liked. So I piped up. That was the day our bit of trouble began.

"It was one of those typical headachy Sandyhill March mornings—house heated to bursting point and a livery sun outdoors. A family gathering was in progress—you and your aunt and your mother had come down for the day. I mouldered off by myself, as I frequently did do, to watch the old clock at its cheering work. Rosanna came in and said, 'You like that, don't you?' to which I said, 'Yes, I should like to have it.' To which she said, 'Yes, I daresay you would.' At which point you came prancing into the room. I suppose you were about six, and your mother had got you up in a perfectly sickening little scarlet coat, like a monkey wears on a barrel organ. The moment was jam for Rosanna; she turned to you and she said, 'Clara; one day I intend *you* to have that clock. Do you know it has never stopped, and it never will?' You registered pleasure, and I went off down the woods.—*None* of this comes back?"

"Nothing," said Clara firmly—with growing fear.

"So that really you don't remember my catching you, later on, in the anteroom, you having glided back for a private gloat at your clock? Or what I said, or we did, or what happened then?"

"No, *no*. Why? What do you mean? Paul, you're simply making me worse.—And what are you *doing*? Leave that alone: *it's mine!*"

"That's just why I'm asking you to step over here," said Paul, who was lifting the dome with becoming care, to place it on the table beside the clock. "Why? To make an experiment. Let's face it. Either this works—which it may not—or I take you by hand tomorrow to a psychiatrist. Blood is thicker than water, after all. Come on—I can't wait all night; I have got a date."

Hooking his arm round Clara's reluctant waist, Paul approached his cousin relentlessly to the clock. After four or five seconds of this enforced staring into the diligent works, Clara began to relax—was she hypnotized? In the absolute nothing behind the clock's anatomy there appeared and began to dilute, like colour dropped into water, the red of the Sandyhill anteroom wallpaper: meanwhile, there crept on another sense the smell of pitched pine exasperated by heating. There could be felt the stare of a draped and open door window, in which, from moment to moment, somebody might appear. The murmur of voices out of the winter garden hung on the hazy terrace behind Paul's voice.

"I'll tell you something, Clara. Have you ever SEEN *a minute? Have you actually had one wriggling inside your hand? Did you know if you keep your finger inside a clock for a minute, you can pick out that very minute and take it home for your own?"* So it is Paul who stealthily lifts the dome off. It is Paul who selects the finger of Clara's that is to be guided, shrinking, then forced wincing into the works, to be wedged in them, bruised in them, bitten into and eaten up by the cogs. *"No, you have got to keep it there, or you will lose the minute. I am doing the counting—the counting up to sixty."* . . . But there is to be no sixty. The ticking stops.

We have stopped the clock.

The hundred years are all angry. *"Stop crying, idiot: that won't start it again!"* . . . But oh, oh but, it won't let my finger go! . . . O-o-h! . . . *"Suck it, be quiet, don't make a noise!"* . . . What have you made me do? *"You wanted to."* You made me want to . . . What shall we, what shall we, what shall we do, do, *do?* . . . *"You go out and skip about on the terrace, make them keep on watching you, then they won't come in."* But what will you do? *"Something."* But it's stopped ticking! . . . *"I tell you, go out and skip about on the terrace."*

For the second time, Paul withdrew Clara's finger, with a painful jerk, from the clock which had stopped ticking. Her finger was bitten, but not so badly: it had grown too big to go in so deep this time. He was, meanwhile, going on smoothly: "We were in luck that Friday—because it *was* a Friday, of course. All I did was put the glass back and walk away. But half an hour later, the regular chap from Southstone turned up to wind it. With a mouth that butter couldn't possibly melt in, I tailed him into the anteroom, just to see. The clock stopped and that half-hour missing made even him turn pale. He sent me to find Rosanna. I was unable to. I came back to watch him put through a long and amazing job. The ladies were upstairs, tying up your finger. By the time he had got the clock set and going, he found he had run things fine for his bus home. He decided, therefore, as Rosanna was missing, not to report the occurrence till the following week. Owing to hurry or worry, the poor brute, he shot out of Sandyhill gate and across the main street in time to be flattened out by a bus coming the other way. Any evidence perished with him: Rosanna was spared the knowledge. In gratitude, you and I subscribed sixpence each towards the funeral wreath. But of course you would never remember *that*?"

"I remember giving the sixpence for the wreath," said Clara slowly, not looking up from her finger.

"But only that?"

"No, *not* only that—thank you, Paul." There ensued an unavoidable pause, at the end of which Clara said: "I expect you would like to go now? I think I heard you say you had got a date?"

"Nothing need stand, if you'd rather not be alone?"

"Thank you very much; I, I shall sit with my memories. I expect to spend some time getting to know them." Turning away, with all the detachment possible, she occupied herself in emptying Paul's ash from the shell into a more suitable tray. "Oh, by the way, Paul," she added, "do by all means have the clock. Aunt Addie ought to have known that you wanted it. And, apart from any sentiment of Rosanna's, it means nothing to me. Won't you take it along now?"

"Thanks, that is nice of you, Clara," said Paul promptly. "Actually, under the circumstances, I could not very easily take it along this evening; and in fact I have nowhere to put it for the duration. Could you keep it for me, or would it be in your way?"

"There is no reason why it should be in my way; as I say, I expect to move to a larger flat. It is not very useful at present to tell the time by, but apart from that I should never know it was there."

QUESTIONS

1. Why does Cousin Rosanna make Paul and Clara "no allowances and few presents" while she is alive, even though she has made them her heirs? (192)

2. In continuing her futile affair with Henry Harley, what reason does Clara have for becoming "increasingly grateful to Cousin Rosanna for either her resolute ignorance or her tolerance"? (193)

3. If "there was nothing, no single thing, in the history of Clara at Sandyhill that she could not remember," why doesn't Clara remember the clock? (197)

4. Why doesn't Clara dispose of the clock, even though its presence torments her?

5. Why does Paul seem to see Cousin Rosanna's motives more clearly than Clara?

6. What are Paul's motives in forcing Clara to remember when, as children, he persuaded her to put her finger into the clock?

7. At the end of the story, why doesn't either Clara or Paul seem interested in possessing the clock?

FOR FURTHER REFLECTION

1. Why does Bowen set "The Inherited Clock" during wartime?

2. Are Cousin Rosanna's intentions in making Paul and Clara her heirs fulfilled or thwarted at the end of the story?

3. Why can the anticipation of a great inheritance prevent people from living a satisfying life?

Gluttony

RAYMOND CARVER

Raymond Carver (1938–1988) was born in Oregon and grew up in Yakima, Washington. He married and had two children by the age of twenty and worked at a series of menial jobs until he was nearly thirty. While enrolled at Chico State College in California, Carver came under the tutelage of John Gardner. "Will You Please Be Quiet, Please?" was included in *The Best American Short Stories 1967,* and by the 1970s, Carver's fame brought him teaching appointments at various universities, including the University of Iowa's Writers' Workshop. *What We Talk About When We Talk About Love* (1981) and *Cathedral* (1983) are among his most highly praised story collections. Carver's stories employ a spare, plain prose to portray working-class characters groping toward connection and understanding. Carver suffered from severe alcoholism for most of his life and ultimately died of lung cancer.

Fat

$\mathcal{I}$ am sitting over coffee and cigarettes at my friend Rita's and I am telling her about it.

Here is what I tell her.

It is late of a slow Wednesday when Herb seats the fat man at my station.

This fat man is the fattest person I have ever seen, though he is neat-appearing and well dressed enough. Everything about him is big. But it is the fingers I remember best. When I stop at the table near his to see to the old couple, I first notice the fingers. They look three times the size of a normal person's fingers—long, thick, creamy fingers.

I see to my other tables, a party of four businessmen, very demanding, another party of four, three men and a woman, and this old couple. Leander has poured the fat man's water, and I give the fat man plenty of time to make up his mind before going over.

Good evening, I say. May I serve you? I say.

Rita, he was big, I mean big.

Good evening, he says. Hello. Yes, he says. I think we're ready to order now, he says.

He has this way of speaking—strange, don't you know. And he makes a little puffing sound every so often.

I think we will begin with a caesar salad, he says. And then a bowl of soup with some extra bread and butter, if you please. The lamb chops, I believe, he says. And baked potato with sour cream. We'll see about dessert later. Thank you very much, he says, and hands me the menu.

God, Rita, but those were fingers.

I hurry away to the kitchen and turn in the order to Rudy, who takes it with a face. You know Rudy. Rudy is that way when he works.

As I come out of the kitchen, Margo—I've told you about Margo? The one who chases Rudy? Margo says to me, Who's your fat friend? He's really a fatty.

Now that's part of it. I think that is really part of it.

I make the caesar salad there at his table, him watching my every move, meanwhile buttering pieces of bread and laying them off to one side, all the time making this puffing noise. Anyway, I am so keyed up or something, I knock over his glass of water.

I'm so sorry, I say. It always happens when you get into a hurry. I'm very sorry, I say. Are you all right? I'll get the boy to clean up right away, I say.

It's nothing, he says. It's all right, he says, and he puffs. Don't worry about it, we don't mind, he says. He smiles and waves as I go off to get Leander, and when I come back to serve the salad, I see the fat man has eaten all his bread and butter.

A little later, when I bring him more bread, he has finished his salad. You know the size of those caesar salads?

You're very kind, he says. This bread is marvelous, he says.

Thank you, I say.

Well, it is very good, he says, and we mean that. We don't often enjoy bread like this, he says.

Where are you from? I ask him. I don't believe I've seen you before, I say.

He's not the kind of person you'd forget, Rita puts in with a snicker.

Denver, he says.

I don't say anything more on the subject, though I am curious.

Your soup will be along in a few minutes, sir, I say, and I go off to put the finishing touches to my party of four businessmen, very demanding.

When I serve his soup, I see the bread has disappeared again. He is just putting the last piece of bread into his mouth.

Believe me, he says, we don't eat like this all the time, he says. And puffs. You'll have to excuse us, he says.

Don't think a thing about it, please, I say. I like to see a man eat and enjoy himself, I say.

I don't know, he says. I guess that's what you'd call it. And puffs. He arranges the napkin. Then he picks up his spoon.

God, he's fat! says Leander.

He can't help it, I say, so shut up.

I put down another basket of bread and more butter. How was the soup? I say.

Thank you. Good, he says. Very good, he says. He wipes his lips and dabs his chin. Do you think it's warm in here, or is it just me? he says.

No, it is warm in here, I say.

Maybe we'll take off our coat, he says.

Go right ahead, I say. A person has to be comfortable, I say.

That's true, he says, that is very, very true, he says.

But I see a little later that he is still wearing his coat.

My large parties are gone now and also the old couple. The place is emptying out. By the time I serve the fat man his chops and baked potato, along with more bread and butter, he is the only one left.

I drop lots of sour cream onto his potato. I sprinkle bacon and chives over his sour cream. I bring him more bread and butter.

Is everything all right? I say.

Fine, he says, and he puffs. Excellent, thank you, he says, and puffs again.

Enjoy your dinner, I say. I raise the lid of his sugar bowl and look in. He nods and keeps looking at me until I move away.

I know now I was after something. But I don't know what.

How is old tub-of-guts doing? He's going to run your legs off, says Harriet. You know Harriet.

For dessert, I say to the fat man, there is the Green Lantern Special, which is a pudding cake with sauce, or there is cheesecake or vanilla ice cream or pineapple sherbet.

We're not making you late, are we? he says, puffing and looking concerned.

Not at all, I say. Of course not, I say. Take your time, I say. I'll bring you more coffee while you make up your mind.

We'll be honest with you, he says. And he moves in the seat. We would like the Special, but we may have a dish of vanilla ice cream as well. With just a drop of chocolate syrup, if you please. We told you we were hungry, he says.

I go off to the kitchen to see after his dessert myself, and Rudy says, Harriet says you got a fat man from the circus out there. That true?

Rudy has his apron and hat off now, if you see what I mean.

Rudy, he is fat, I say, but that is not the whole story.

Rudy just laughs.

Sounds to me like she's sweet on fat-stuff, he says.

Better watch out, Rudy, says Joanne, who just that minute comes into the kitchen.

I'm getting jealous, Rudy says to Joanne.

I put the Special in front of the fat man and a big bowl of vanilla ice cream with chocolate syrup to the side.

Thank you, he says.

You are very welcome, I say—and a feeling comes over me.

Believe it or not, he says, we have not always eaten like this.

Me, I eat and I eat and I can't gain, I say. I'd like to gain, I say.

No, he says. If we had our choice, no. But there is no choice.

Then he picks up his spoon and eats.

What else? Rita says, lighting one of my cigarettes and pulling her chair closer to the table. This story's getting interesting now, Rita says.

That's it. Nothing else. He eats his desserts, and then he leaves and then we go home, Rudy and me.

Some fatty, Rudy says, stretching like he does when he's tired. Then he just laughs and goes back to watching the TV.

I put the water on to boil for tea and take a shower. I put my hand on my middle and wonder what would happen if I had children and one of them turned out to look like that, so fat.

I pour the water in the pot, arrange the cups, the sugar bowl, carton of half and half, and take the tray in to Rudy. As if he's been thinking about it, Rudy says, I knew a fat guy once, a couple of fat guys, really fat guys, when I was a kid. They were tubbies, my God. I don't remember their names. Fat, that's the only name this one kid had. We called him Fat, the kid who lived next door to me. He was a neighbor. The other kid came along later. His name was Wobbly. Everybody called him Wobbly except the teachers. Wobbly and Fat. Wish I had their pictures, Rudy says.

I can't think of anything to say, so we drink our tea and pretty soon I get up to go to bed. Rudy gets up too, turns off the TV, locks the front door, and begins his unbuttoning.

I get into bed and move clear over to the edge and lie there on my stomach. But right away, as soon as he turns off the light and gets into bed, Rudy begins. I turn on my back and relax some, though it is against my will. But here is the thing. When he gets on me, I suddenly feel I am fat. I feel I am terrifically fat, so fat that Rudy is a tiny thing and hardly there at all.

That's a funny story, Rita says, but I can see she doesn't know what to make of it.

I feel depressed. But I won't go into it with her. I've already told her too much.

She sits there waiting, her dainty fingers poking her hair.

Waiting for what? I'd like to know.

It is August.

My life is going to change. I feel it.

QUESTIONS

1. What is the significance of the fat man's use of "we" when referring to himself?

2. Why does the fat man assure the narrator that he doesn't "eat like this all the time" and has "not always eaten like this"? (219, 221)

3. When the narrator says she likes to "see a man eat and enjoy himself," why does the fat man say, "I don't know. . . . I guess that's what you'd call it"? (219)

4. What is the "something" that the narrator knows she was "after" but is unable to identify? (220)

5. Does the narrator consider the fat man gluttonous?

6. When the narrator is in bed with Rudy, why does she feel "terrifically fat, so fat that Rudy is a tiny thing and hardly there at all"? (222)

7. Why and how does the narrator think that her life is going to change?

FOR FURTHER REFLECTION

1. Why do we associate certain character traits with certain eating habits?

2. What distinguishes a pleasure whose satisfaction induces guilt from one that does not?

3. Why do we sometimes feel guilty about telling a story such as the one that the narrator tells Rita?

XU XI

A Chinese-Indonesian native of Hong Kong, Xu Xi (1954–) is the author of three novels, including *The Unwalled City* (2001), and three collections of stories and essays. She has also coedited two anthologies of Hong Kong literature in English. Xu Xi began writing and publishing stories and essays in English while still a child, but worked for eighteen years in international marketing and management before devoting herself full-time to writing. Much of her work chronicles the contradictions of modern-day Hong Kong. She divides her time between New York, Hong Kong, and New Zealand. "Famine" was first published in *Ploughshares* and was selected for *The O. Henry Prize Stories 2006*.

Famine

*I*escape. I board Northwest 18 to New York, via Tokyo. The engine starts, there is no going back. Yesterday, I taught the last English class and left my job of thirty-two years. Five weeks earlier, A-Ma died of heartbreak, within days of my father's sudden death. He was ninety-five, she ninety. Unlike A-Ba, who saw the world by crewing on tankers, neither my mother nor I ever left Hong Kong.

Their deaths rid me of responsibility at last, and I could forfeit my pension and that dreary existence. I am fifty-one and an only child, unmarried.

I never expected my parents to take so long to die.

This meal is *luxurious*, better than anything I imagined.

My colleagues who fly every summer complain of the indignities of travel. Cardboard food, cramped seats, long lines, and these days, too much security nonsense, they say. They fly Cathay, our "national" carrier. This makes me laugh. We have never been a nation; "national" isn't our adjective. *Semantics,* they say, dismissive, just as they dismiss what I say of debt, that it is not an inevitable state, or that children exist to be taught, not spoilt. My colleagues live in overpriced, new, mortgaged flats and indulge 1 to 2.5 children. Most of my students are uneducable.

Back, though, to this in-flight meal. Smoked salmon and cold shrimp, endive salad, strawberries and melon to clean the palate. Then, steak with mushrooms, potatoes au gratin, a choice between a shiraz or cabernet sauvignon. Three cheeses, white chocolate mousse, coffee, and port or a liqueur or brandy. Foods from the pages of a novel, perhaps.

My parents ate sparingly, long after we were no longer impoverished, and disdained "unhealthy" Western diets. A-Ba often said that the only thing he really discovered from travel was that the world was hungry, and that there would never be enough food for everyone. It was why, he said, he did not miss the travel when he retired.

I have no complaints of my travels so far.

My complaining colleagues do not fly business. This seat is an *island* of a bed, surrounded by air. I did not mean to fly in dignity, but having never traveled in summer, or at all, I didn't plan months ahead, long before flights filled up. I simply rang the airlines and booked Northwest, the first one that had a seat, only in business class.

Friends and former students, who do fly business when their companies foot the bill, were horrified. *You* paid *full fare? No one does!* I have money, I replied, why shouldn't I? *But you've given up your "rice bowl." Think of the future.*

I hate rice, always have, even though I never left a single grain, because under my father's watchful glare, A-Ma inspected my bowl. Every meal, even after her eyes dimmed.

The Plaza Suite is nine hundred square feet, over three times the size of home. I had wanted the Vanderbilt or Ambassador and would have settled for the Louis XV, but they were all booked, by those more important than I, no doubt. Anyway, this will have to do. "Nothing unimportant" happens here at the Plaza is what their website literature claims.

The porter arrives, and wheels my bags in on a trolley.

My father bought our tiny flat in a village in Shatin with his disability settlement. When he was forty-five and I one, a falling crane crushed his left leg and groin, thus ending his sailing and procreating career. Shatin isn't very rural anymore, but our home has denied progress its due. We didn't get a phone till I was in my thirties.

I tip the porter five dollars and begin unpacking the leather luggage set. There is too much space for my things.

Right about now, you're probably wondering, along with my colleagues, former students, and friends, *What on earth does she think she's doing?* It was what my parents shouted when I was twelve and went on my first hunger strike.

My parents were illiterate, both refugees from China's rural poverty. A-Ma fried tofu at Shatin market. Once A-Ba recovered from his accident, he worked there also as a cleaner, cursing his fate. They expected me to support them as soon as possible, which should have been after six years of primary school, the only compulsory education required by law in the sixties.

As you see, I clearly had no choice but to strike, since my exam results proved I was smart enough for secondary school. My father beat me, threatened to starve me. *How dare I,* when others were genuinely hungry, unlike me, the only child of a tofu seller who always ate. *Did I want him and A-Ma to die of hunger just to send me to school? How dare I risk their longevity and old age?*

But I was unpacking a Spanish leather suitcase when the past, that country bumpkin's territory, so rudely interrupted.

Veronica, whom I met years ago at university while taking a literature course, foisted this luggage on me. She runs her family's garment enterprise, and is married to a banker. Between them and their three children, they own four flats, three cars, and at least a dozen sets of luggage. Veronica invites me out to dinner (she always pays) whenever she wants to complain about her family. Lately, we've dined often.

"Kids," she groaned over our rice porridge, two days before my trip. "My daughter won't use her brand-new Loewe set because, she says, that's passé. All her friends at Stanford sling these canvas bags with one fat strap. Canvas, imagine. Not even leather."

"Ergonomics," I told her, annoyed at this bland and inexpensive meal. "It's all about weight and balance." And cost, I knew, because the young overspend to conform, just as Veronica eats rice porridge because she's overweight and no longer complains that I'm thin.

She continued. "You're welcome to take the set if you like."

"Don't worry yourself. I can use an old school bag."

"But that's barely a cabin bag! Surely not enough to travel with."

In the end, I let her nag me into taking this set, which is more bag than clothing.

Veronica sounded worried when I left her that evening. "Are you *sure* you'll be okay?"

And would she worry, I wonder, if she could see me now, here, in this suite, this enormous space where one night's bill would have taken my parents years, no, *decades*, to earn and even for me, four years' pay, at least when I first started teaching in my rural enclave (though you're thinking, of course, quite correctly, *Well, what about inflation*, the thing economists cite to dismiss these longings of an English teacher who has spent her life instructing those who care not a whit for our "official language," the one they never speak, at least not if they can choose, especially not now when there is, increasingly, a choice).

My unpacking is done; the past need not intrude. I draw a bath, as one does in English literature, to wash away the heat and grime of both cities in summer. *Why New York?* Veronica asked, at the end of our last evening together. Because, I told her, it will be like nothing I've ever known. For the first time since we've known each other, Veronica actually seemed to envy *me*, although perhaps it was my imagination.

The phone rings, and it's "Guest Relations" wishing to welcome me and offer hospitality. The hotel must wonder, since I grace no social register. I ask for a table at Lutèce tonight. Afterwards, I tip the concierge ten dollars for successfully making the reservation. As you can see, I am no longer an ignorant bumpkin, even though I never left the schools in the New Territories, our urban countryside now that no one farms anymore. Besides, Hong Kong magazines detail lives of the rich and richer so I've read of the famous restaurant and know about the greasy palms of New Yorkers.

I order tea and scones from Room Service. It will hold me till dinner at eight.

The first time I ever tasted tea and scones was at the home of my private student. To supplement income when I enrolled in Teacher Training, I tutored Form V students who needed to pass the School Certificate English exam. This was the compromise I agreed to with my parents before they would allow me to qualify as a teacher. Oh yes, there was a second hunger strike two years prior, before they would let me continue into Form IV. That time, I promised to keep working in the markets after school with A-Ma, which I did.

Actually, my learning English at all was a stroke of luck, since I was *hardly* at a "name school" of the elite. An American priest taught at my secondary school, so I heard a native speaker. He wasn't a very good teacher, but he paid attention to me because I was the only student who liked the subject. A little attention goes a long way.

Tea and scones! I am *supposed* to be eating, not dwelling on the ancient past. The opulence of the tray Room Service brings far surpasses what that pretentious woman served, mother of the hopeless boy, my first private student of many, who only passed his English exam because he cheated (he paid a friend to sit the exam for him), not that I'd ever tell since he's now a wealthy international businessman of some repute who can hire staff to communicate in English with the rest of the world, since he still cannot, at least not with any credibility. That scone ("from Cherikoff," she bragged) was cold and dry, hard as a rock.

Hot scones, oozing with butter. To ooze. I like the lasciviousness of that word, with its excess of vowels, the way an excess of wealth allows people to waste kindness on me, as my former student still does, every lunar New Year, by sending me a *laisee* packet with a generous check which I deposit in my parents' bank account, the way I surrender all my earnings, as any filial and responsible unmarried child should, or so they said.

I eat two scones oozing with butter and savor tea enriched by cream and sugar, here at this "greatest hotel in the world," to vanquish, once and for all, my parents' fear of death and opulence.

Eight does not come soon enough. In the taxi on the way to Lutèce, I ponder the question of pork.

When we were poor but not impoverished, A-Ma once dared to make pork for dinner. It was meant to be a treat, to give me a taste of meat, because I complained that tofu was bland. A-Ba became a vegetarian after his accident and prohibited meat at home; eunuchs are angry people. She dared because he was not eating with us that night, a rare event in our family (I think some sailors he used to know invited him out).

I shat a tapeworm the next morning—almost ten inches long—and she never cooked pork again.

I have since tasted properly cooked pork, naturally, since it's unavoidable in Chinese cuisine. In my twenties, I dined out with friends, despite my parents' objections. But friends marry and scatter; the truth is that there is no one but family in the end, so over time, I submitted to their way of being and seldom took meals away from home, meals my mother cooked virtually till the day she died.

I am distracted. The real question, of course, is whether or not I should order pork tonight.

I did not expect this trip to be fraught with pork!

At Lutèce, I have the distinct impression that the two couples at the next table are talking about me. Perhaps they pity me. People often pitied me my life. *Starved of affection,* they whispered, although why they felt the need to whisper what everyone could hear I failed to understand. All I desired was greater gastronomic variety, but my parents couldn't bear the idea of my eating without them. I ate our plain diet and endured their perpetual skimping because they did eventually learn to leave me alone. That much filial propriety was reasonable payment. I just didn't expect them to *stop* complaining, to fear for what little fortune they had, because somewhere someone was less fortunate than they. That fear made them cling hard to life, forcing me to suffer their fortitude, their good health, and their longevity.

I should walk over to those overdressed people and tell them how things are, about famine, I mean, the way I tried to tell my students, the way my parents dinned it into me as long as they were alive.

Famine has no menu! The waiter waits as I take too long to study the menu. He does not seem patient, making him an oxymoron in his profession. My students would no more learn the oxymoron than they would learn about famine. *Daughter, did you lecture your charges today about famine?* A-Ba would ask every night before dinner. *Yes,* I learned to lie, giving him the answer he needed. This waiter could take a lesson in patience from me.

Finally, I look up at this man who twitches, and do not order pork. *Very good,* he says, as if I should be graded for my literacy in menus. He returns shortly with a bottle of the most expensive red available, and now I *know* the people at the next table are staring. The minute he leaves, the taller of the two men from that table comes over.

"Excuse me, but I believe we met in March? At the U.S. Consulate cocktail in Hong Kong? You're Kwai-sin Ho, aren't you?" He extends his hand. "Peter Martin."

Insulted, it's my turn to stare at this total stranger. I look *nothing* like that simpering socialite who designs wildly fashionable hats that are all the rage in Asia. Hats! We don't have the weather for hats, especially not those things, which are good for neither warmth nor shelter from the sun.

Besides, what use are hats for the hungry?

I do not accept his hand. "I'm her twin sister," I lie. "Kwai-sin and I are estranged."

He looks like he's about to protest, but retreats. After that, they don't stare, although I am sure they discuss me now that I've contributed new gossip for those who are nurtured by the crumbs of the rich and famous. But at least I can eat in peace.

It's my outfit, probably. Kwai-sin Ho is famous for her cheongsams, which is all she ever wears, the way I do. It was my idea. When we were girls together in school, I said the only thing I'd ever wear when I grew up was the cheongsam, the shapely dress with side slits and a neck-strangling collar. She grimaced and said they weren't fashionable, that only spinster schoolteachers and prostitutes wore them, which, back in the sixties, wasn't exactly true, but Kwai-sin was never too bright or imaginative.

That was long ago, before she became Kwai-sin in the cheongsam once these turned fashionable again, long before her father died and her mother became the mistress of a prominent businessman who whisked them into the strato-sphere high above mine. For a little while, she remained my friend, but then we grew up, she married one of the shipping Hos, and became the socialite who refused, albeit politely, to recognize me the one time we bumped into each other at some function in Hong Kong.

So now, vengeance is mine. I will not entertain the people who fawn over her and possess no powers of recognition.

Food is getting sidelined by memory. This is unacceptable. I cannot allow all these intrusions. I must get back to the food, which is, after all, the point of famine.

This is due to a lack of diligence, as A-Ma would say, this lazy meandering from what's important, this succumbing to sloth. My mother was terrified of sloth, almost as much as she was terrified of my father.

She used to tell me an old legend about sloth.

There once was a man so lazy he wouldn't even lift food to his mouth. When he was young, his mother fed him, but as his mother aged, she couldn't. So he marries a woman who will feed him as his mother did. For a time, life is bliss.

Then one day, his wife must return to her village to visit her dying mother. "How will I eat?" he exclaims in fright. The wife conjures this plan. She bakes a gigantic cookie and hangs it on a string around his neck. All the lazy man must do is bend forward and eat. "Wonderful!" he says, and off she goes, promising to return.

On the first day, the man nibbles the edge of the cookie. Each day, he nibbles further. By the fourth day, he's eaten so far down there's no more cookie unless he turns it, which his wife expected he would since he could do this with his mouth.

However, the man's so lazy he lies down instead and waits for his wife's return. As the days pass, his stomach growls and begins to eat itself. Yet the man still won't turn the cookie. By the time his wife comes home, the lazy man has starved to death.

Memory causes such unaccountable digressions! There I was in Lutèce, noticing that people pitied me. Pity made my father livid, which he took out on A-Ma and me. Anger was his one escape from timidity. He wanted no sympathy for either his dead limb or useless genitals.

Perhaps people find me odd rather than pitiful. I will describe my appearance and let you judge. I am thin but not emaciated and have strong teeth. This latter feature is most unusual for a Hong Kong person of my generation. Many years ago, a dentist courted me. He taught me well about oral hygiene, trained as he had been at an American university. Unfortunately, he was slightly rotund, which offended A-Ba. I think A-Ma wouldn't have minded the marriage, but she always sided with my father, who believed it wise to marry one's own physical type (illiteracy did not prevent him from developing philosophies, as you've already witnessed). I was then in my mid-thirties. After the dentist, there were no other men and, as a result, I never left home, which is our custom for unmarried women and men, a loathsome custom but difficult to overthrow. We all must pick our battles, and my acquiring English, which my parents naturally knew not a word, was a sufficiently drastic defiance to last a lifetime, or at least till they expired.

This dinner at Lutèce has come and gone, and you haven't tasted a thing. It's what happens when we converse overmuch and do not concentrate on the food. At home, we ate in the silence of A-Ba's rage.

What a shame, but never mind, I promise to share the bounty next time. This meal must have been good because the bill is in the thousands. I pay by traveler's checks because, not believing in debt, I own no credit cards.

Last night's dinner weighs badly, despite my excellent digestion, so I take a long walk late in the afternoon and end up in Chelsea. New York streets are dirtier than I imagined. Although I did not really expect pavements of gold, in my deepest fantasies, there did reign a glitter and sheen.

No one talks to me here.

The air is fetid with the day's leftover heat and odors. Under a humid, darkening sky, I almost trip over a body on the corner of Twenty-fourth and Seventh. It cannot be a corpse! Surely cadavers aren't left to rot in the streets.

A-Ma used to tell of a childhood occurrence in her village. An itinerant had stolen food from the local pig trough. The villagers caught him, beat him senseless, cut off his tongue and arms, and left him to bleed to death behind the rubbish heap. In the morning, my mother was at play, and while running, tripped over the body. She fell into a blood pool beside him. The corpse's eyes were open.

He surely didn't mean to steal, she always said in the telling, her eyes burning from the memory. *Try to forget,* my father would say. My parents specialized in memory. They both remained lucid and clearheaded till they died.

But this body moves. It's a man awakening from sleep. He mumbles something. Startled, I move away. He is still speaking. I think he's saying he's hungry.

I escape. A taxi whisks me back to my hotel, where my table is reserved at the restaurant.

The ceiling at the Oak Room is roughly four times the height of an average basketball player. The ambience is not as seductive as promised by the Plaza's literature. The problem with reading the wrong kind of literature is that you are bound to be disappointed.

This is a man's restaurant, with a menu of many steaks. Hemingway and Fitzgerald used to eat here. Few of my students have heard of these two, and none of them will have read a single book by either author.

As an English teacher, especially one who was not employed at a "name school" of the elite, I became increasingly marginal. Colleagues and friends converse in Cantonese, the only official language out of our three that people live as well as speak. The last time any student read an entire novel was well over twenty years ago. English literature is not on anyone's exam roster anymore; to desire it in a Chinese colony is as irresponsible as it was of me to master it in our former British one.

Teaching English is little else than a linguistic requirement. Once, it was my passion and flight away from home. Now it is merely my entrée to this former men's club.

But I must order dinner and stop thinking about literature.

The entrées make my head spin, so I turn to the desserts. There is no gooseberry tart! Ever since *David Copperfield*, I have wanted to taste a gooseberry tart (or perhaps it was another book, I don't remember). I tell the boy with the water jug this.

He says, "The magician, madam?"

"The orphan," I reply.

He stands, open-mouthed, without pouring water. What is this imbecility of the young? They neither serve nor wait.

The waiter appears. "Can I help with the menu?"

"Why?" I snap. "It isn't heavy."

But what upsets me is the memory of my mother's story, which I'd long forgotten until this afternoon, just as I hoped to forget about the teaching of English literature, about the uselessness of the life I prepared so hard for.

The waiter hovers. "Are you feeling okay?"

I look up at the sound of his voice and realize my hands are shaking. Calming myself, I say, "Au jus. The prime rib, please, and escargots to start," and on and on I go, ordering in the manner of a man who retreats to a segregated club, who indulges in oblivion because he can, who shuts out the stirrings of the groin and the heart.

I wake to a ringing phone. Housekeeping wants to know if they may clean. It's already past noon. This must be jet lag. I tell Housekeeping, Later.

It's so *comfortable* here that I believe it is possible to forget.

I order brunch from Room Service. Five-star hotels in Hong Kong serve brunch buffets on weekends. The first time I went to one, Veronica paid. We were both students at university. She wasn't wealthy, but her parents gave her spending money, whereas my entire salary (I was already a working teacher by then) belonged to my parents. The array of food made my mouth water. *Pace yourself,* Veronica said. *It's all you can eat.* I wanted to try everything, but gluttony frightened me.

Meanwhile, A-Ba's voice. *After four or more days without food, your stomach begins to eat itself,* and his laugh, dry and caustic.

But I was choosing brunch.

Mimosa. Smoked salmon. Omelet with swiss cheese and chives. And salad, the expensive kind that's imported back home, crisp romaine in a caesar. Room Service asks what I'd like for dessert, so I say chocolate ice-cream sundae. Perhaps I'm more of a bumpkin than I care to admit. My colleagues, former students, and friends would consider my choices boring, unsophisticated, lacking in culinary imagination. They're right, I suppose, since everything I've eaten since coming to New York I could just as easily have obtained back home. They can't understand, though. It's not *what* but *how much.* How opulent. The opulence is what counts to stop the cannibalism of internal organs.

Will that be all?

I am tempted to say, Bring me an endless buffet, whatever your chef concocts, whatever your tongues desire.

How long till my money runs out, my finite account, ending this sweet exile?

Guest Relations knocks, insistent. I have not let anyone in for three days. I open the door wide to show the manager that everything is fine, that their room is not wrecked, that I am not crazy even if I'm not on the social register. If you read the news, as I do, you know it's necessary to allay fears.

So I do, because I do not wish to give the wrong impression. I am not a diva or an excessively famous person who trashes hotel rooms because she can.

I say, politely, that I've been a little unwell, nothing serious, and to please have Housekeeping stop in now. The "please" is significant; it shows I am not odd, that I am, in fact, cognizant of civilized language in English. The manager withdraws, relieved.

For dinner tonight, I decide on two dozen oysters, lobster, and filet mignon. I select a champagne and the wines, one white and one red. Then, it occurs to me that since this is a suite, I can order enough food for a party, so I tell Room Service that there will be a dozen guests for dinner, possibly more. *Very good*, he says, and asks how many extra bottles of champagne and wine, to which I reply, As many as needed.

My students will be my guests. They more or less were visitors during those years I tried to teach. You mustn't think I was always disillusioned, though I seem so now. To prove it to you I'll invite all my colleagues, the few friends I have, like Veronica, the dentist who courted me and his wife and two children, even Kwai-sin and my parents. I bear no grudges; I am not bitter towards them. What I'm uncertain of is whether or not they will come to my supper.

This room, this endless meal, can save me. I feel it. I am vanquishing my fear of death and opulence.

There was a time we did not care about opulence and we dared to speak of death. You spoke of famine because everyone knew the stories from China were true. Now, even in this country, people more or less know. You could educate students about starvation in China or Africa or India because they knew it to be true, because they saw the hunger around them, among the beggars in our streets, and for some, even in their own homes. There was a time it was better *not* to have space, or things to put in that space, and to dream of having instead, because no one had much, except royalty and movie stars and they were *meant* to be fantasy—untouchable, unreal—somewhere in a dream of manna and celluloid.

But you can't speak of famine anymore. Anorexia's fashionable and desirably profitable on runways, so students simply *can't see the hunger*. My colleagues and friends also can't, and refuse to speak of it, changing the subject to what they prefer to see. Even our journalists can't seem to see, preferring the reality they fashion rather than the reality that is. I get angry, but then, when I'm calm, I am simply baffled. Perhaps my parents, and friends and colleagues and memory, are right, that I *am* too stubborn, perhaps even too slothful, because instead of *seeing* reality, I've hidden in my parents' home, in my life as a teacher, even though the years were dreary and long, when what I truly wanted, what I desired, was to embrace the opulence, forsake the hunger, but was too lazy to turn the cookie instead.

I mustn't be angry at them, by which I mean all the "thems" I know and don't know, the big impersonal "they." Like a good English teacher I tell my students, you *must* define the "they." Students are students and continue to make the same mistakes, and all I can do is remind them that "they" are you and to please, please, try to remember because language is a root of life.

Most of the people can't be wrong all the time. Besides, whose fault is it if the dream came true? Postdream is like postmodern; no one understands it, but everyone condones its existence.

Furthermore, what you can't, or won't see, *doesn't* exist.

Comfort, like food, exists, *surrounds* me here.

Not wishing to let anger get the better of me, I eat. Like the Romans, I disgorge and continue. It takes hours to eat three lobsters and three steaks, plus consume five glasses of champagne and six of wine, yet still the food is not enough.

The guests arrive and more keep coming. Who would have thought all these people would show up, all these people I thought I left behind. Where do they come from? My students, colleagues, the dentist and his family, a horde of strangers. Even Kwai-sin and her silly hats, and do you know something, we *do* look a little alike, so Peter Martin wasn't completely wrong. I changed my language to change my life, but still the past throngs, bringing all these people and their Cantonese chatter. The food is not enough, the food is never enough.

Room Service obliges round the clock.

Veronica arrives and I feel a great relief, because the truth is, I no longer cared for her anymore when all we ate was rice porridge. It was mean-spirited, I was ungrateful, forgetting that once she fed me my first buffet, teasing my appetite. *Come out, travel,* she urged over the years. It's not her fault I stayed at home, afraid to abandon my responsibility, traveling only in my mind.

Finally, my parents arrive. My father sits down first to the feast. His leg is whole, and sperm gushes out from between his legs. *It's not so bad here,* he says, and gestures for my mother to join him. This is good. A-Ma will eat if A-Ba does, they're like that, those two. My friends don't understand, not even Veronica. She repeats now what she often has said, that my parents are "controlling." Perhaps, I say, but that's unimportant. I'm only interested in not being responsible anymore.

The noise in the room is deafening. We can barely hear each other above the din. Cantonese is a noisy language, unlike Mandarin or English, but it is alive. This suite that was too empty is stuffed with people, all needing to be fed.

I gaze at the platters of food, piled in this space with largesse. What does it matter if there *are* too many mouths to feed? A phone call is all it takes to get more food, and more. I am fifty-one and have waited too long to eat. They're right, they're all right. If I give in, if I let go, I will vanquish my fears. *This* is bliss, truly.

A-Ma smiles at the vast quantities of food. This pleases me because she so rarely smiles. She says, *Not like lazy cookie man, hah?*

Feeling benevolent, I smile at my parents. *No, not like him,* I say. *Now, eat.*

QUESTIONS

1. When the narrator's tea and scones arrive, why does she say, "I am *supposed* to be eating, not dwelling on the ancient past"? (229)

2. Why is the narrator unable to keep herself from recalling her past?

3. What does the narrator believe are her rightful responsibilities toward her parents?

4. Why does the narrator claim to be the twin sister of Kwai-sin?

5. Why does the narrator fail to describe the meal at Lutèce?

6. Does the narrator succeed in vanquishing her fear of opulence and death?

7. What, if anything, does the narrator achieve through her indulgence in gluttony while in New York?

FOR FURTHER REFLECTION

1. Why do food and memory seem to be so deeply connected to each other?

2. Why can a hunger strike be an effective means of making a point?

3. What motivates us, as adults, to want to "vanquish" those aspects of our parents that we found objectionable as children?

Lust

PERRI KLASS

Perri Klass (1958–), a pediatrician and assistant professor of pediatrics in Boston, was born in Trinidad and raised in New York City and New Jersey. After graduating from Radcliffe College at Harvard with a field concentration in biology, she began to write and also did graduate work in zoology at the University of California, Berkeley. She entered Harvard Medical School in 1982, completing her degree in 1986. Klass has published novels, collections of short stories, and works of nonfiction addressing various aspects of health, nutrition, and medical practice. "Not a Good Girl," first published in *Mademoiselle* in 1983, won the O. Henry Award.

Not a Good Girl

en nowadays can be very strange, if you ask me. I went to bed with one I had just met when I was up in Boston for two days. This is not something I do ferociously often, jump into bed with men I've just met. In fact, for the last six months or so, I haven't jumped into bed with anyone. Not that I've been celibate on principle, or anything like that. It's just that I've been pretty busy lately.

This man I went to bed with in Boston was a graduate student in biochemistry at Harvard who had come to my seminar, the first of the two I was going to give. (You would never say, would you, "the man with whom I went to bed"? I suppose the whole phrase has its roots in such a cute, euphemistic view of things that it has to be kept schoolgirlish and ungrammatical.) Anyway, he was a graduate student in my field, which is immunology. That, of course, lends itself easily to crude sexual analogies, since it is concerned with the body's defenses against foreign intruders, but never mind all that now. I didn't take any particular notice of him at my seminar, except when he asked a reasonably intelligent question. Then he turned up again that evening, when the people who were "hosting" me took me to an Italian restaurant; there was a big group of junior-faculty types and graduate students, including this one, Eric. After dinner, which was extremely so-so and which seemed to leave everyone feeling a little discouraged, my hosts wanted to take me out drinking, but I said I thought I would just go back to the hotel, and Eric said he had a car and would drop me off. In his car I was conscious of our different clothes, me in my give-a-seminar outfit, blazer and wool skirt and stockings, Eric in very worn corduroy pants and a workshirt frayed at the cuffs. We stopped for a traffic light, he put his hand, ragged cuff and all, on my stockinged knee, and asked perfectly straightforwardly if I wanted "company for the night." As simple as that. I considered for a minute, maybe less, aware that I wanted his hand to travel further up my leg, and said okay, appropriately nonchalant.

I could not possibly have been more than four or five years older than he, though, of course, there was that infinite spiritual distance between still-in-school and out-of-school-and-working. Still, I was inclined to put his lack of romantic finesse down to his callow youth. I don't mean the come-on in the car; that seemed to me very acceptable and even sweet and disarming. And of course I wasn't expecting genuine romantic feeling and wouldn't have welcomed it if it had materialized, but once we were in the hotel room, I was less than thrilled when he kissed me and said, "Well, why don't you take your clothes off?" then started to pull off his own. It would frankly have done more for me if he'd unbuttoned even one or two of the buttons on my shirt. He did switch off the light, which might have indicated a romantic awareness of the full moon coming through the window, but more likely just meant he wanted the conventional darkened room. Anyway, we had sex on the professionally large and accommodating hotel double bed, in the romantic silver splash of the full moon.

It just knocked me out how good he was, which shows that she who doesn't expect much is sometimes richly rewarded. But then, afterward, when we were exchanging bits of information to give our mutual nakedness some small base of intimacy (how we had no boyfriends, girl-friends, husbands, wives, how much he respected my work, that kind of thing), he said to me, "Women nowadays can be very strange, if you ask me." And he went on to tell me that women nowadays expect men to be gentle and tender but still to go on filling all the traditional male roles, by which he meant, for example, expecting the man to get out of bed and investigate noises in the night. I was protesting halfheartedly that I personally could imagine nothing worse than being left alone in bed to listen to night noises, when it occurred to me that this "complaint" was Eric's way of letting me know how sensitive he was, that he took seriously what he thought were feminist expectations of men, at least seriously enough to complain about them. A scientist who truly cared about his human relationships. I felt, with some irritation, that we had omitted all the traditional first-night trappings; there had been no false tenderness, no ersatz romance, and neither had there been any hard-bitten bedpost notching. Eric and I seemed to have skipped emotionally to some point later on in a relationship (and not a very appealing relationship), when sweeping generalizations about "men" and "women" were just another way of attacking each other.

But I didn't want to worry about any of this. Isn't the point of a one-night stand that you get off on the novelty and the adventure without having to worry about the other person?

In any case, it didn't turn out to be exactly a one-night stand. It turned out to be a two-night stand, though something should be said about the day between the two nights. I was supposed to go visit some labs, but it was a beautiful morning, and as Eric was driving me past the Boston Common, he suggested that we stop and enjoy the sunshine. So we got out of the car and went to the Public Gardens. I sat on Eric's wool lumberjack jacket, which he had spread for me in deference to my costume, stockings again, and a different wool skirt and a different shirt, the same blazer. He, of course, was wearing exactly the same clothes he had worn the day before. I was feeling tension about the seminar I had to give that afternoon, and mindless pleasure in the sun and the smell of the earth, and I had half-forgotten the details of Eric's after-sex conversation, except that something about it had been faintly disagreeable. I also retained somewhere, between my legs perhaps, the impression that the preconversation sex had been distinctly agreeable. Overall, though, I was finding Eric, today, rather less attractive than I had the day before.

Mentally, I redesigned him, giving him truly curly hair instead of vaguely wavy tendrils, making him taller and thinner to entitle him to his awkwardness, while knitting his body more carefully so that the awkwardness would be more superficial. Though, in all fairness, I had to admit that he hadn't been the least bit awkward in bed. Just then, he put his arms around me and kissed me. I let him, first amused, then aroused, though I don't really believe in making out in public. Soon, we had gotten each other pretty thoroughly worked up, and then without any apparent reason, certainly nothing as definite as anyone's orgasm, we slacked off and began to relax. I began thinking about my seminar again. Then, three boys, who apparently had been watching us climb all over each other, began to call things out at us, encouraging us to finish what we had started. They couldn't have been more than ten years old, maybe less, and they were all three small and thin and pale and should have been in school. One of them carried an enormous portable radio, a ghetto blaster, as they say, though they were as white as Eric and I. After a moment, when they still hadn't gone away, Eric got to his feet and ran toward them, running with rather surprising grace, for someone engaged in such an awkward and ridiculous bit of behavior. I supposed that his motive was simple irritation and a desire to protect me from the jibes of these children, but he must have realized almost immediately, finding himself running across the grass, that he could only look sillier and sillier. The children retreated, slightly scared but triumphant in having provoked him, and he gave up the chase, veering around in a would-be-casual semicircle, as if he had just been running a little ways to work off his exuberance at the feeling of spring in the air.

Needless to say, I was not fooled. I was annoyed with his silliness and more annoyed because I had just discovered a run in my stocking, which I attributed to our making out. Now, I would have to stop at a drugstore sometime before my seminar and replace the stockings. Again I felt, watching him lope shamefacedly back to me, that we were somewhere deep into a relationship, maybe someone else's relationship, certainly not mine. The man making a fool of himself in public, attempting to defend his woman's honor against the onslaughts of smart-ass ten-year-olds. Someone else's relationship, someone else's man.

I might not have slept with Eric again if my second seminar had not gone so exceptionally well. I had been much more nervous about this one than the first, since I'd given the first one many times before. The second seminar, though, explained my very recent work, including work still in progress. I felt vulnerable and a little unconvinced about some of the material, but it went almost devastatingly well, the applause at the end was genuine, and the questions had a slightly awestruck air, even the challenging questions, the ones that were meant to suggest major gaps in my thinking. I had no trouble with the questions. And I felt that one reason it had gone so well was Eric's presence; I was showing off particularly for him and also trying to intimidate him and dazzle him and so on. And so then I felt a little in his debt; also I enjoyed the tentativeness of his offer: "Do you want me to come with you tonight?" It was much more tentative than you would expect, considering that I had slept with him the night before. It took us out of the middle of all those other relationships.

Once again, things turned out very well in bed, and we were both satiated and asleep at 2:30 in the morning, when the phone by the bed rang and it turned out to be my friend Eleanora, calling from New York to say she'd broken my big blue platter. Eleanora and her husband lived two floors up from me, and I had given her my key when I left for Boston and asked her to feed my cat. She had had company that night and had needed a big serving platter and had taken mine and broken it while she was washing it. Then she cried and drank steadily, until she was drunk and miserable enough to call me at the hotel in Boston.

She was crying over the phone. Don't cry, it doesn't matter, I told her, aware that it mattered, that I would not forgive her. I had not told her she could take the platter. Eleanora, I kept saying, why are you carrying on like this, it doesn't matter, I'll buy a new platter. The rhyme was becoming a refrain. Eric was awake and had turned on the bedside lamp. The sight of him was reassuring; he was calm, and we were not emotionally mixed up with each other. I wanted to hang up on Eleanora and see if Eric could get it up again. I was angry about the platter and angry with myself for caring about the platter, and angry with Eleanora for having judged me so correctly that she knew I would be angry about it.

I'm so messy, she was saying. Everything I touch turns out to be a mess. My life is one mess after another. After the platter broke, she had a fight with her husband, a plump and pompous man. He had gone to sleep without forgiving her, she told me, and she was in the living room, with, I assumed, an empty bottle of Southern Comfort in front of her. I know Eleanora's tastes. Why did you have a fight, I asked wearily. Eric was lying back against his pillow, watching me, looking a little surprised. Eleanora said something incoherent, dinner had not gone well, things had not come out right, important guests. For heaven's sake, Eleanora, I said, this is right out of some TV sitcom when the husband's boss comes to dinner. Don't take it so seriously. But then I had to listen to a long speech about how awful her life was and how I couldn't understand. I had no husband, after all. Immunology. Fancy hotels.

Are you alone? she asked suddenly. Well, no, as a matter of fact, I'm not, I said. But it's okay. By which I meant, go ahead and keep me on the phone, we were only sleeping when you called, the sex was over and done with. Immediately, Eleanora's voice took on a giggly quality. She assured me that she hadn't meant to interrupt, that clearly I had more important things to worry about than a broken platter. I'll tell you all about it when I get home, I said. Eric raised his eyebrows; I shrugged. You just bet you will, Eleanora giggled, I'm not going to let you off without a full description. And she said goodbye in high spirits, so I guess I really did manage to do a good turn and cheer up a friend in distress.

I explained a little to Eric, feeling he deserved it. He seemed a bit off balance. It was the sudden awareness of my real, tangled life, which he did not know anything about, in which he had no place. He had asked me all the wrong questions, it seemed—did I have a husband, a boyfriend? —and should have asked, instead, if I had a cat and if I had a friend named Eleanora who broke things.

"What's your cat's name?" he asked me, after I explained why Eleanora had the key to my apartment; then, after I told him, he said, "You have a cat named Carmen?" I wondered if he thought that was a ridiculous name, if he would, after all, turn out to be some kind of kindred sensibility, so I said, "Someone else named her," leaving him free to make fun of the name. But he had no particular opinion; he had perhaps begun to wonder who had named my cat—an ex-lover, someone I used to live with—and I thought of telling him that my little sister had chosen the name; giving me one of her own cat's kittens, she had thought to please me, knowing I like music. I didn't say it. Instead, Eric and I investigated and discovered that he could indeed get it up again, though, to be honest, it took him so damn long to reach orgasm that I lost interest. But I kept my eyes wide open; it is very bad manners to fall asleep in such a situation.

As if in return for his unexpected glimpse into my life, he offered me a confidence the next morning as he drove me to the airport to catch the air shuttle to New York. He told me that sometimes he was afraid he wouldn't be able to write his dissertation. All I could say was that I was sure he would be fine. I wondered whether he actually would be fine and whether I would see his name on articles or run into him in the future at scientific meetings. "Can I ask you something?" he said. I nodded. "If we lived near each other, would you have an affair with me?" I was silent too long to make it convincing before saying that we'd certainly give it a try, didn't he think? Fortunately, we got to the airport very soon after that and, instead of letting him park, I just got out in front of the terminal and kissed him goodbye and escaped.

Later, on the plane, I was thinking about all the little pieces of far-advanced and none-too-pleasant relationships that I had sensed between myself and Eric. I was wondering what my two-night stand might have to teach me; in science, of course, you have to learn from your experiments, and one valuable lesson is that you can never control all the variables. It can be scary when an experiment gets out of hand, and back at the airport, I'd had the distinct feeling that Eric was ready for all sorts of complications. I suspected there was something to be learned from this interlude with him about the nature of entanglements that occur between lives, the extremely fine line between no relationship and all relationships. And then suddenly, I began to smile to myself, almost to giggle, because it occurred to me that Eric had wanted to follow this experiment to wherever it might lead us, but that I had prevented it. I'd kept it to something more like a seminar—short, controlled, ending neatly on schedule. But it had been educational, I decided; it's hard to learn major lessons in quick little seminars, but they can serve to expose you to new ideas, to start you thinking. The most important thing about seminars is that they should surprise you a little. You shouldn't know, walking in, exactly how you'll feel walking out. And if, in addition, you enjoy them while they last, then you have to consider them successful, I suppose.

QUESTIONS

1. Why does the narrator comment on the grammatical contrast between "this man I went to bed with" and "the man with whom I went to bed"? (245)

2. Why is the narrator dismissive of the sexual analogies that her medical specialty (immunology) suggests?

3. Does the narrator desire romantic feeling?

4. If the narrator does not plan to forgive Eleanora for breaking the blue platter, why does she tell Eleanora that "it doesn't matter"? (250)

5. What do the narrator's descriptions of relationships reveal about her attitude toward them?

6. When the narrator indicates that Eric seemed ready for "all sorts of complications," what complications is she referring to? (252)

7. In what way has this "seminar" been a "surprise" to the narrator? How has it started her "thinking"? (252)

FOR FURTHER REFLECTION

1. Is this narrator in control of her life?

2. Is the narrator "not a good girl"?

3. Does the narrator use good judgment in remaining emotionally uninvolved with Eric?

NATHAN ENGLANDER

Born in New York City and raised in an Orthodox Jewish family,
Nathan Englander (1970–) graduated from the State University of
New York at Binghamton and received his MFA in creative writing
from the Iowa Writers' Workshop. He published a collection of short
stories, *For the Relief of Unbearable Urges*, in 1999. Englander's
stories—like those of Bernard Malamud and Isaac Bashevis Singer—
often possess the qualities of myths or fables. With pathos and
touches of surrealism, Englander presents characters struggling
mightily, and comically, with moral dilemmas.

For the Relief of
Unbearable Urges

The beds were to be separated on nights forbidden to physical intimacy, but Chava Bayla hadn't pushed them together for many months. She flatly refused to sleep anywhere except on her menstrual bed and was, from the start, impervious to her husband's pleading.

"You are pure," Dov Binyamin said to the back of his wife, who—heightening his frustration—slept facing the wall.

"I am impure."

"This is not true, Chava Bayla. It's an impossibility. And I know myself the last time you went to the ritual bath. A woman does not have her thing—"

"Her thing?" Chava said. She laughed, as if she had caught him in a lie, and turned to face the room.

"A woman doesn't menstruate for so long without even a single week of clean days. And a wife does not for so long ignore her husband. It is Shabbos, a double mitzvah tonight—an obligation to make love."

Chava Bayla turned back again to face her wall. She tightened her arms around herself as if in an embrace.

"You are my wife!" Dov Binyamin said.

"That was God's choice, not mine. I might also have been put on this earth as a bar of soap or a kugel. Better," she said, "better it should have been one of those."

That night Dov Binyamin slept curled up on the edge of his bed—as close as he could get to his wife.

After Shabbos, Chava avoided coming into the bedroom for as long as possible. When she finally did enter and found Dov dozing in a chair by the balcony, she went to sleep fully clothed, her *sheitel* still on top of her head.

As he nodded forward in the chair, Dov's hat fell to the floor. He woke up, saw his wife, picked up his hat, and, brushing away the dust with his elbow, placed it on the nightstand. How beautiful she looked all curled up in her dress. Like a princess enchanted, he thought. Dov pulled the sheet off the top of his bed. He wanted to cover her, to tuck Chava in. Instead he flung the sheet into a corner. He shut off the light, untied his shoes—but did not remove them—and went to sleep on the tile floor beside his wife's bed. Using his arm for a pillow, Dov Binyamin dreamed of a lemon ice his uncle had bought him as a child and of the sound of the airplanes flying overhead at the start of the Yom Kippur War.

Dov Binyamin didn't go to work on Sunday. Folding up his *tallis* after prayers and fingering the embroidery of the tallis bag, he recalled the day Chava had presented it to him as a wedding gift—the same gift his father had received from his mother, and his father's father before. Dov had marveled at the workmanship, wondered how many hours she had spent with a needle in hand. Now he wondered if she would ever find him worthy of such attentions again. Zipping the prayer shawl inside, Dov Binyamin put the bag under his arm. He carried it with him out of the shul, though he had his own cubby in which to store it.

The morning was oppressively hot; a *hamsin* was settling over Jerusalem. Dov Binyamin was wearing his lightest caftan, but in the heat wave it felt as if it were made of the heaviest wool.

Passing a bank of phones, he considered calling work, making some excuse, or even telling the truth. "Shai," he would say, "I am a ghost in my home and wonder who will mend my tallis bag when it is worn." His phone card was in his wallet, which he had forgotten on the dresser, and what did he want to explain to Shai for, who had just come from a Shabbos with his spicy wife and a house full of children.

Dov followed Jaffa Street down to the Old City. Roaming the alleyways always helped to calm him. There was comfort in the Jerusalem stone and the walls within walls and the permanence of everything around him. He felt a kinship with history's Jerusalemites, in whose struggles he searched for answers to his own. Lately he felt closer to his biblical heroes than to the people with whom he spent his days. King David's desires were far more alive to Dov than the empty problems of Shai and the other men at the furniture store.

Weaving through the Jewish Quarter, he had intended to end up at the Wall, to say Tehillim, and, in his desperate state, to scribble a note and stuff it into a crack just like the tourists in their cardboard yarmulkes. Instead, he found himself caught up in the crush inside the Damascus Gate. An old Arab woman was crouched down behind a wooden box of cactus fruit. She peeled a sabra with a kitchen knife, allowing a small boy a sample of her product. The child ran off with his mouth open, a stray thorn stuck in his tongue.

Dov Binyamin tightened his hold on the tallis bag and pushed his way through the crowd. He walked back to Mea Shearim along the streets of East Jerusalem. Let them throw stones, he thought. Though no one did. No one even took notice of him except to step out of his way as he rushed to his rebbe's house for some advice.

Meir the Beadle was in the front room, sitting on a plastic chair at a plastic table.

"Don't you have work today?" Meir said, without looking up from the papers that he was shifting from pile to pile.

Dov Binyamin ignored the question. "Is the Rebbe in?"

"He's very busy."

Dov Binyamin went over to the kettle, poured himself a mug of hot water, and stirred in a spoonful of Nescafé. "How about you don't give me a hard time today?"

"Who's giving a hard time?" Meir said, putting down the papers and getting up from the chair. "I'm just telling you Sunday is busy after a day and a half without work." He knocked at the Rebbe's door and went in. Dov Binyamin made a blessing over his coffee, took a sip, and, being careful not to spill, lowered himself into one of the plastic chairs. The coffee cut the edge off the heat that, like Dov, sat heavy in the room.

The Rebbe leaned forward on his *shtender* and rocked back and forth as if he were about to topple.

"No, this is no good. Very bad. Not good at all." He pulled back on the lectern and held it in that position. The motion reminded Dov of his dream, of the rumbling of engines and a vase—there had been a blue glass vase—set to rocking on a shelf. "And you don't want a divorce?"

"I love her, Rebbe. She is my wife."

"And Chava Bayla?"

"She, thank God, has not even raised the subject of separation. She asks nothing of me but to be left alone. And this is where the serpent begins to swallow its tail. The more she rejects me, the more I want to be with her. And the more I want to be with her, the more intent she becomes that I stay away."

"She is testing you."

"Yes. In some way, Rebbe, Chava Bayla is giving to me a test."

Pulling at his beard, the Rebbe again put his full weight on the lectern so that the wood creaked. He spoke in a Talmudic singsong:

"Then you must find the strength to ignore Chava Bayla, until Chava Bayla should come to find you—and you must be strict with yourself. For she will not consider your virtues until she is calm in the knowledge that her choices are her own."

"But I don't have the strength. She is my wife. I miss her. And I am human, too. With human habits. It will be impossible for me not to try and touch her, to try and convince her. Rebbe, forgive me, but God created the world with a certain order to it. I suffer greatly under the urges with which I have been blessed."

"I see," said the Rebbe. "The urges have become great."

"Unbearable. And to be around someone that I feel so strongly for, to look and be unable to touch—it is like floating through heaven in a bubble of hell."

The Rebbe pulled a chair over to the bookcases that lined his walls. Climbing onto the chair, he steadied himself, then removed a volume from the top shelf. "We must relieve the pressure."

"It is a fine notion. But I fear that it's impossible."

"I'm giving you a *heter*," the Rebbe said. "A special dispensation." He went over to his desk and flipped through the book. He began to scribble on a pad of onionskin paper.

"For what?"

"To see a prostitute."

"Excuse me, Rebbe?"

"Your marriage is at stake, is it not?"

Dov bit at his thumbnail and then rushed the hand, as if it were something shameful, into the pocket of his caftan.

"Yes," he said, a shake entering his voice. "My marriage is a withered limb at my side."

The Rebbe aimed his pencil at Dov.

"One may go to great lengths in the name of achieving peace in the home."

"But a prostitute?" Dov Binyamin asked.

"For the relief of unbearable urges," the Rebbe said. And he tore, like a doctor, the sheet of paper from the pad.

Dov Binyamin drove to Tel Aviv, the city of sin. There he was convinced he would find plenty of prostitutes. He parked his Fiat on a side street off Dizengoff and walked around town.

Though he was familiar with the city, its social aspects were foreign to him. It was the first leisurely walk he had taken in Tel Aviv and, fancying himself an anthropologist in a foreign land, he found it all quite interesting. He was usually the one under scrutiny. Busloads of American tourists scamper through Mea Shearim daily. They buy up the stores and pull tiny cameras from their hip packs, snapping pictures of real live Hasidim, like the ones from the stories their grandparents told. Next time he would say "Boo!" He laughed at the thought of it. Already he was feeling lighter. Passing a kiosk, he stopped and bought a bag of pizza-flavored Bissli. When he reached the fountain, he sat down on a bench among the aged new immigrants. They clustered together as if huddled against a biting cold wind that had followed them from their native lands. He stayed there until dark, until the crowd of new immigrants, like the bud of a flower, began to spread out, to open up, as the old folks filed down the fountain's ramps onto the city streets. They were replaced by young couples and groups of boys and girls who talked to each other from a distance but did not mix. So much like religious children, he thought. In a way we are all the same. Dov Binyamin suddenly felt overwhelmed. He was startled to find himself in Tel Aviv, already involved in the act of searching out a harlot, instead of home in his chair by the balcony, worrying over whether to take the Rebbe's advice at all.

He walked back toward his car. A lone cabdriver leaned up against the front door of his Mercedes, smoking. Dov Binyamin approached him, the heat of his feet inside his shoes becoming more oppressive with every step.

"Forgive me," Dov Binyamin said.

The cabdriver, his chest hair sticking out of the collar of his T-shirt in tufts, ground out the cigarette and opened the passenger door. "Need a ride, Rabbi?"

"I'm not a rabbi."

"And you don't need a ride?"

Dov Binyamin adjusted his hat. "No. Actually no."

The cabdriver lit another cigarette, flourishing his Zippo impressively. Dov took notice, though he was not especially impressed.

"I'm looking for a prostitute."

The cabdriver coughed and clasped a hand to his chest.

"Do I look like a prostitute?"

"No, you misunderstand." Dov Binyamin wondered if he should turn and run away. "A female prostitute."

"What's her name?"

"No name. Any name. You are a taxi driver. You must know where are such women." The taxi driver slapped the hood of his car and said, "Ha," which Dov took to be laughter. Another cab pulled up on Dov's other side.

"What's happening?" the second driver called.

"Nothing. The rabbi here wants to know where to find a friend. Thinks it's a cabdriver's responsibility to direct him."

"Do we work for the Ministry of Tourism?" the second driver asked.

"I just thought," Dov Binyamin said. His voice was high and cracking. It seemed to elicit pity in the second driver.

"There's a cash machine back on Dizengoff."

"Prostitutes at the bank?" Dov Binyamin said.

"No, not at the bank. But the service isn't free." Dov blushed under his beard. "Up by the train station in Ramat Gan—at the row of bus stops."

"All those pretty ladies aren't waiting for the bus to Haifa." This from the first driver, who again slapped the hood of his car and said, "Ha!"

The first time past, he did not stop, driving by the women at high speed and taking the curves around the cement island so that his wheels screeched and he could smell the burning rubber. Dov Binyamin slowed down, trying to maintain control of himself and the car, afraid that he had already drawn too much attention his way. The steering wheel began to vibrate in Dov's shaking hands. The Rebbe had given him permission, had instructed him. Was not the Rebbe's heter valid? This is what Dov Binyamin told his hands, but they continued to tremble in protest.

On his second time past, a woman approached the passenger door. She wore a matching shirt and pants. The outfit clung tightly, and Dov could see the full form of her body. Such immodesty! She tapped at the window. Dov Binyamin reached over to roll it down. Flustered, he knocked the gearshift, and the car lurched forward. Applying the parking brake, he opened the window the rest of the way.

"Close your lights," she instructed him. "We don't need to be onstage out here."

"Sorry," he said, shutting off the lights. He was comforted by the error, not wanting the woman to think he was the kind of man who employed prostitutes on a regular basis.

"You interested in some action?"

"Me?"

"A shy one," she said. She leaned through the window, and Dov Binyamin looked away from her large breasts. "Is this your first time? Don't worry. I'll be gentle. I know how to treat a black hat."

Dov Binyamin felt the full weight of what he was doing. He was giving a bad name to all Hasidim. It was a sin against God's name. The urge to drive off, to race back to Jerusalem and the silence of his wife, came over Dov Binyamin. He concentrated on his dispensation.

"What would you know from black hats?" he said.

"Plenty," she said. And then, leaning in farther, "Actually, you look familiar." Dov Binyamin seized up, only to begin shaking twice as hard. He shifted into first and gave the car some gas. The prostitute barely got clear of the window.

When it seemed as if he wouldn't find a suitable match, a strong-looking young woman stepped out of the darkness.

"Good evening," he said.

She did not answer or ask any questions or smile. She opened the passenger door and sat down.

"What do you think you're doing?"

"Saving you the trouble of driving around until the sun comes up." She was American. He could hear it. But she spoke beautiful Hebrew, sweet and strong as her step. Dov Binyamin turned on his headlights and again bumped the gearshift so that the car jumped.

"Settle down there, Tiger," she said. "The hard part's over. All the rest of the work is mine."

The room was in an unlicensed hostel. It had its own entrance. There was no furniture other than a double bed and three singles. The only lamp stood next to the door.

The prostitute sat on the big bed with her legs curled underneath her. She said her name was Devorah.

"Like the prophetess," Dov Binyamin said.

"Exactly," Devorah said. "But I can only see into the immediate future."

"Still, it is a rare gift with which to have been endowed." Dov shifted his weight from foot to foot. He stood next to the large bed unable to bring himself to bend his knees.

"Not really," she said. "All my clients already know what's in store."

She was fiery, this one. And their conversation served to warm up the parts of Dov the heat wave had not touched. The desire that had been building in Dov over the many months so filled his body that he was surprised his skin did not burst from the pressure. He tossed his hat onto the opposite single, hoping to appear at ease, as sure of himself as the hairy-chested cabdriver with his cigarettes. The hat landed brim side down. Dov's muscles twitched reflexively, though he did not flip it onto its crown.

"Wouldn't you rather make your living as a prophetess?" he asked.

"Of course. Prophesying's a piece of cake. You don't have to primp all day for it. And it's much easier on the back, no wear and tear. Better for *you*, too. At least you'd leave with something in the morning." She took out one of her earrings, then, as an afterthought, put it back in. "Doesn't matter anyway. No money in it. They pay me to do everything *except* look into the future."

"I'll be the first then," he said, starting to feel almost comfortable. "Tell me what you see."

She closed her eyes and tilted her head so that her lips began to part, this in the style of those who peer into other realms. "I predict that this is the first time you've done such a thing."

"That is not a prophecy. It's a guess." Dov Binyamin cleared his throat and wiggled his toes against the tops of his shoes. "What else do you predict?"

She massaged her temples and held back a naughty grin.

"That you will, for once, get properly laid."

But this was too much for Dov Binyamin. Boiling in the heat and his shame, he motioned toward his hat.

Devorah took his hand.

"Forgive me," she said, "I didn't mean to be crude."

Her fingers were tan and thin, more delicate than Chava's. How strange it was to see strange fingers against the whiteness of his own.

"Excluding the affections of my mother, blessed be her memory, this is the first time I have been touched by a woman that is not my wife."

She released her grasp and, before he had time to step away, reached out for him again, this time more firmly, as if shaking on a deal. Devorah raised herself up and straightened a leg, displayed it for a moment, and then let it dangle over the side of the bed. Dov admired the leg, and the fingers resting against his palm.

"Why are we here together?" she asked—she was not mocking him. Devorah pulled at the hand and he sat at her side.

"To relieve my unbearable urges. So that my wife will
be able to love me again."

Devorah raised her eyebrows and pursed her lips.

"You come to me for your wife's sake?"

"Yes."

"You are a very dedicated husband."

She gave him a smile that said, You won't go through
with it. The smile lingered, and then he saw that it said
something completely different, something irresistible. And
he wondered, as a shiver ran from the trunk of his body
out to the hand she held, if what they say about American
women is true.

Dov walked toward the door, not to leave, but to shut
off the lamp.

"One minute," Devorah said, reaching back and remov-
ing a condom from a tiny pocket—no more than a slit in
the smooth black fabric of her pants. Dov Binyamin knew
what it was and waved it away.

"Am I really your second?" she asked.

Dov heard more in the question than was intended.
He heard a flirtation; he heard a woman who treated the
act of being second as if it were special. He was sad for
her—wondering if she had ever been anyone's first. He did
not answer out loud, but instead nodded, affirming.

Devorah pouted as she decided, the prophylactic held
between two fingers like a quarter poised at the mouth of
a jukebox. Dov switched off the light and took a half step
toward the bed. He stroked at the darkness, moving forward until he found her hair, soft, alive, without any of the
worked-over stiffness of Chava's wigs.

"My God," he said, snatching back his hand as if he
had been stung. It was too late, though. That he already
knew. The hunger had flooded his whole self. His heart was
swollen with it, pumping so loudly and with such strength
that it overpowered whatever sense he might have had. For
whom then, he wondered, was he putting on, in darkness,
such a bashful show? He reached out again and stroked her

hair, shaking but sure of his intent. With his other arm, the weaker arm, to which he bound every morning his tefillin, the arm closer to the violent force of his heart, he searched for her hand.

Dov found it and took hold of it, first roughly, as if desperate. Then he held it lightly, delicately, as if it were made of blown glass—a goblet from which, with ceremony, he wished to drink. Bringing it toward his mouth, he began to speak.

"It is a sin to spill seed in vain," he said, and Devorah let the condom fall at the sound of his words.

Dov Binyamin was at work on Monday and he was home as usual on Monday night. There was no desire to slip out of the apartment during the long hours when he could not sleep, no temptation, when making a delivery in Ramot, to turn the car in the direction of Tel Aviv. Dov Binyamin felt, along with a guilt that he could not shake, a sense of relief. He knew that he could never be with another woman again. And if it were possible to heap on himself all the sexual urges of the past months, if he could undo the single night with the prostitute to restore his unadulterated fidelity, he would have them tenfold. From that night of indulgence he found the strength to wait a lifetime for Chava's attentions—if that need be.

When Chava Bayla entered the dining room, Dov Binyamin would move into the kitchen. When she entered the bedroom, he would close his eyes and feign sleep. He would lie in the dark and silently love his wife. And, never coming to a conclusion, he would rethink the wisdom of the Rebbe's advice. He would picture the hairy arm of the cabdriver as he slapped the hood of his taxi. And he would chide himself. Never, never would he accuse his wife of faking impurity, for was it not the greater sin for him to pretend to be pure?

It was only a number of days from that Sunday night that Chava Bayla began to talk to her husband with affection. Soon after, she touched him on the shoulder while handing him a platter of *kasha varnishkes*. He placed it on the table and ate in silence. As she served dessert, *levelesh*, his favorite, Dov's guilt took on a physical form. What else could it be? What else but guilt would strike a man so obviously?

It began as a concentrated smoldering that flushed the whole of his body. Quickly intensifying, it left him almost feverish. He would excuse himself from meals and sneak out of bed. At work, frightened and in ever-increasing pain, he ran from customers to examine himself in the bathroom. Dov Binyamin knew he was suffering from something more than shame.

But maybe it was a trial, a test of which the Rebbe had not warned him. For as his discomfort increased, so did Chava's attentions. On her way out of the shower, she let her towel drop in front of him, stepping away from it as if she hadn't noticed, like some Victorian woman waiting for a gentleman to return her hankie with a bow. She dressed slowly, self-consciously, omitting her undergarments and looking to Dov to remind her. He ignored it all, feeling the weight of his heart—no longer pumping as if to burst, but just as large—the blood stagnant and heavy. Chava began to linger in doorways so that he would be forced to brush against her as he passed. Her passion was torturous to Dov, forced to keep his own hidden inside. Once, without any of the protocol with which they tempered their lives, she came at the subject head-on. "Are you such a small man," she said, "that you must for eternity exact revenge?" He made no answer. It was she who walked away, only to return sweeter and bolder. She became so daring, so desperate, that he wondered if he had ever known the true nature of his wife at all. But he refused, even after repeated advances, to respond to Chava Bayla in bed.

She called to him from the darkness.

"Dovey, please, come out of there. Come lie by me and we'll talk. Just talk. Come Doveleh, join me in bed."

Dov Binyamin stood in the dark in the bathroom. There was some light from the street, enough to make out the toilet and the sink. He heard every word his wife said, and each one tore at him.

He stood before the toilet, holding his penis lightly, mindful of halacha and the laws concerning proper conduct in the lavatory. Trying to relieve himself, to pass water, he suffered to no end.

When he began to urinate, the burning worsened. He looked down in the half darkness and imagined he saw flames flickering from his penis.

He recalled the words of the prostitute. For his wife's sake, he thought, as the tears welled in his eyes. This couldn't possibly be the solution the Rebbe intended. Dov was supposed to be in his wife's embrace, enjoying her caresses, and instead he would get an examination table and a doctor's probing hands.

Dov Binyamin dropped to his knees. He rested his head against the coolness of the bowl. Whatever the trial, he couldn't bear it much longer. He had by now earned, he was sure, Chava Bayla's love.

There was a noise; it startled him; it was Chava at the door trying to open it. Dov had locked himself in. The handle turned again, and then Chava spoke to him through the door's frosted-glass window.

"Tell me," she said. "Tell me: When did I lose my husband for good?"

Every word a plague.

Dov pressed the lever of the toilet, drowning out Chava Bayla's voice. He let the tears run down his face and took his penis full in his hand.

For Dov Binyamin was on fire inside.

And yet he would not be consumed.

QUESTIONS

1. Why does the Rebbe give Dov Binyamin a special dispensation to see a prostitute?

2. Why does Dov follow the Rebbe's advice?

3. Why are we told that Devorah is American?

4. What is the significance of Devorah sharing the name of a prophetess?

5. Why does Chava Bayla's affection for Dov return a few days after his night with Devorah?

6. Why does Dov not respond to Chava's advances?

7. According to the story, is Dov's physical suffering a random occurrence or punishment for his night with Devorah?

FOR FURTHER REFLECTION

1. Are there circumstances in which adultery is justifiable?

2. In considering whether an act is immoral or sinful, should it make any difference if it is sanctioned by someone who possesses moral authority?

3. Do those who do wrong ultimately suffer for their actions in some way?

ACKNOWLEDGMENTS

All possible care has been taken to trace ownership and secure permission for each selection in this anthology. The Great Books Foundation wishes to thank the following authors, publishers, and representatives for permission to reprint copyrighted material:

A Rose for Emily, from COLLECTED STORIES OF WILLIAM FAULKNER, by William Faulkner. Copyright © 1930 by William Faulkner, renewed 1958 by William Faulkner. Reprinted by permission of Random House, Inc.

Good Country People, from A GOOD MAN IS HARD TO FIND AND OTHER STORIES, by Flannery O'Connor. Copyright © 1955 by Flannery O'Connor, renewed 1983 by Regina O'Connor. Reprinted by permission of Harcourt, Inc.

Roman Fever, from ROMAN FEVER AND OTHER STORIES, by Edith Wharton. Copyright © 1934 by *Liberty Magazine*, renewed 1962 by William R. Tyler. Reprinted by permission of Scribner, an imprint of Simon & Schuster Adult Publishing Group.

Smokers, from IN THE GARDEN OF THE NORTH AMERICAN MARTYRS: A COLLECTION OF SHORT STORIES, by Tobias Wolff. Copyright © 1981 by Tobias Wolff. Reprinted by permission of the Ecco Press, an imprint of HarperCollins Publishers.

Hairball, from WILDERNESS TIPS, by Margaret Atwood. Copyright © 1991 by O. W. Toad Limited. Reprinted by permission of Doubleday, a division of Random House, Inc.

The House with the Mezzanine, from STORIES, by Anton Chekhov, translated by Richard Pevear and Larissa Volokhonsky. Translation copyright © 2000 by Richard Pevear and Larissa Volokhonsky. Reprinted by permission of Bantam Books, a division of Random House, Inc.

Shiloh, from SHILOH AND OTHER STORIES, by Bobbie Ann Mason. Copyright © 1982 by Bobbie Ann Mason. Reprinted by permission of International Creative Management, Inc.

The Rocking-Horse Winner, from THE COMPLETE SHORT STORIES, vol. 3, by D. H. Lawrence. Copyright © 1933 by the Estate of D. H. Lawrence, renewed 1961 by Anthony Ravagli and C. M. Weekley, executors of the Estate of Frieda Lawrence. Reprinted by permission of Viking Penguin, a division of Penguin Group (USA) Inc.

The Inherited Clock, from THE COLLECTED STORIES OF ELIZABETH BOWEN, by Elizabeth Bowen. Copyright © 1981 by Curtis Brown Limited, Literary Executors of the Estate of Elizabeth Bowen. Reprinted by permission of Alfred A. Knopf, a division of Random House, Inc.

Fat, from WHERE I'M CALLING FROM: NEW AND SELECTED STORIES, by Raymond Carver. Copyright © 1976, 1977, 1981, 1983, 1986, 1987, 1988 by Raymond Carver. Reprinted by permission of Grove/Atlantic, Inc.

Famine, by Xu Xi, from THE O. HENRY PRIZE STORIES 2006. Copyright © 2004 by Xu Xi (S. Komala). Reprinted by permission of Harold Matson Company, Inc.

Not a Good Girl, by Perri Klass, from PRIZE STORIES 1984: THE O. HENRY AWARDS. Copyright © 1983 by Perri Klass. First published in *Mademoiselle*. Reprinted by permission of the Elaine Markson Literary Agency.

For the Relief of Unbearable Urges, from FOR THE RELIEF OF UNBEARABLE URGES, by Nathan Englander. Copyright © 1999 by Nathan Englander. Reprinted by permission of Alfred A. Knopf, a division of Random House, Inc.